HOLLY SMALE wanted to write from the age of five when she discovered that books didn't grow on trees like apples. Her passion for stories led her on a number of adventures, including modelling, teaching children in Japan, PR and backpacking across dozens of countries around the world. She has a degree in English literature and an MA in Shakespeare from Bristol University.

The Valentines series is the much anticipated follow-up to the number-one, internationally bestselling Geek Girl series, which sold over three million copies in thirty languages and won the Teen and Young Adult category of the Waterstones Children's Book Prize.

Love Me Not is the third and final book that follows the famous Valentine sisters.

This is Mercy's story.

smale.

ries.

THE Valentines

LOVE ME NOT

HOLLY SMALE

HarperCollins Children's Books

First published in Great Britain by
HarperCollins *Children's Books* in 2021
HarperCollins *Children's Books* is a division of HarperCollins*Publishers* Ltd
HarperCollins Publishers
1 London Bridge Street
London SE1 9GF

www.harpercollins.co.uk

HarperCollins*Publishers*
1st Floor, Watermarque Building, Ringsend Road
Dublin 4, Ireland

1

ISBN 978–0–00–839352–6

Holly Smale asserts the moral right
to be identified as the author of the work.

Typeset in Plantin Std by
Palimpsest Book Production Ltd, Falkirk, Stirlingshire
Printed and bound in England by
CPI Group (UK) Ltd, Croydon, CR0 4YY

MIX
Paper from
responsible sources
FSC™ C007454

This book is produced from independently certified FSC™ paper
to ensure responsible forest management.

For more information visit: www.harpercollins.co.uk/green

For my sister, Tara,
always and unconditionally

1

You're not going to like me.

I'm not *nice*, I'm not *relatable*, you'll find it difficult to *empathise* with the snarky daughter of Hollywood royalty yada yada, and frankly you can bore right off.

It is not a girl's job to be *liked*.

I'm not your mentor or your confidante. I didn't ask to be an inspiration or an aspiration; to make you feel *seen* and cosy inside. If you want saccharine sweetness and a tenuous grasp on the English language, go see my little sister Hope. Looking for a beautiful pushover? Check out my other sister Faith. Maverick charm from the brains of a moron? My brother Max has it in spades.

But me: Mercy Valentine? I don't need your validation and I don't want it, so keep moving.

I am not your hero.

★

'They're called *iceberg* houses,' Dior breathes as she leads me down winding marble stairs. 'Daddy says they're all the rage in South Ken, so we just *had* to have one.'

She flicks her blonde hair and beams at me.

Already irritated – and I've been at this party six minutes – I pick the painful scab on my knuckle.

'I *think*,' my friend adds thoughtfully, popping the end of a highlighted strand in her mouth, 'it's because you mostly find icebergs in rich places, like the Arctic, and they cost *lots* of money to visit? So, it's, like, the *most* expensive type of house?'

Dior, in case you haven't worked it out yet, is an idiot.

'You're an idiot,' I tell her as she leads me round the corner into a heaving, screaming corridor and past a full-size gym, complete with real palm trees and a floor-to-ceiling climbing wall. 'It's because they're bigger in the basement than they are on top. Like *icebergs*.'

Maybe it's all the bleach she gets put in her hair every six weeks.

Maybe she should stop chewing on it.

'Oh duh!' Dior laughs loudly at her stupidity, as

only the daughter of a billionaire tech start-up who will never need a job can. 'Am I not just the *silliest*? But look!'

She gestures proudly at a half-million-pound packed wine cellar to our right – locked, obviously – and then swishes past a darkened mini cinema (Make-out Room), a spa (Nap Area), a large exotic indoor garden, and – oh for the love of—

'Dior, is that a flaming *bowling alley*?'

'Sure is.' She nods proudly as we go down another level and it stretches out in full neon to our left. 'Mummy *really* likes to bowl now and then, so we thought – why not make our own? Then we don't have to rent icky shoes.'

Yup: I am in the house of a family who built an entire subterranean Megabowl instead of just *purchasing bowling footwear*. That's the problem with new-money families: you can't buy class, common sense isn't genetic and wealth is totally wasted on the wealthy.

'Bowling is for losers,' I tell her calmly. 'Congratulations.'

Mercy.

Dior's face falls momentarily – punctured – then she spots someone behind me and perks up again.

'*OhmyGodohmyGodohmyGODDDDD!*' The shriek is piercing and uncomfortable, like chewing on a ball of cotton wool. 'Cee! Ceeeeee, you came! What do you think? Isn't it just the *best* birthday party? Aren't I *the luckiest*?'

I cringe as Amethyst – sorry, *Mee* – wraps her skinny tanned arms round my neck.

'Don't touch me,' I say, extricating myself.

'Sorry, Cee.' Amethyst is the glossy daughter of a supermodel and an international surgeon: her nose has already been edited, her lips are scheduled next. 'I'm just so, *so* excited. Eighteen today! *Eighteen! A legit adult!* And such a *good* idea to have the party here, Vee! Dee's house is just *so* much cooler than mine.'

'Vee' – Nova – progeny of a celeb musician and an oh my God I can't be bothered to even finish this sentence – grabs her arm and shakes it fondly. 'You're worth it, gorgeous bestie.'

'No, *you're the gorgeous one*,' Amethyst trills.

'*You are.*'

'No, *you are.*'

'You're both minging trolls,' I conclude flatly, taking a drink from a random passing boy. 'And I'll have that.'

Yup. Cee, Mee, Vee, Dee: together we're like a freaking vocal warm-up for *The Sound of Music*.

With distaste, I smooth down my waist-length dark red wig and stare around the basement. It's carnage. Palm trees are being scaled, shoes thrown, songs bellowed, some dimwit has pulled a T-shirt up over his head and drawn a face on his belly.

Girls are fluttering, boys are peacocking.

'Why, *hello* there,' a shiny orange guy with black hair twinkles, sliding a bronzed hand around my waist. 'My name is Dylan Harris, TV Star from Netflix. How do you—'

'I will rip your arm off at the shoulder,' I say without looking at him. 'I will rip it off, I will sharpen it with my teeth, then I will shove it into your mouth so hard your ears fall off.'

'O-kay,' he says slowly, backing away.

What does a girl have to do around here to be left alone?

Then why come to a party in the first place?

'Cee, are you coming?' Dior squeaks into my face, wiggling her bottom like she's constipated. 'There's a special *dancefloor*; it's glass and it lights up when you stand on it!'

'Ohmygoshohmygosh,' Amethyst exhales. 'Dancing is, like, *compulsory* on your birthday!'

'Totally,' Vee nods, pulling us all towards a crowded room filled with shimmering turquoise light, as shockingly bad music bursts into the air. 'Oh my gosh, Daddy wrote this song for my sweet sixteenth!'

And I just nearly dry-gagged up my dinner.

The girls grab hands in a circle and attempt to grab mine too. I shake them off and stick my hands in my pockets.

'I just wish,' Dee says, with an elaborately sad face, 'that Tee was here to celebrate with us.'

'Me too,' Vee pouts. 'To Tee!'

'To Tee!' Mee cheers as they clap hands together.

The three Birdbrains twirl off across the room like dropped pennies and I scowl at the crowd. Beautiful faces are lit with the kind of happiness that comes from being unable to conceive of a time when they won't be perfect, when their lives won't be perfect, when everything around them won't be the epitome of flawless, priceless perfection.

All I want to do is rip my eyes out and shove them up my nostrils just for something else to focus on.

Look at the floor.

Blinking, I stare at my feet. Beneath them, the solid-glass floor is turquoise and flickering because – I narrow my eyes – underneath it is . . . *water?* This moronic family have put a *swimming pool* under a transparent dancefloor. Which means—

Yes! Do it. Do it. Do it.

Obviously I'm doing it. With nobody looking, I make my way to the edge of the room.

Do it!

Subtly, I slide my hands over the marble walls until I feel a little lever tucked away behind yet another fairy-lit imported palm tree. Pausing, I pick at the scab on my hand while I watch the crowds for a few minutes: full of joy and so very, very dry.

For the first time tonight, I smile.

NOW, Mercy!

'I'm *doing* it,' I say out loud.

And I pull the lever.

2

See? I'm distinctly unpleasant.

'Give me a kiss.'

'Only if you give me a kiss first.'

'I'm going to kiss your gorgeous chin.' *Mwah.* 'Look at it!' *Mwah.* 'Have you ever seen anything more adorable?' *Mwah.* 'I ask you. Does Ben not have the best chin you have ever seen on a human being?'

The goldfish-sucking sound pauses.

Apparently it's not rhetorical: my little sister Hope is asking everyone for their opinion on the pointy end of her new boyfriend's stupid face. I've only been awake twenty minutes but I'd rather be rubbed all over by a waiter with a cheese-grater than witness any more of this pathetic budding romance.

'It looks like an elbow,' I say shortly, picking at a slice of toast. 'And if you don't stop cooing, I'm going to puke my breakfast onto the table and rub both your faces in it.'

'Mercy!' Ben's mum (our housekeeper) frowns at me.

'Don't be mad, Mags,' I add equitably. 'I'll make sure to leave some for you to clean up.'

Sure, Benjamin may be hotter than when we were kids, but my little sister is looking at the dude like my entire family hasn't seen him shove a finger in his ear, examine the wax and then wipe it on his jeans.

'Don't listen to the devil-child,' Max says, leaning over and scruffing up my hair. 'Mermaid is just upset that she accidentally made a party *more* fun last night, instead of less.'

I hit him, hard. 'Did not.'

'Did so,' my brother grins, rubbing the top of his bicep. 'You sent everyone crashing into a swimming pool, just like in *It's a Wonderful Life*. Bit derivative, but everyone loved the drama. It's already gone viral.'

'One girl cried,' I grumble defensively.

'Only one? You're losing your Machiavellian touch.' Max laughs, getting his phone out and pointing it at me. 'Better luck spreading unhappiness next time, sis. Comments on your failure?'

I glare at him, then at the empty seat.

By the time I got back from Dior's, Faith had gone. Four weeks ago, my middle sister broke up with her dullard pop-star boyfriend, had a meltdown and shaved her head. She then reached a compromise with our parents. She's allowed to rent her friend Scarlett's scabby studio flat in Brixton during the day, as long as she returns to our mansion every night. My party schedule is the opposite, so we now rarely see each other.

Not that I care. Effie's absence makes no difference to me at all.

I kick her chair with my foot.

'Oh my goodness,' Hope breathes at Ben, her cheeks flushed. She kisses him again. *Mwah.* 'Ben-jamin-o, I swear you are pacifically –' *mwah* – 'the most handsome guy –' *mwah* – 'I have ever seen in my life.'

Mwah mwah mwah.

Ben laughs – 'Finally you've noticed.' – and kisses her back. Max and I glance at each other. Either of us going to tell the nitwit it's *specifically*?

She starts at her new school soon – they can deal with it.

'That's strange,' I say, standing up and folding my arms. 'Because, Hope, that's exactly what you said about Jamie, isn't it?'

There's a chunky silence.

'You *do* remember Jamie, don't you?' I make my face innocent. 'The Californian? Tall, blond, ripped, total narcissist? You were madly in love with him? Said he was your perfect guy? Ran away to America to be with him and everything?'

Everyone is looking at the table. Maggie slams some plates into the sink.

'Oh, *whoops,*' I exhale, putting a hand over my mouth. 'Were we not supposed to talk about him? My bad.'

All the light has trickled out of Hope. Guilt pinches my stomach.

There was no need for that, Mercy.

'Just saying it as it is,' I shrug defensively.

'You can be a heartless cow sometimes, Mer,' Ben says quietly, squeezing Hope's hand. 'You know, just saying it as it is.'

'Guess that's why Merciless got her new job,' Max

growls, taking our little sister's side as always. 'Playing a gobby nightmare is hardly a stretch.'

'Jamie was a mistake,' Po mumbles. 'I know that now.'

There's another solid silence.

This is the bit where Faith would say something sweet to break the tension, or my twin Charity would make a joke; Dad would be loud and American or Mum would swoop in, playful and wry.

But they're not here and the whole family tilts somehow.

'Whatever,' I sigh, walking out of the kitchen. 'Love is pathetic and so are all of you.'

And I slam the door behind me.

Four years ago

'Timing is everything.' Charity wraps a family photograph in silver. 'We must work together seamlessly.'

'Like in a battle,' I nod, swaddling a pillow.

'Indeed,' my twin agrees, smoothing out the newly shiny dresser. 'Strategised for ultimate hilarious impact.'

We grin at each other and survey our handiwork.

Every single thing in Hope's room is covered in tinfoil. The cushions, the books, the beloved Hollywood posters, the pencils, the rug, the entire bed and its posts. Even her favourite cuddly toy dog Rocket has been given a miniature silver suit, although we've left his face out because we don't want him to suffocate. It took all morning and cost literally our entire allowance, but it was totally worth it. Our little sister's bedroom looks like an oven-ready jacket potato.

'Mischief approved,' Charity nods in satisfaction. 'Time?'

I look at my watch. 'Twelve fourteen.'

'Sixteen minutes left.'

As always, Tee is the architect of this prank. She's gleaming, her pupils are dilated, her breath has quickened. It's weird how I notice these details on her; how I know her better than I know me.

'Ready?'

'Always.'

'Army of two,' Charity grins at me.

'Army of two,' I echo back.

And I remember – as I do sometimes, in surprising little lurches – that apart from a tiny scar in Charity's left eyebrow, to most of the world we are one person doubled: copied and pasted next to each other as if by some giant, genetic computer.

'GO!' my twin shouts, and we split: careering haphazardly around the Valentine mansion like matching pinballs.

I take care of Mum first: a huge spider goes in her closet while she's in her en-suite bathroom. Then Little Miss Perfect Faith gets a motion-activated fart machine in her backpack. In the meantime, Tee prepares the prank for Grandma (a life-size movie poster of her looming behind the front door), Dad (foghorn attached under his office chair) and Max (fake loo-roll in the downstairs toilet).

Breathless, we leg it back to our bedroom. Technically, we have two bedrooms – hers is yellow, mine navy – but as with everything in our lives, we have always considered them both *ours*.

'Mission complete?' Charity whispers as we hop conspiratorially on top of the primrose duvet.

'Mission achieved,' I confirm warmly.

Huddled together, we listen to Mum's shower-pump switch off, Eff's bedroom door open, Grandma and Hope return in the limo, Dad come in from taking a break in the garden, Max lock himself into the toilet.

'Ten,' Tee whispers solemnly.

'Nine,' I intone.

'Eight.'

'Seven.'

'You *know*,' my sister says, holding her fingers in the air. 'It's less like a *battle* and more like a *symphony*. The right notes in the right places, blending perfectly. A cacophony of chaos.'

I laugh. 'You're evil. Six.'

'Five.' Charity makes little horns, closes her eyes and smiles blissfully. 'I prefer the term Mistress of Mayhem.'

'Four. Debatable.'

'Three. Certifiable.'

'Two. We'll see.'

'We will. *One*.' A fraction of a pause, my sister breathes in and swings her hands out like a conductor, and a honk blasts out—

'AAAAAAAAAAAGGGHHHHHHHHHHH HHHHHHHH!!!!'

'Oh goodness gracious!'

'What the actual—'

'That's not me!' *Fart.* 'It's not!' *Fart. Fart.* 'I swear it's not me!' *Fart fart fart.*

'I AM GOING TO STRING YOU UP! GET BACK HERE, YOU LITTLE—'

Thump, thump, thump . . .

'Yay, *aliens*!'

Satisfied, Charity collapses on the bed, and I crumple with her: snorting and giggling, scrambled together. Like the framed sonograph in Mum's bedroom, it's not always easy to know where one of us ends and the other begins.

'Now for the chorus,' my other half chuckles.

Beaming, Tee raises her hands like a conductor again and we hold our breath.

We wait a few seconds.

Then – from around the massive house – all we hear, yelled in unison, is: 'CHARRRIIITYYYYY!!!'

4

'Mistress of Mayhem'? Idiot.

What kind of ridiculous thirteen-year-old casually uses the word 'cacophony' anyway?

Scowling, I fling a black Gucci dress over my shoulder.

'Are you *kidding me*,' I growl as I chuck a pair of black Prada trousers on top of it and continue wading angrily through my giant walk-in closet. 'All I ask for is some *respect*.'

I check the label of a black jumpsuit: nope.

'The common *decency* to leave my stuff alone.' Another jumpsuit: nope. 'To be able to walk into my own wardrobe and get ready for my first day at my brand-new job without having my carefully curated possessions missing.'

I rifle through a pile of stinking, night-club steeped clothes on the floor. Why can't Maggie just come directly into my closet and source my dirty laundry for herself? What kind of housekeeper is she, anyway?

'But no, the airhead poo-bag feels free to waltz in –' a black shirt gets thrown into the corner – 'and take whatever she wants –' then a black corset-top, 'and run away with it –' a black scarf. 'Then when I need my silk Yves Saint Laurent jumpsuit, my *thief* of a sister has gone and—'

Oh. There it is.

Look a bit stupid now, dontcha.

I snort. 'It probably didn't fit her, so whatever.'

Glowering, I yank the jumpsuit on. Then I pull my straightened, thick black hair into a smooth bun, tug on spike-heeled black boots – the kind you can use as weapons should the need arise – rim my eyes with black liner and dab on dark purple lipstick.

I need to make sure I look suitably off-putting. There are enough muppets in my life already without accidentally collecting more of them at work.

That's a lot of black, Mer.

'I like black. It's my favourite colour.'

No, it's not.

'It is. It's sophisticated and brutal and makes me look like a fierce warrior goddess.'

It's joyless and boring. Your favourite colour is red.

'Pfff.' I tidy up the edge of a lip with a black-painted nail. 'Maybe when I was little. Red like *blood.*'

Red like roses. Like lipsticks. Like HEARTS.

'Like danger,' I correct sharply. 'Stay away from me, that's what red says.'

Red like carpets. Like I'm going to be a famous actress one day, loved by the whole world, just like my mummy.

'Ha!' I roll my eyes. 'Nobody wants to be like that crazy locked-up nightmare. She's an embarrassment to the Valentines.'

And you're talking to yourself in the mirror.

'Shut your face.'

Only because it's your face too, hahaha.

Scowling, I flip the mirror so it reflects the ceiling, grab my black Gucci handbag, shove my script in along with some random makeup and swing it over my shoulder.

Purple doesn't really suit you either, FYI.

I'm not going to even dignify that with a response. Double-locking my bedroom door behind me, I march crossly down the stairs. My baby sister's already lurking. The audacity is almost impressive.

'Don't,' I say sharply as Po emerges from the library.

'Huh?'

'I'm warning you, little girl, I will unleash a *universe* of pain. I will rip open the fires of hell and pour them over your head until your brain boils.'

Hope blinks and cocks her head to the side. She has such a sweet, pretty face: heart-shaped and wide-eyed. Who would guess that underneath it is a ruthless sartorial plunderer?

'Gosh,' she says in her eternally positive voice. 'How dramatic! Would a brain boil, do you think? Or fry? How can we find out without hurting anyone?'

Seriously, I might as well try to threaten a baby hedgehog.

'Don't steal my clothes,' I conclude uselessly.

'Okay!' Hope nods and beams at me. 'Oooh, can we gossip for a second, Mer? I happen to have *information.*'

For the love of—

'No.' I grab my keys off the table as Po follows

me through the hallway anyway, bouncing on her tiptoes.

'*Well,*' she breathes with a hasty glance to either side, like a cartoon spy, 'I have reason to believe that our big brother has a *very important secret.*'

She waits expectantly for her news to make impact.

I open the front door. 'Don't care.'

'And after some thorough investigation . . .' Hope continues proudly – 'which started at breakfast and finished just now –' so fifteen minutes total, move over Sherlock Holmes – 'I have certained that—'

'*As*certained.'

'No, Mercy, I have become *certain.*' Hope's expression is patient, as if I'm a challenging but rewarding student. 'So, the word we're looking for is *certained.*'

'Actually, the word we're looking for right now is *ass.*'

The Valentine family limousine is waiting for me in the driveway, and I've got an important script to scan in the luxurious silence of a chauffeur intelligent enough to stay quiet. Instead, I'm inexplicably listening to the ramblings of a sister who clearly is not.

Sighing, I stomp down the stone porch steps.

'He's got a secret girlfriend!' Hope squeaks after me, unable to contain the 'surprise' any longer. 'Max is in a relationship!!! I worked it out all by myself! He keeps disappearing and taking selfies and making videos of himself! It's love!'

Don't say it. Don't say it. Come on, don't—

'Congratulations,' I snap over my shoulder. 'Me and Faith worked that out about a month ago. Well done, Einstein.'

Disappointment flickers over my little sister's face.

Nice one, Mercy.

'And you didn't tell . . .' Hope swallows and rallies as I open the limo door. 'Well, it's okay! Because I'm going to find out exactly who Max loves, then I'll know more than you do!'

Just say something nice. Or smile. Just a quick—

'That's highly unlikely, you simpering moron.'

Climbing in and shutting myself away with a *click,* I close my eyes and pick at the painful scab on my hand until the guilt has passed.

Then I open my eyes again.

'Well?' I snap. 'What are you looking at? Drive.'

5

I do know what happiness feels like.

When I'm on stage or in front of a camera, Mercy Valentine dissolves and I become someone else: a different person with a different life and a different past. Suddenly my words aren't mine any more, my thoughts and emotions are replaced. Even my memories belong to someone else.

My decisions have different consequences.

So, yeah, I think you get where I'm going with this little soliloquy.

Happiness is . . . not being me.

'She's here!' Verity Ramirez glances pointedly at her watch as I stomp into the Globe Theatre, demanding attention with my razor heels. 'Just on time! Everyone, I am delighted to introduce you to our brand-new heroine, Mercy Valentine!'

With no theatrical glamour whatsoever, the entire cast and crew are stuffed into a tired back room. Temporary trestle tables have been pushed together like some kind of cheap wedding buffet, scripts laid out in place of cutlery, and roughly twenty sets of eyes are fixed curiously on me.

I hold my hand up briefly by way of greeting.

'And *yes*,' my new director adds brightly, black bob and thick-rimmed cliché tortoiseshell glasses shining under faintly flickering neon. 'I appreciate that as *thespians* we're *big fans* of the Valentine family, but let's try to keep it professional, shall we?'

I slam my bag on one of two spare chairs.

'Are you suggesting I got this job because my family is famous?' I sit down with my arms folded and scowl at her. 'You're lucky to have me. I'd like to see another actor lead *Much Ado* at the last minute.'

A few days ago, the retro loser playing Beatrice in *Much Ado About Nothing* smashed her ankle roller-skating, two weeks before opening night. Frankly – as I told my agent – taking the expression 'break a leg' literally is so pathetic I could cry.

'Oh, gosh, no! No nepotism here!' Verity turns to

the rest of the cast. 'Mercy is an incredibly skilled actress and we're very grateful to get someone of her media visibility in at such late notice!' She laughs tightly. 'We certainly paid through the nose for the honour, hahaha!'

Ego smoothed, I nod faux-graciously.

The rest of the cast smiles warmly, so I do one of those creepy smiles back: the kind where you stretch your mouth out tightly and briefly widen your eyes so nobody knows for sure if it's real or sarcastic even though it's pretty clearly the latter.

'Obviously *we* know each other,' Verity continues with forced enthusiasm. 'But as this run through is specifically to settle Mercy in, why don't we all introduce ourselves?'

The very pretty redhead playing Hero – so let's call her 'Hero' because I cannot be bothered to start learning IRL names – starts chattering about her hopes, dreams, visions for the future or whatever. Then governor 'Leonato' jumps in, followed by waiting woman 'Margaret' and the play's villain 'Don John'.

One by one, everyone says something so irrelevant I end up slumped on the table with my chin on my arm, picking at my nails and flicking flakes of black nail varnish across the room. They're secondary characters: who gives a furry bum-hat about their back stories?

'I'mmm Daisssssyyyyy but youuuuu can callll me Dayyyy.'

The voice is so slow I am forced to glance up through lowered eyelashes, just to see what kind of moron it's coming from. Daiiissssyyy is roughly my age and has a long face, long fringe, long eyes, long nose, long fingers, long arms, as if she's been stretched out like warm toffee. Also, how hard is it to dye your hair? Keeping your natural colour when it's that colour is just arrogant, if you ask me.

'I'm playing the Second Watchman,' she explains over a period of three hundred years, smiling shyly. 'I know it's just a tiiiiiiiinnnyyyy part but it's my fiiiirrrrsssssst acting role and I can't waaaaaiiiiit to—'

'Awfully sorry, old beans!' An attractive blond dude I suppose – if you like men with their own family crest, which I do not – slinks into the circle wearing jeans, a crisp white shirt and a baby-pink *pashmina*. 'Traffic was dastardly! Apols!' Posh-Boy grins at me with porcelain veneers so large he looks like a pastel zebra. 'Well, hallo thar! You must be my new paramour!'

Obviously, I know of Eli Bickford-Goggins: swishing his blond curtains in the sunshine like a pedigree pony any time the paps are near.

I give him my favourite blank, dead-eyed expression, then roll my eyes slightly. The girl playing 'Margaret' has blushed neon-pink and is staring in visible mortification at the floor. Clearly these two have already had their little failed on-set romance.

What absolute amateurs.

'Our very own hero!' Verity waves Eli towards the other empty chair and I begrudgingly dump my bag on the trestle table instead. 'Always a joy, Elijah! But, and please don't think I'm singling you out, we absolutely *must* arrive on time for rehearsals. I'll have to start locking the doors!'

Everyone but me giggles nervously.

'No, really, I've had enough.' Her smile stretches to breaking point. 'I'll be locking the doors. You won't be let in. Let's crack on, shall we?'

Within seconds Eli Bilbo-Baggins is reciting his full biography – including the hospital he was born in – so I lean back in my chair and gaze at the ceiling of one of the world's most iconic theatres. In the next room, on the other side of this wall, is the most famous stage ever walked upon. This was where Mum's career truly began, twenty years ago. Or whatever you call it when it's over.

A light tapping noise starts behind one of the back-room walls.

I narrow my eyes at it.

'So *that*, in a nut-shellio,' Eli Dingo-Daggins concludes in a voice so posh it could rip the skin off monkeys, 'is the story of how little old me managed to . . .'

Tap tap tap TAP.

'. . . potted history, a *soupçon* of my past some might say . . .'

TAP TAP TAP TAP TAP.

'Oh, I'm *sorreh*,' Posh-Boy swishes his pashmina at the tapping. 'Am I *interrupting* someone?'

The whole cast turns towards the continued noise, and it abruptly becomes that of a very loud electric drill – *DRRRRRRRRRRR* – then stops.

'Oh, hahaha!' Verity's laughter sounds literally nothing like laughter. 'Don't mind Finneas! He practically lives here! Technically stage crew but will do just about anything for a chocolate biscuit!'

Silence, then—

Tap.

Trying not to smile, I stare down at my script.

'Okay, so wharrr was I?' Eli Dunkin-Donut clears his throat in irritation, and then recommences his monologue. 'Ah, yes, as a whipper-snapper I—'

I let out a loud bored sigh.

From across the circle, Hero smiles and lifts an eyebrow at me, so I look away quickly and slump back onto the table. I can sense my new colleagues watching me eagerly, waiting for the slightest opportunity to welcome me to this exciting collective experience with open arms.

What does Don John say? *I cannot hide what I am.*

But why the hell would I want to?

6

Also, I thought this play was supposed to be a comedy.

The cast clearly didn't get the memo.

'Did he break out into tears?' 'Leonato' asks as we finally begin to limp along the actual read-through.

'In great measure,' a messenger nods.

'A kind overflow of kindness.' The old man smiles warmly. 'There are no faces truer than those that are so washed. How much better is it to weep at joy than to joy at weeping!'

The entire cast looks keenly at me for my first line.

'Blimey,' I mutter under my breath. '*I'm* going to start weeping if you don't liven this dross up.'

'I'm sorry?' Verity glances across with a frown. 'Mercy, can you speak a little louder?'

'I SAID,' I shout pettily. 'I PRAY YOU, IS SIGNIOR MOUNTANTO RETURNED FROM THE WARS OR NO?'

'Umm, lovely!' My director clears her throat, unsure what to do with me already. 'Just a tiny note: *remember* that Beatrice is asking after Benedict because she's already crazy about him before the play starts, so try to add a smidge of *nuance* to these lines if you can.'

I eyeball my director flatly.

'Who the bat-bottom is *Benedict*?'

'Ah.' Verity coughs. 'We had to . . . change his name to fit in with a younger cast and audience, move with the times, remain appropriate and so on.'

'Shame.' I glance at Eli, who is now examining a loose thread at the end of his pashmina with an expression of genuine fascination. 'The original name suited him perfectly.'

There's a snigger from somewhere in the rest of the cast.

Honestly, while I'm genuinely delighted to be working at the Globe, I can't believe I've landed my Big Break with a *romance*. I'd have much preferred a tragedy: I'd make a fabulous Goneril, or a kickass, albeit very young, Lady Macbeth. Instead, I'm stuck with some sap about Hero and Claudio, who fall in love without a single decent conversation, and Benedick and Beatrice, who hate each other but are tricked by 'friends' into believing they're in love and getting married.

Shakespeare seems to think that 'romance' means either emotionally committing to someone you barely know or spending forever with someone you can't stand.

At least Beatrice has her head screwed on at the start.

'I wonder that you will still be talking, Signior Benedict,' I sigh at Eli tiredly. 'Nobody marks you.'

'What?' He laughs. 'My dear Lady Disdain! Are you yet living?'

'Is it possible—'

I glance up sharply: Daiiiissssssyyyy is whispering along with my line. I don't know why the world's slowest girl is so invested in this play. The Second Watchman could go for a mani-pedi in the middle of it and nobody would notice.

'*Is it possible*,' I repeat pointedly, 'disdain should die while she hath such meet food to feed it as

Signior Benedict? Courtesy itself must convert to disdain if you come in her presence.'

'. . . I would I could find in my heart that I had not a hard heart.' Eli grins with those impossibly giant teeth. 'For, truly, I love none . . .'

Finally, my *favourite* line. 'I had rather hear my dog bark at a crow, than a man swear . . .'

Except I suddenly feel a bit . . . prickly.

'Mercy?' The director prompts.

'Umm.' I glance at my script again, scratching the back of my neck with my fingernails. 'I had rather hear my dog bark at a crow, than a man swear he loves me.'

I look at my arms: all the hairs are standing on end. Frowning, I glance round the table, but the rest of the cast are focused on their scripts.

And – just like that – the prickle disappears.

I blink.

'Well, you are a *rare parrot-teacher*,' Eli Poopy-Piggins snorts. I'm really not looking forward to our love scenes. He's disturbingly smooth and poreless – it'll be like making out with a hairless cat.

Beatrice isn't present for the rest of the scene, so I get my phone out. Dior has posted a photo of us at last night's party. She looks perfect; I have one eye half shut and a double chin.

Scowling, I write underneath:

Party times are good times. <3 <3

Then I text her:

DELETE IT RIGHT NOW OR I WILL DELETE YOU

My phone *beeps*:

But I look so pretty. :(

Jaw tight, I reply:

Not for much longer if you don't TAKE IT DOWN.

The photo immediately disappears. This is *exactly* why I fought my grandmother for independent control of my social media.

Then I type out a text:

SUP

Beep.

Stand Up Paddleboarding? X

My nostrils twitch.

Yes. I am communicating via the world's most
boring watersport.

Beep.

It's actually really fun. Good for the core. X

Quickly, I smash out:

I am not an apple.

I smile because I know Effie is smiling too, then
add:

Everything okay? I'm worried. I haven't seen
you in ages.

Beep.

Yes! I'm really good! Xx

I frown, unconvinced.

You sure? I saw the headlines about Noah and
his new g—

'Mercy?' I look up briefly: our director's face looks
like a plastic Lego man with a smile drawn on. 'I
know you're not on stage right *now*, but perhaps
you could continue your phone conversation when
everyone in the room isn't having a read-through
purely for your benefit?'

The whole cast is staring at me with slightly open
mouths.

Great first impression, Mer.

'Family emergency,' I snap, sticking my phone
back in my handbag. 'But fine. I guess I'll just leave
my younger sister to battle through her emotional
breakdown on her own, as long as it'll keep you
guys happy.'

Mercy!

What?! I am concerned about Faith! Using her as an excuse for rudeness is a convenient by-product.

'Ooh.' Eli Buzzard-Bullock leans forward, interested in someone other than himself for the first time today. 'And by "sister" are you, per chance, referring to the exquisite angel that is Faith Valentine?'

I narrow my eyes. 'Maybe.'

'Could you possibly get me an *intro*, old bean?' He bares enormous gums at me. 'I read that she was recently dumped, very sad, and I am quite smitten, I tell you.'

'I *would* –' I grimace flatly, holding my hands in the air – 'But we put her in a nunnery as punishment for Not Holding On To Her Man.'

There's that prickle again. Did someone just . . . laugh?

Verity slams the edges of her script on the table unnecessarily hard – 'Right, let's crack on, shall we?' – and we shamble endlessly to the final scene, a full two hours later than supposed to.

'Strike up, pipers!' Benedict concludes, and I push my chair back, stand up and sling my bag over my shoulder.

Hero jumps up simultaneously and follows me out.

'Hey!' She taps me on the shoulder, as if I'm not still pointedly ignoring her. 'Mercy?'

I nod, looking at my watch, even though I know the time.

'A bunch of us go out for a quick burger when we run late like this.' She smiles with alarmingly earnest blue eyes. 'We were wondering if you'd like to join us?'

A handful of cast are lurking behind her, holding their coats and staring at me with friendly, hopeful, slightly awestruck expressions. I stare back for a few seconds, then start laughing.

'Absolutely not,' I chuckle, pushing open the theatre door. 'I'm *Mercy Valentine*. As if I haven't got somewhere better to be.'

Best line I've heard all day.

7

RIDE OR DIE GANG

Dior
Mercy your late!

Nova
YOU'RE late, Dee.

Dior
I am not, I'm standing right next to you!

Nova
rolls eyes

Amethyst
What are you DOING, Cee? This party is LIT,

they've got mini vegan hot dogs! Are you still stuck at that little play?

Mercy
Outside now. Stop calling it a Little Play.

Dior
Much ado about NOTHING, amiright hahahahaha

Amethyst
LOL

Nova
Yasssssssssssssss

Mercy
That's literally the point of the title.

Angling my body sharply, I smooth out my shoulder-length blue wig and lift my chin as imperiously as possible. I'm already regretting the 'pull-you-in' bodysuit underwear. It seemed like a good idea earlier but now it feels like I'm wearing the restrictive swimming costume of a Victorian prude who has little interest in breathing.

'Mercy!' *Flash.* 'Mercy Valentine! Over here!'

'Mercy!' *Flash. Flash.* 'Look this way!'

'Mercy!'

With fierce eyes, I stare at the paparazzi and they stare straight back: the attention warm and addictive on my skin.

'Mercy!' One pap holds his camera up higher. 'Mercy Valentine! How's the new role?'

I admit a small lurch of pride.

'Amazing,' I announce, re-angling myself, putting a hand on one hip and pushing my clavicles out so I look high-fashion. 'I am honoured to follow in my mother's footsteps by playing Shakespeare's iconic Beatrice at the Globe.' I pause for effect. 'Although hopefully I will not follow her all the way to rehab.'

A collective shocked laugh from the paps.

Anything for a headline, huh?

You betcha, baby.

'Any news about Faith?' *Flash.* 'Is she all right? She hasn't been seen for weeks!'

My stomach twists. Tell me about it. They probably know about as much as I do.

'I am not at liberty to discuss my family's personal business,' I answer firmly, turning a different way. 'I can only speak for myself.'

A short, disappointed silence.

'Although,' I add – switching my expression to tearful and brave – 'I hope that my sister's recent emotional difficulty has gone some way to destigmatising the mental health problems of even the most successful and beautiful.'

Mercy! Stop using Faith for attention!

Effie doesn't want the fame, so why can't I take hers instead?

'And, Mercy, how are—'

'Why, hello there!' A semi-dressed Dee sidles up and hooks on to my arm, wearing what appear to be clothes designed for a small dog. 'I'm Dior Nguyen, *best friend* of party girl Mercy Valentine!'

Irritated – there goes my big solo interview opportunity – I smile for the cameras: *five, four, three, two* . . .

Then I peel the muppet off me.

'You know,' Dior whispers as we head towards

the lift of the ludicrously named Gherkin. (What next? Crisp Steeple? Nugget Tower?) 'Mummy and Daddy were *fuming* about the water trampled through our house after the party! They were, like, "That Mercy, she's a bad egg, huh? I blame absent parents." And I was, like, our house is soooooo famous now – you should be stoked! Haha!'

The lift doors *ping* open halfway up and I frown at a snogging couple with a sizable age gap. Ah, the culturally accepted exchange of looks and youth for power and money.

Or maybe they just really like each other.

'Cute,' I say flatly. 'Babysitting can be just *so* rewarding, huh.'

They abruptly peel apart.

Why do you always have to be so cynical?

'I think you mean *realistic*.'

'Huh?' Dior frowns as the doors close again. 'What did you say?'

'Nothing.'

Arms folded, I lean against the wall of the lift until the doors finally swing open to reveal the domed, bright purple-lit fortieth floor. The room is packed full to its exposed steel rafters. Everyone here is either recognisable or trying very hard to be.

Dior squeezes my arm again with a hand that she's going to lose if she's not very careful.

I shake her off and look for the other two.

'*Babes!!!!*' Amethyst and Nova immediately appear, looking achingly try-hard in their matching, frothy layers. '*At last!* Oh my goodness, you missed *all* the drama! He –' they nod at an A-list actor – 'just hit on *her* –' they nod at a model – 'even though everyone knows she's secretly dating—'

'Stop talking,' I interrupt, picking at my knuckle. 'You're boring me.'

Dee, Mee and Vee glance at each other.

'You know,' Nova pouts, sticking her bottom lip out. 'You can be really hurtful sometimes, Cee.' She lifts her chin. 'Tee would never have spoken to us the way you do.'

'Well, Tee's not here,' I snap, spotting Faith's pathetic ex-boyfriend holding court in the corner. 'She died two years ago. Remember?'

Shoulders back, I stomp across the room towards Noah. He pretends not to see me, so I ignore my inner loathing, stand realllllllly close and breathe hard through my nose until he acknowledges my intense and creepy presence.

Okay, you're being super weird.

It's a party. I'm allowed to keep myself entertained, aren't I?

'Mercy,' Noah snaps. 'I don't want to talk to you.'

'Oh no.' From out of the corner of my eye, a curious journalist with an eye for a headline is already swinging towards us. 'The deprivation of your famously tedious conversational skills will be a great loss to me, Mediocre Pop Star. How's getting over my beautiful sister going?'

Noah goes pink. 'For your information, I'm seeing a very nice—'

'Yeah, I saw the pic. Downgrade!'

'Screw—' Noah spots the journalist and forces a fake smile. He clearly knows now that I put on a wig, broke into his after-show party and intentionally snogged him while he was dating Faith, then sent the photos to the papers so she'd find out. 'Screw you, it's none of your business,' he hisses through a charming grin, putting his arm round me for a photo as I try not to flinch.

'Of course it is.' I smile brightly. *Flash*. 'Eff is my sister.'

'You're a bad sister and a bad person,' Noah whispers, kissing my cheek. Ugh. *Flash*. 'You destroyed our relationship because you can't bear to see anyone happy. Do you even know what love is?'

'Does anyone?' I shrug off his arm and we beam at each other and clink glasses. *Flash*. 'And Faith *wasn't* happy, you total cretin, that's why she's not with you any more.'

Noah flushes and looks away. 'How do you sleep at night?'

'On my back,' I hiss. 'Like a vampire.'

A quick last shared grin for the camera – *flash* – and I march off: temporarily sated, like I've poked at an itch I couldn't quite reach.

Was that fun?

'Absolutely,' I confirm cheerfully, taking two glasses from a waiter and glancing around the room. 'Ten out of ten, highly recommend, would do again. Who's next?'

There's a failed TV presenter with a famous anger-management problem: I could poke that and see what happens. Or a guy wearing so much hair gel I could completely destr—

'Ceeeeeee!' The Birdbrains are back. 'You won't *believe* who just said hi to Dee! The guy that was the face of—'

Are they really this boring now?

Yup.

What happened to them?

Dunno. Boobs?

Hahaha.

Distractedly, I scan the room again looking for a weak link: a football player, his girlfriend, a radio DJ—

'So Mee said—'

'And then Vee said—'

'So then Dee said—'

Narrowing my eyes, I spot a lost-looking redhead teenage model. Rolling my shoulders back, I lick my canine teeth and prepare to pounce. A flicker of familiar, mean excitement rushes through me. It's time to get this party mov—

There's a tiny *ping* and something forces me to turn round just as the lift doors slide open. A middle-aged woman shambles into the room. She's skeletal and pale with ratty hair, and is wearing an enormous floor-length manky fur coat that swallows her whole.

My throat closes until I can't breathe.

MUM?

8

Two and a bit years ago

The hot boy scrolls through his phone.

'Hey, snuggle pup,' Charity says, leaning over him and stroking his cheek with her fluffy white coat sleeve. 'Whatcha got there? Looks kinda ritzy to me.'

My nostrils flare; she's off script already.

'Why, honey-bear,' my sister whispers, sticking her ghost finger in poor Blake's ear while he tries to stay in character. 'You know I got a pigeon on my ping-pong table?'

'CUT! CUT CUT CUT!'

'Soo-rrreeeeee!' Charity chuckles at our director. 'Did I do something wrong?'

'Yes,' he sighs. 'And you know that because you've done it wrong fourteen takes in a row.'

My twin shrugs and twinkles at me.

Alarmed, I slide down in my chair, tucked into the darkness at the back of the set. I don't want anyone to think I'm encouraging Charity's screw-ups or that she's doing it to impress me. For once, I'm not the intended audience.

'But I'm a ghost!' Tee explains faux-innocently. 'He can't see me!'

'It doesn't give you licence to stick your fingers wherever you want to,' the director says in frustration. 'And 1920s slang is historically accurate; you can't just make it up as you go along.'

'Oh, oh, here's a goody, why don't scientists trust atoms?' My sister does an eyebrow wiggle and holds out her hands. 'Because they *make up everything*.'

Blake laughs and *boom*: target achieved. My sister has had a crush on our cute co-star for ages. If there's a way to make him laugh she'll do it, even at the expense of her career.

Correction. *Our* career.

'I give up.' The director holds his hands out in affectionate exasperation. 'Where's your sister? Mercy?'

'Here!' I spring from the shadows. 'I'm here!'

I'm already dressed and made-up in an identical 1920s costume: silver-fringed flapper dress, ashy hair and ghostly greyed skin.

'Mercy, please take Charity's place. *Again.*'

I glance guiltily at Tee, but she winks – completely unfazed – and my shoulders loosen.

The director assesses me. 'You know the lines?'

'Yes.'

'Good.' He sighs. 'As always, that makes one of you.'

Charity flings me the huge white fur coat and blows a jubilant kiss to Blake. He blushes pink, and – giddy with her romantic success – my sister takes the seat I've just left. She sits there grinning with her elbows on her knees, chin propped in her hands like an adorable, mischievous elf.

I pull the ginormous fur coat on, affection blending with irritation. *My Boo* has only been on air a few months, but it's already watched by millions.

Why can't Charity, for *once*, take something seriously?

'Places,' the director barks as I stand exactly where my twin stood five minutes ago. 'Quiet on set.'

Tee nods and makes an elaborate zipping motion with her fingers.

I clear my throat and focus on the scene.

'Roll sound.'

'Sound is speeding.'

'Episode thirty-six, scene one, take fifteen.'

'Set.'

'Action!'

And I melt into character: a wave of happiness pulsing through me like an electric current.

'Hey,' I say as a hundred-year-old dead, lonely and lovesick teenager, crossing the room towards Blake. 'Snuggle pup, whatcha got there? Looks kinda ritzy to me.'

The scene plays out perfectly: done in one take.

'CUT! Break for lunch. Superb as always.'

Glowing, I turn towards my twin to exchange a jubilant air-five. Then I frown, blinded by the set lights. Someone is standing next to Tee but it's neither Maggie nor Mr Gilbert, our normal chaperones. In fact, it looks like—

'*Mum?*'

'Hello, darling.' My mother gives me her world-famous, mega-watt smile as I attempt to nonchalantly saunter over so fast I nearly trip on a camera wire. 'I see I got here just in time.'

'But . . .' I'm so excited to see her my voice has gone all pitchy. I cough and attempt to lower it. 'I thought you were shooting again today?'

'We finally got a day off.' She's so beautiful. 'And I thought I'd spend it watching my girls in action. Weren't you amazing?'

My glow gets brighter. 'Really? I was?'

'Oh my gosh.' My mother beams at me, her grey eyes dazzling. 'Even better than I was at your age. That is a lovely coat, by the way. It really suits you, my darling. I'll put a word in, see if we can take it home with us.'

I'm about to burst with pride like a pigeon on antacid.

'She was quite good, right?' my sister agrees solemnly, her eyebrow scar covered by makeup. She nods at the empty chair with *Charity Valentine* written on it. 'I guess Tee's the most talented actress in the family, huh?'

My glow flickers, my stomach falls. Mum laughs and reaches forward to hug Charity.

'Nice try,' she says, kissing her hair and smiling

at me over Tee's shoulder. 'But I know the difference between my twins. Good job, *Mercy*.'

And, just like that, the glow is back.

9

'Mum?'

I try to move towards her, but my heels feel bolted to the floor.

'And would you *believe* that then Dee said—'

'I did not!'

'You so did! It was totally—'

How has nobody noticed my mother yet? Why are conversations continuing? Why is music still playing, as if one of the most famous women in the world hasn't just stumbled into the room after months of hiding away in the dark?

Because she doesn't look like Mum any more.

I swallow.

'He definitely fancied me because you know what they say about eye contact and he was totally – Cee? Are you listening? Cee?'

What's she doing here?

I dunno, finishing off the Valentine name once and for all?

'Cee? What are you—'

Do something! Go over and—

I'm going to!

Now! Before she—

'FOR THE LOVE OF CAT BUMS, FOR ONCE IN YOUR LIFE WILL YOU JUST SHUT THE HELL UP?'

Vee, Mee and Dee stare at me with round eyes.

'I . . . that's not what I—'

'Whatever.' Dior links arms with the other two. 'Come on, girls. I suggest we leave Her Royal Highness to her own fascinating company for an evening and see how much she likes it.'

The Birdbrains march away to the other side of the room and stand pointedly with their backs to me. I don't have time to deal with them; I've got a mother to hide before anyone sees what she's turned into.

With effort, I unscrew myself from the floor, slip round the edge of the room and grab Mum's furry arm. Then I drag her without ceremony behind an enormous vase of purple-lit flowers.

Be gentle, Mercy. Be kind. Try to remember she—

'*Mother*,' I hiss under my breath. 'What the *hell* do you think you're playing at?'

'Oh, hello, darling.' Mum blinks, her thin face empty and drawn. 'It's the *Vanity Fair* party, isn't it? I usually come to the *Vanity Fair* party, don't I?'

'You usually shower and wear deodorant too, but clearly they're not regular habits you're as keen to stick to.'

Alarm is steadily rising. Up close, Juliet Valentine is a mess: deep lines are etched in her skin like dried-out concrete and she has the flaky, porous texture of someone who hasn't been to see our family dermatologist for quite some time.

The white fur coat we were gifted from set years ago is now clumped and yellowed, stinking of dust and mothballs.

And her hair . . . It's greasy, rooted, turning *white*.

My stomach twists.

'Mum,' I say more gently. 'How did you get here? Did the media see you? Where did you get the coat?' I look down and my stomach lurches. 'Where are your *shoes*?'

'There's a secret side door.' My famously stylish mother looks down in faint surprise at her dirty bare toes. 'I found the coat in the back of . . . a cupboard.'

No need to ask which room she's been foraging through like a half-crazed squirrel.

'What are you wearing underneath it?' Another bolt of alarm. 'Mum, *tell me there's something underneath the coat.*'

'Of course there is.' My mother smiles and gently touches my face. 'I just . . . can't remember precisely what, that's all.'

I automatically knock her hand away, brain lurching.

'Right, come with me.'

Holding her fluffy shoulders, I steer her towards the toilets: rotating with careful spins and turns like we're trying to hide a pregnancy on a TV show. Somehow, I manage to squeeze us into the same cubicle without anyone spotting her.

Then I lock the door, breathing hard.

'You look tired, darling.' My mother assesses with a soft but distant expression. 'Are you looking after yourself properly?'

'Shouldn't really have to,' I snap, pulling makeup out of my handbag. 'Hold still.'

With emergency wet-wipes, I scrub my mother's face and feet, then brush her hair and paint her face. There's not much I can do about how skinny she is, but it's a fashion party: everyone will probably ask for tips.

Mum submits to my furious makeover in silence, like a small admonished child.

Finally, I stare at the ratty fur coat.

'Right,' I snap tiredly, rubbing my face. 'Let's see what's underneath this monstrosity.'

Obediently, my mother unbuttons. She's still wearing the disgusting lace nightie she's been floating around in for weeks. Making an abrupt decision, I pull off my boots and Louis Vuitton jumpsuit so I can help her slip into them.

The nightie goes straight into the sanitary bin.

Then, with a twisting sensation in my chest, I tug the coat I once shared with my sister on over my granny unitard, pull the blue wig off and stuff it into my handbag. Suffice it to say, this is not a look I want to draw attention to any more.

'Did you spot Mercy Valentine?' A familiar voice

floats out of the cubicle next to us. 'I cannot *believe* she has the guts to show up here, after what she did to you last time.'

'I *know*, right? You know she's doing *theatre* now? How the mighty have fallen.'

'She's definitely got a *stage* face, if you catch my drift. Better from a distance, hahaha.'

As they giggle, a flush of sweet, liquid rage sweeps through me, and I hang on to it gratefully like a drowning person thrown an unexpected life ring.

'Okay!' I smile fixedly at my mother, click open the cubicle door and lead her out. 'Ready to party?'

Then I spin us both to face the mirrors.

On the upside, Juliet Valentine looks quite wonderful now: elegant, cool, fierce, sophisticated.

On the downside, I look like a homeless polar bear.

'Oh!' My mother blinks at herself in the glass. 'Lovely!'

With another *click*, the TV presenters emerge from their cubicles at the same time, see me and freeze on the spot, blood abruptly draining out of their faces.

Okay, this time I'm on board.

'Girls!' I take a menacing, bare-footed step towards them. 'Or, I should say, *women* ten years older than you pretend on Wikipedia? Next time you see this stage face, you'd better make sure you're much, *much* further away. Do you understand?'

I snarl, lurch forward and – with terrified squeaks – they *meep* and scrabble inelegantly out of the bathroom like two panicked gerbils trapped in one toilet roll tube.

Grinning – that's much better – I turn back to my mother.

She's still clocked out, vague, confused. I realise with a pang that it doesn't matter if she looks like Juliet Valentine, World-famous Movie Star and British Sweetheart, if she still can't *act* like her. Because that's what being famous really is: an eternal performance that you can never put down.

'Mum,' I say gently, staring into her glowing and glossy face. 'You're Juliet Valentine.'

She blinks at me. 'I'm Juliet Valentine.'

'Yes,' I repeat firmly. 'You are *Juliet Valentine*, A-list celebrity and cultural icon. Valentines Always Act With Class.'

Some kind of light goes on at the back of my mother's head.

And she smiles, accepting the role.

10

It's the performance of a lifetime.

Within seconds of re-entering the room, the party has fallen silent. Juliet Valentine is no longer an invisible middle-aged woman, without weight or importance. She is the bright star these planets gravitate towards and spin round.

Aka the power of lipstick and a decent jumpsuit.

'Juliet!' A beauty editor races over. 'Oh my goodness, you're here! How wonderful to see you again! Aren't you *glowing*?'

Not for nothing has my mother been trained by my grandmother for forty years. I watched Faith struggle against those steel-like rules until they nearly broke her, but now I'm watching the same commandments prop my mother up like scaffolding.

Numb to the stomach, I watch as my mother's face softens.

'How sweet of you to say!' Mum smiles beatifically, taking the editor's hand and squeezing it. 'It's a privilege to be here, Cassidy. Thank you so much for inviting me again.'

The floodgates have opened and here comes the tide.

'If it isn't Juliet Valentine! My darling! You've come back to us!'

'How *are* you?'

'You *brave* thing! What tragedy, what strength!'

'I saw *Pinnacle* and it is *your best* work, without a shadow of a doubt! A masterpiece! You're going to win all the big ones, mark my words! Don't call it a comeback!'

Mesmerised, I watch my mother's lovely face: poised, friendly and in control. This is the same woman who ripped our house apart a few weeks ago, looking for a dead girl's baby blanket to sell at public auction.

Now she says: 'I would love to come to your gallery opening!'

She says: 'And how is your handsome son, Charles?'

She says: 'What a beautiful dress you're wearing,

Jessica. *Do* tell me where you got it from, so I can get one *just* like it.'

For a few minutes, I am so in awe of her astonishing performance I actually forget I'm standing chunkily behind her, looking like an oversized Russian hat.

'And you've brought your daughter this year, I see!' A doddery actress – one of Grandma's ancient friends – holds a heavily bejewelled hand out to me. 'Following in the family footsteps, I hear! How *glorious.*'

Her intense eye contact indicates that my bare feet are literally all she can see.

'It's easier to follow people without shoes on,' I grin conspiratorially. 'They can't hear you coming.'

'Haha!' Mum gives a sweet, high laugh, which sounds nothing like her real, throaty one. 'This is Mercy. She has always been the most talented of my girls.'

Then there's a long, awkward silence.

My girls.

And into the gap race Faith, Hope, Charity and me: running around the garden after Mum, climbing into her bed, hanging on to her legs, tweaking her nose, pulling on her hair.

I can see my mother faltering, spiralling, stumbling. The scaffolding loosening.

'I'm afraid we must go,' I say as Mum begins to glaze over: emptying quietly out of her own head like the cinema audience at the end of a film. 'Lots of lovely parties to attend, as I'm *sure* you can imagine.'

I grab my mother's arm and pull her into a waiting lift. I don't know how much longer we have.

I jab at the ground-floor lift buttons.

Jab. Jab. Jab.

'Juliet!' Another actress chases after us breathlessly. *Jab*. 'I just wanted to say that—'

'The Valentines are closed,' I snap. 'Come back tomorrow.'

The doors slide shut, and there's a silence as the lift glides towards the ground. I glance sideways at my mother; she's staring blankly at nothing. And all I can think of is the last time we were alone together. Who am I kidding? I think about it all the time.

Impulsively, I hit every other floor button too.

Jab. Jab. Jab. Jab. Jab.

The lift glides to the thirty-ninth floor, stops and the doors swing open, pause, swing shut again. The lift continues to descend: open, pause, close. Thirty-eighth: open, pause, close. Thirty-seventh . . .

Swallowing, I clear my throat and try to remember what a conversation with my mother even sounds like. She seems faintly present for the first time in a very long time, and this is my big chance. There's a question I desperately need to ask her before she disappears again.

'Mum,' I say finally. Open, pause, close. 'Do you—Ah. I mean, do you ever . . .' Open, pause, close. My cheeks are hot, my stomach churning. 'What I'm trying to say is—'

'*Enunciate*, darling,' Mum says glassily. '*Project*. Remember, the audience must hear *every word*.'

I scowl, then realise she's just reciting Grandma's dumb lessons on autopilot. 'I guess I just want to know . . .'

Anxious, I take a deep breath and hold it as the lift drops another four floors: eighteenth . . . seventeenth . . . sixteenth . . . fifteenth . . .

Then I burst out: 'Do you ever feel like a part of you is gone?'

Mum continues to stare ahead – unmoving and unblinking – and I wait, tensely, hoping she heard me, as the lift continues to drop: fourteenth, thirteenth . . .

Finally, she whispers: 'Your child is always a part of you.'

'Yeah.' I nod, swallowing. 'Of course. But I mean more . . . literally. Like . . . a part of *you* is gone. A part that wasn't . . . Charity. Like she . . . took it with her when she went.'

Silence again. Twelfth, eleventh—

I try again.

'It's just . . .' We drop to floor ten, and my voice feels raw and weightless. 'I thought grief was this temporary thing, Mum. I thought it was something you healed from, you know? Dealt with, moved on from, left behind eventually. But I'm starting to think that maybe something inside you dies too and never comes back.'

Silence. Ninth floor. Eighth floor. Seventh floor. Sixth, and I'm suddenly so full of white-hot sadness and disappointment I feel like I'm about to shatter.

'Mum, *please*,' I sob in a shaky voice. 'I saw you in there. You can switch back on for everyone else, can't you do it for me? Just for a minute? *Please?*'

Turning, I stare directly at Mum's perfect profile.

She blinks once, very slowly, and opens her mouth, and it feels like maybe this is it, maybe there's a tiny bridge forming between us, maybe she understands in a way that nobody else can, so I take a deep breath and blurt—

'Do you ever feel like now you're just—'

Ping.

The doors swing open and a bleached-blonde woman walks in, freezes and stares at my mother speechlessly.

I'm going to destroy her. I'm going to rip this silent stranger apart and smear her internal organs across the inside of this lift because that's it: the first real conversation I've had with my mother in two years, over.

In silence, the three of us sink to the ground.

Ping.

The doors swing open and the world lights up.

'Bad,' I finally finish as my mother walks out.

Flash. 'Juliet Valentine!' *Flash.*

'Juliet!' *Flash flash.* 'Does this appearance mark your public return?' *Flash.* 'Have you recovered from your breakdown?' *Flash flash.* 'Are you still divorcing Michael Rivers?'

'Juliet!' *Flash.* 'Smile for us!'

'You look amazing!' *Flash.* 'Do you have a response to the recently emerged images of your husband with an unknown American in her forties?'

Flash flash flash flash.

In horror, I watch as my mother holds her breath and glides towards them. She attempts to straighten her thin shoulders, lifts her chin and faces the paparazzi.

They wait, the air solid with anticipation.

'I,' Mum says. 'Am. Very.'

And that's it: end of sentence. My mother fades into silence and stands there, blinking, and I realise she's run out of steam, the scaffolding has collapsed, the performance is over.

Mercy, help her!

Impulsively, I run out of the lift with no real plan.

'Blimey,' one of the paps whispers as I throw myself bodily in front of my mother and hold my arms out. 'What rancid ditch did Mercy Valentine roll out of this time?'

Blinking, I stare down at the gross fur coat.

Do it.

What am I wearing underneath again?

Half a wetsuit.

Swallowing, I lift my gaze and stare directly at the paps.

'I am the greatest actress that has ever lived!' I scream. 'Everybody, look at MEEEEEEE!'

And I unbutton the coat and drop it to the floor.

Hours later, I crawl into Effie's bed.

Here's your summary: I chaperoned Mum home, apologised to the Birdbrains over text and convinced them to meet me at a nightclub. Stuck the blue wig back on, danced on a few tables. Climbed into the DJ booth to redirect flagging party vibes. Got thrown out and given yet another life-ban. Threw a box of chips across the road at a wolf-whistler. Ran down the pavement with bare feet, the girls giggling, ripping their shoes off too and chasing after me.

You know, standard Tuesday night.

Now the morning light is coming up and Eff is still fast asleep: knees tucked up, back curled, hands gripped into fists like a kid. Only Faith Valentine could look this angelic while dribbling.

Too tired to take the bodysuit off, I gently lie next to my sister. She stirs and I turn towards her, studying her gorgeous face for some kind of clue as to how she's really feeling. Faith hides beneath a veneer of icy perfection, and I'm scared she's doing it again. I'm scared I'll wake up to more smashed mirrors, that she hasn't really forgiven me for what I did to her, that I'm losing her too.

'Faith?' I whisper. 'Are you awake?'

'No,' she mumbles back.

'Is everything okay?' I study her outline in the darkness. 'We've not really hung out much since . . .' I destroyed her relationship with Noah because I felt like it.

Eff's eyes open sleepily and she smiles. 'I'm good.'

'You promise?'

'Promise.'

Her beautiful cat-shaped hazel eyes shut again and I don't know if I believe her. 'You'd tell me if you weren't, wouldn't you, Eff? This time, you'd tell me? You wouldn't try to go through it on your own?'

'Yes.' Her voice is blurry. 'Talktomorrowsleepnow.'

Faith throws a long, graceful arm across her face and after a couple of seconds her breathing becomes deep and regular, a tiny rattle at the base of her throat. And there's nothing left for me to do but lie still as the remainder of the night stretches and expands and closes round me like a dark mouth.

It always does this.

It always swallows me.

'Hey,' I whisper when I can't bear any more. 'Are you still there?'

And as always I hear Charity, clear as a bell.

Yes.

VALENTINES ACT WITH ASS!!!

Mercy Valentine hits rock bottom (pictured, left). The actress and it-girl (17) showed off her ample ass-ets last night by dancing in her underwear outside the glitzy *Vanity Fair* London bash, in a cheeky display some have called 'trashy', 'attention seeking' and 'kind of pathetic'.

The solo burlesque coincided with the public return of her mother, Juliet Valentine (41) in stylish black Yves Saint Laurent (pictured, right). Dignified Juliet was a stark contrast to her eldest daughter.

'Mercy can't stand the attention on anyone else,' a close friend of the socialite's claimed afterwards. 'She's always like that! If it's not about Mercy Valentine, she's just not interested. Me, me, me! It's kind of sad, really.'

Class clearly doesn't run in the Valentine family!

Oh, bite me.

'Lights! Cameras! Action! Heeerrrrrre she comes! The most classless of the Valentines! Move aside, guys, so we can get more atrocious bum puns through the door!'

I can murder Max with impunity now, right?

Totally. Vase?

'Screw you.' I pick up a priceless piece of porcelain and lob it hard at my brother's head. It smashes with a satisfying crash on the kitchen wall behind him. 'You're just jealous that it's me on the front pages this morning and not you.'

Max shakes his head in mock sadness. There are the remnants of sandwiches, crisps and half-eaten doughnuts scattered all over the papers. Yet again, I appear to have slept straight through to lunch.

I glance at the clock: nope, nearly dinner.

'Sure.' My brother scratches his head. 'I mean, is it *underwear*, though? Because they *say* it is, but it looks like something plumbers use to insulate boilers.'

I throw an empty mug at him and sit down as it hits the wall too.

'Well, *I* think you look fierce and brave,' Hope says

staring at the photos with unabashed admiration. 'Like a shiny, courageous eel.'

My nose twitches. There's a rustling sound in the pantry, and I turn just in time to see Faith emerging with a handful of Coco Pops that she's delicately popping in her mouth one by one, even though they look exactly like rabbit poop.

'Eff!' I jump up eagerly from the table. 'You're still here!'

Then I flush and cough.

'What I meant was—' I sit back down again, folding my arms tightly and lifting my chin. 'Why are you still here? Aren't you normally ensconced in your dirty little squat all day?'

I study her face carefully, but as always it's serene and closed.

'Meh.' Effie shrugs nonchalantly. 'Free food.'

Then she glances quickly at the papers and lifts her eyebrows. She's wearing her cycling gilet, which I'm guessing means Eff biked to her flat this morning, saw the papers, realised what happened last night, biked back again and waited hours for me to roll out of her bed to see if I'm okay. Ugh, she's such a nice person.

I blink once, slower than usual: I'm fine.

Faith's chin twitches: did you do it to distract the paps from Mum?

I scratch my nose: maybe.

She shortens her upper lip: I love you.

'Greedy muppet,' I snap: I love you too.

'I'm a monster for the carbs.' Eff smiles and throws a Coco Pop at me as I pick the nearest tabloid off the table.

'Or,' Hope mutters as I scan the article again and grit my teeth, 'maybe, Faith, you're the kind of monster who *sells* things that don't belong to you without asking anyone else first if they mind?'

Jaw tight, I get my phone out and type:

Mercy
GUYS STOP TALKING TO THE FLAMING PRESS ABOUT ME

Nova
Wasn't me. But all publicity is good publicity, right?

Amethyst
Not me either. You should be happy, they made you look sort of skinny in the photos. ;)

I stare at the screen impatiently.

Dior is typing, Dior is typing, Dior is typing, Dior is typing.

Mercy
 . . . Spit it out Dior.

Dior
They said they were going to put my name in. :(

My friends, ladies and gentlemen.

'What are you talking about, Po?' Faith asks Hope as I put my phone back in my pocket and look up. 'Baby, are you okay?'

'Mmm-hmm.'

'Hope?'

'Mmm.'

'Talk to me, sweetheart.'

'Of course I'm not okay!' Hope unexpectedly bursts out: 'I am mad in matter of fact, Effie! You sold Elaine! She was my best friend and you *sold* her at auction!'

'Hang on.' Faith frowns and glances at me and Max. We both shrug. 'Your best friend? Are you talking about that little old painting that used to be in our library?'

'Yes!' Hope squeaks with her fists clenched. 'I am! Perch ants I am *obviously* talking about that painting!'

Max, Faith and I glance at each other again, our nostrils flaring.

'Poodle, what's a "perch ant"?'

'It's an ant that doesn't know which way to— Stop laughing at me!' Hope jumps up, incandescent and shiny. 'I can see you all laughing at me! Stop it!'

The three of us collapse in giggles on the table.

Ping.

'You're an idiot,' I snort as I grab my phone and open my email. 'You can't be best mates with an inanimate object – that's the most ridiculous thing I've ever hea—'

My eyes open wide.

From: Finneas O'Connor
To: Mercy Valentine

Mercy,

I hope you had a good evening – it certainly appears so.

I have been given the exhilarating job of informing you that you missed your first full rehearsal of *Much Ado About Nothing* this morning. The director was keen to highlight this genuine mistake – which she's sure it was – but HR was busy and I walked past at the wrong moment so it fell to me; yay, joy, thrilled by this illustrious opportunity, etc.

Please see attached the schedule of future rehearsals, all of which are compulsory. Your agent should have sent you this already. As you can see, you have a costume fitting tomorrow. It is neither voluntary nor optional, as per the nature of most full-time employment.

I do hope you find a way to wake up for it in time.

Best, Finn (stage crew)

I can feel my cheeks burning.

Okay, how was I supposed to know I had a rehearsal today? My agent never sent me a schedule. Or maybe she did, but I was dancing on a table at the time. Regardless, how dare this *Finn* dude berate me? He's not even cast: he's *stage crew*.

'I am *so* sorry,' Effie says gently, reaching out for Hope's arm as she snatches it away. 'Darling, I had no idea. Honestly. What can I do to fix this?'

'Crikey,' my brother laughs loudly. 'Calm down, both of you. We'll get you a new painting, Hope. What would you like? Bunnies? Kittens? Ben on the back of a horse?'

Frowning, I look at my phone again.

I am *Mercy Valentine*. This random clearly doesn't know how to communicate with a real-life star.

'You can't just replace friends, Max!'

With a scowl, I hit REPLY.

From: Mercy Valentine
To: Finneas O'Connor

I don't know what kind of plebeians you are used to dealing with, but I will *not* be spoken to like that. I am a VALENTINE. I am playing BEATRICE. You hack wood and bang nails. Stay in your lane.

And, for the record, I did NOT 'miss' the rehearsal. I am SICK.

Mercy

SEND.

It's not lying because I've got a mild headache actually. So it's simply manipulating the truth for my own purposes, which is what actors are trained to do. *Ping.*

From: Finneas O'Connor

Very sorry to hear about your sickness. I'd imagine you caught a cold by dancing around in your underwear in the middle of the night. And actually you are NOT playing Beatrice. You are in bed. Hence my email.

As for hacking wood and banging nails, I also sometimes glue things.

Finn

'Mercy?'

Hastily, I type:

From: Mercy Valentine

Apparently you are unable to distinguish between—

'Mer?'

'Mermaid? *Mercy Valentine?*'

Blinking, I look up. My siblings are staring at me.

'Whoa.' My brother frowns. 'What's happening to Mercy's face? Is it . . . melting? Or . . . No way! That must be what a smile looks like!'

'What?' I snap, quickly straightening my face. 'No. It's not my fault you can't read basic body language, moron.'

Hope's eyes narrow, then widen. 'Oh my gosh! Mercy, that's an "I'm Flirting With A Boy" face! You like someone!'

I snort loudly. 'Please. I don't like *anyone.*'

'We all know *you* like someone.' My little sister points at Max, then she turns to examine Faith's face carefully. 'And you like someone too! Oh my gosh, is everyone at this table in love?! I just *knew* it was contagious! Did I pass it on to everyone?'

Faith and Max open their mouths; I start laughing.

'Hope,' I point out with a genuinely amused chuckle, 'just because you "fall in love" or whatever with any human who shows you the slightest bit of attention, doesn't mean the rest of us are desperate too. We've got standards.'

Mercy, that was completely uncalled for.

Hope's face crumples like a wet paper bag, and my stomach pinches hard.

'I just meant—' I clarify quickly.

'I know what you meant,' Po says, standing up so abruptly her chair falls over with a *bang*. 'And I feel sorry for you, Mercy. I do. You think you're so tough and unreachable but *I* think you locked up your heart somewhere safe years ago and now you can't reach it.'

Something cold shoots through me. 'That's not—'

'I *love* Ben,' she continues fiercely, fists clenched. 'I love him and I always have, since I was tiny. He's the kindest, most genuine guy in the world. And so what if I seem desperate? I'd rather chase love *desperately* than shut myself down like you have.'

Faith and Max are staring, eyes wide.

'Hope,' I say slowly, bewildered. 'I—'

'WHAT'S ALL THIS ABOUT CHASING LOVE?' a loud American voice booms behind me. 'I'VE TOLD YOU ALL: NO DATING UNTIL YOU'RE FORTY.'

13

Valentines know how to make an entrance.

Still reeling, I spin towards my enormous father, who's taking up the entire kitchen doorway.

'Dad!' Hope yelps in delight, lobbing herself at him.

'What's going on?' Dad chuckles, kissing the top of her fluffy head. 'Po, what have you said to make this lot so uncharacteristically quiet? Are you wreaking havoc again?'

'A bit,' she admits proudly.

'That's my girl.' My father turns towards Faith. 'Sticking to our agreement, sweetheart? Coming home every evening?' She holds a silent thumb up, so Dad turns his attention to Max. 'Make me one of those disgusting sandwiches, Mr Inexplicably Topless on YouTube. Anyone would think we don't give you a decent T-shirt allowance. Where's Maggie?'

Max grimaces and hands our father a limp PB and J.

'Out with her son, my *boyfriend*,' Hope answers, her mood already shifted back to sunny again. 'Also, it's a big secret but Max has a new girlfriend and he's totally crazy about her!'

'Excuse me?' Max's eyes pop as Hope sticks her tongue out at him. 'Where are you getting this information from?'

'Sources,' she says airily.

Frowning bemusedly, Dad turns towards me but my head is still buzzing: I feel like I've unexpectedly had a chunk torn out of my face by a cute kitten. Quickly, I try to recalibrate.

'What?' I snap. 'What's that expression for?'

'I'll get to you in a minute,' my father says in a low warning tone, and my stomach sinks. 'But first, there's somebody I'd like you all to meet.'

We look simultaneously at the doorway.

A short, smiling woman is standing there: dull brown hair, brown eyes and brown *cargo pants*. My eyes widen. This has got to be a joke. *This* is her? Dad's new conquest? This is who all the drama and headlines have been about?

'Love' apparently makes you turn your life and family upside down for a woman wearing multiple storage options and *Crocs*.

'New house help?' I smirk quickly. 'How wonderful. Do you do laundry?'

'MERCY!'

'What?' I mime innocence. 'What did I do?'

Hope has already wrapped herself round the American like needy ivy. Fingers crossed Mum snaps to and comes downstairs in time to turn this into fisticuffs complete with rubberised kicks.

'Guys, this is *Roz*!' My little sister inexplicably winds herself a little more tightly. 'I met her in California and she's a psychotic *genius*.

She means 'psychological'.

'Dad.' I lift my eyebrows. 'Why are you dating our new housekeeper? That's a bit sad.'

'SHE IS NOT THE HOUSEKEEPER, MERCY!' Dad explodes. 'STOP BEING SO FLAMING RUDE!'

'I'm actually a therapist,' Roz dimples, holding her hand out. 'It's good to meet you. I know it's somewhat sudden, me being in England, but I'm hoping to take the chance to get to know you all a bit better here.'

'Not professionally, I hope.' I fake interest in my phone, now I've made her feel suitably unwelcome. 'I've destroyed more than my fair share of shrinks. Happy to add you to the list.'

I click on my draft to Finneas:

From: Mercy Valentine
To: Finneas O'Connor

Apparently you are unable to distinguish between THE TALENT and THE CREW, so please—

I can be more cutting. *Delete.*

'MERCY!' Weirdly, Dad's still furious. 'PUT YOUR PHONE DOWN. THAT IS EXACTLY WHY I AM HERE.'

I keep typing. 'Extreme reaction to a small problem, Father.'

Faith puts a hand over her mouth and I grin at her smugly.

'I am *here*,' Dad fumes, snatching my phone and slamming it on the table, 'to discuss your behaviour, Mercy. Ever since I returned to the UK, I have been waking up to new, increasingly alarming trashy headlines about my eldest daughter. You're an actor, not a reality-TV wannabe. It stops now, do you read me?'

'Michael,' Roz says warningly. 'I don't think—'

'Stay out of it, Little Miss Gap,' I snap, then turn back to my father. 'You abandoned your children to a crazy woman so you could run away to America with your army-trousered bit of fluff. So, exactly whose behaviour is under fire here?'

Dad opens his mouth and shuts it again, like a fish.

'I was making a *movie*.' He rubs his face. 'But that doesn't excuse you—'

'Doing whatever I want? You see, that's the perk of having no parents, *Dad*. You get total freedom from their hypocrisy. I get photographed once in my underwear, you kick off. Max shoots topless videos every day, and you make a joke about it.'

My father's mouth flaps uselessly.

'Michael,' Roz says quietly, taking a step forward. 'Mercy has a point, and I know it's not my place but perhaps this isn't the best way to—'

'You're right,' I snap, waving a dismissive hand. 'It's *not* your place. So keep it schtum, Little Miss

Khaki Casual. I don't need you sticking up for me in a faux-bonding ritual.'

Faith, Max and Hope are all staring at me.

'MERCY!' Dad has completely lost it, which is great because battle instantly makes me sharper and clearer. 'STOP TALKING TO PEOPLE LIKE THAT! THIS CONSTANT ATTENTION SEEKING IS NOT HOW YOU WERE BROUGHT UP!'

'I'm a Valentine – it's *exactly* how I was brought up.' I stand up and fake an exaggerated yawn. 'Plus it worked, didn't it? You've finally made a cameo.'

Kaboom.

'Listen.' Dad rubs an exhausted hand over his face. 'Mercy, I understand why you're angry and I appreciate –' he says something about unhappiness, something about grief, loss, pain, whatever – 'but I am *here* for you now, okay? And actually, I bought a peace-offering to help us move forward, allow you to be more independent and responsible—'

'Oooh.' I roll my eyes. 'Did you buy me a *gift*, Father? Is it a chicken's egg? You gonna make me carry it around like a baby for a week? You're so lame.'

'RIGHT,' Dad yells, crossing his arms. 'MERCY, ENOUGH!!! YOU'RE NOT GETTING IT ANY MORE! GIFT RETRACTED!'

Okay, now I kind of want it. 'What is it?'

'Yeah,' Max chimes in. 'What d'you get her? Because if she's getting presents, maybe I should be a gobby nightmare too.'

Dad instinctively moves to block the back door so in one swift movement, I lunge towards the table, snatch my phone and charge out of the front door. I'm feeling quite curious in spite of myself.

What do you think it is?

Some kind of pet to teach me to love again? To soften my hard, hard heart? I wouldn't say no to a snake.

You'd love a puppy, admit it.

A tarantula. A lizard. Something cold and scary that everyone hates.

A fluffy little bunny rabbit. A tiny little ball of—

WILL YOU SHUT UP?

With my siblings hot on my heels, I run into the back garden and then stop abruptly. Something is sitting quietly on the gravel behind the house, wearing a big pink bow.

It's enormous. It's black. It can kill people.

It is definitely not a bunny.

'Oh, no way!' Max yells at the top of his voice. 'This is the unfairest thing that has ever happened in my entire life!'

My father has bought me a car.

14

Not a car: a *Beast*.

My stomach rolls over and I swallow, hard. There's a high chance I'm going to vomit.

'A Land Rover,' I state as my father arrives, puffing, behind me. 'You went out and bought me a Land Rover.'

Dad is visibly chuffed by his own generosity.

'Every girl of a certain age needs an SUV!' He hesitates, then makes his mind up and hands me the keys. 'You're nearly eighteen, so, I thought it might make you a bit more accountable. You'll have to look after it, check for gas and oil and coolant, keep it maintained—'

'Michael . . .' Roz interrupts quietly.

'I'm American, cars are a rite of passage!' He looks so pleased with himself I want to karate-kick him in the shin. 'Maybe it'll stop you calling the limousine for a drive-thru milkshake at three in the morning!'

Oh, come on. I did that *once*. It's normally a kebab.

'I. Don't. Drive,' I remind him.

'Thought of that too!' Dad grins. 'I've arranged lessons! Here's their business card, all paid up for as long as it takes. Ring them and start learning whenever you want!'

I stare at the rectangle of cardboard he's thrust into my hand.

I feel like I'm going to puke, scream, cry, throw things and laugh hysterically before vomiting again. It's extremely disconcerting, trying to work out which order it's all going to come in.

'I CANNOT BELIEVE THIS!' Max is still yelling. 'She gets an SUV*?* Mercy behaves like an ass for years and you buy her a brand-new *Land Rover*? I'm a total ass too – where is my car*?*! I demand you even this out right now, Father! Sibling equality!'

'Oooh!' Hope is jumping up and down in excitement. 'If we're all getting cars can I have one? Obvs, I'm too young to drive but I'll just hang out in it with Ben and kiss lots.'

Only Faith is silent, studying my face.

'For the love of—' Dad looks at the sky. 'Max, for the last few years I have paid for a penthouse apartment in Knightsbridge that you rarely if ever stay at because you are constantly here, eating whatever crosses your path. I also give you a very healthy allowance so you can *follow your dreams,* whatever they eventually transpire to be.'

'Well.' Max abruptly stops yelling. 'If we're *counting the pennies,* Dad.'

'Po.' My father turns to Hope. 'I paid for a five-star trip for you to California, including the first-class return flights that you upgraded for yourself, plus you're enrolled in one of the most expensive private schools in this country. I think we're even.'

Po frowns. 'Perhaps you could buy me a bike?'

Dad chuckles slightly. 'Faith is currently renting a Brixton studio from a friend, but I am under the distinct impression that this is what she wants. Correct?'

Faith nods.

'So, yes, I bought Mercy a car.' Dad gives my siblings a warning look. 'Is that all right with you grabby little monsters?'

Max and Hope stare at the floor.

'Sorry, Dad.'

'Sorry, Dad.'

Slowly, I turn to stare at The Beast again. I've not really looked it in the face yet – or bonnet, whatever – and it's hard to do so without flinching. It is beyond me how *anyone* could have thought that this was a fitting gift for me.

For us.

Exactly. For us.

'Right.' I swallow and clench my jaw. 'Well. Obviously, Father, I am overjoyed at this extremely generous guilt-gift-hyphen-bribe. I'll be *sure* to behave as instructed by my patriarch now.'

Dad has the gall to look shocked. 'Mercy, that's *not* what—'

'The only foreseeable problem,' I continue, 'is that you seem to have mistaken me for a fat forty-five-year-old divorcee who drives exactly three miles under the speed limit.'

'Mercy! This is a very good SUV! A *safe* car.'

I laugh, shortly. 'So my *gift* is essentially taking away my limo service and making me do the hard work myself, is it? Woohoo! Pinch me! You know, *most* dads usually do the lifts for their teenagers themselves. You realise that, right? Out in the normal world? Where they give a flying fox about their kids?'

'Mercy.' Dad looks crushed and I feel a flash of guilt, but screw him for being so insensitive. 'I genuinely thought that you would be pleased with it.'

'Well, I'm not,' I snort. 'And I'm not driving it.'

Stomach still roiling, I rip the driving lesson card in half and throw it on the floor; then I chuck the keys hard at my father so they whack him in the chest.

Furious, I stomp back into the house.

'Mercy . . .' Faith calls out, jogging after me and reaching for my hand. 'Are you okay? I'm sure that Dad didn't—'

'Not now,' I snap hoarsely, snatching my arm away and running up the winding stairs. 'Take your empathy elsewhere, Eff. I don't have space for it right now.'

Scowling, I reach the hallway. Mum is wandering down the corridor, holding a script and murmuring. For a second, I stare at her in utter bewilderment: she's surfaced again, for the second day in a row?

No warning, nothing? Just boom: I'm present and available again?

Then I see exactly what's clutched in her skinny hand.

My anger surprises even me.

'MOTHER!' Storming forward, I grab *Much Ado About Nothing* away from her. 'That is *my* script! Have you been making notations? This is *not yours!*'

'Oh!' Mum blinks at me, dazed but strangely awake. 'It's such a brilliant play . . . I played Beatrice when I was a little younger. *Such* a fascinating part, are you making sure you . . .'

I shake the script in my mother's face.

'SHE IS MY CHARACTER, I KNOW WHAT SHE IS LIKE! JUST LEAVE MY FLAMING STUFF ALONE! WHAT IS *WRONG* WITH THIS FAMILY?'

I lurch into my bedroom and glare at her until she opens her mouth to say something.

Then I slam the door between us.

Mercy, calm down.

'I *am* calm.' Shaking with rage, I throw the script on my bed and pace the room, looking for something to rip apart, break, smash. 'I'm so calm I'm a freaking zen hippy lying in a field full of flowers making a daisy chain to put on my pet llama.'

With a grunt of fury, I chuck a pillow across the room but it lands with an unsatisfying *flump,* so instead I pick up a hideous china mug featuring a cartoon kitten and hold it in the air.

Not that!

'Fine.' Annoyed, I slam it back down on the dresser, pick up the lamp on my bedside table and lob it against the wall. It cracks, fizzes and sparks out. 'Happy?'

Sure, go ahead and get ready in the dark.

Simmering and irritated with myself along with

everyone else now, I march around the steadily dimming room in circles.

Dad meant well, you know.

'So?' I pick up a crystal glass and hold it in the air for a few seconds then fling it hard. *Crack.* 'Who gives a furry rat-bum what he meant? What's your point?'

They're still healing too.

'Fabulous. When they've worked it out, maybe they can let me know how.'

There's nothing left to break, so I flop on my bed.

Still simmering, I grab my phone and instinctively check my social media. Unbelievably, Max has already posted a faux-crying, heavily filtered selfie with The Beast and tagged me, along with the caption:

When your sister gets your dream wheels :(

With gritted teeth, I check my alerts:

OMG @MercyValentine! Rides tonight? Yay! @Amethystisasuperstar @Diornotthatone

Aaaaagh! Party-time! You can be our designated driver @MercyValentine! @SuperNovababy! @Diornotthatone

But if it's just wheels where's the rest of it? #Questions @MercyValentine @Amethystisasuperstar @SuperNovababy

Yup: exactly as suspected, I'm now expected to ferry my friends around like some kind of unpaid chauffeur.

Brain still fizzing with fury, I ignore them and take my pulsing anger elsewhere. After a little deliberation, I spend some quality time trolling Noah and his new bland, model girlfriend:

@NoahJames Who are you trying so hard to convince?

@NoahJames Please, it's like trading a Ferrari for a Ford Estate.

@NoahJames On second thoughts, you're perfect together. LOL.

A few of his pop-loser mates defend him, so I invest extra time taking them down too, then a half-hour attacking the idiocy of models as a whole. And I'm just deep-diving into the new girlfriend's cheekboneless photos from six years ago – sorry, but puberty does not give you a different face – when my phone pings.

From: Finneas O'Connor
To: Mercy Valentine

App? This must be famous person code. Apple? Appendix? Applause? Approval? The mind boggles.

Confused, I scroll up and flush red.

Instead of deleting my draft, I only deleted the majority of it before sending:

App

I scribble a defiant reply:

From: Mercy Valentine

Don't you have floors to sand? Things to glue together? Why are you still bothering me?

I refresh five or six times.

From: Finneas O'Connor

I glued myself to the sanded floor and this is a desperate cry for help. APPLE! APPENDIX!

I laugh, loudly. Then – suddenly realising how dark my room is – I put my phone on my bedside table, flick on the overhead light and jump up to get ready for yet another night out.

Finn is kinda funny, don't you think?

Without responding, I use a practised hand to layer myself in more heavy, dark makeup. Then I pull on a tight, short black dress and pause in front of my wig collection while I survey my multi-coloured and lace-fronted options.

Ask him how old he is and if he's cute and single.

With a snort, I grab a short pink bob and shake it out.

Go on.

Absolutely not. Are you insane?

Just say 'How old are you and are you perhaps cute and single?'

How subtle.

Subtlety is overrated.

You're obsessed with boys, Charity.

Not obsessed. Dedicatedly interested.

Lifting my eyebrows – 'yeah, okay' – I tie my hair back tightly, fit the wig and assess myself in the mirror again. Too cutesy, too sweet for my current mood. Taking it off, I try a long, dark green one. It makes me look nauseous, so I rip it off immediately.

There's nothing wrong with liking a boy, Cee.

Sure. Look how well it worked out for you.

Ouch.

Sorry.

Just ask Finn how old he is. For me.

No.

Ask him.

Nup.

Ask him. Ask him ask him ask him ask—

'Ugh.' I grab a long, blonde wavy wig with a fringe, slam it on and pick my phone up. 'Only if it'll stop you nagging me.'

From: Mercy Valentine

Is that because your ancient bones were unable to move quickly enough? Have all those years caught up with you?

Then I stare at my phone impatiently. 'He's not replying.'

Why do you care?

'I don't *care*. It's just rude, that's all.' I wait a couple more minutes, then scowl and throw my phone aggressively across the bed. 'If there's one thing in the world I can't stand it's a person with no manners or decorum or sense of general—'

Ping.

Lurching, I grab my phone again.

From: Finneas O'Connor

It is very impolite to try to find out a guy's age with all the delicacy of a tractor driving through a wall.

PS I'm 19. APPETISER!

I laugh: okay, I will *grudgingly* admit he's quite funny, which probably means he's as ugly as a monkfish.

I'd still date him.

Rolling my eyes, I pop my phone in my Gucci handbag, slip into my highest-heeled thigh-high Dolce & Gabbana boots and head down the curved stairs.

'Great,' I say out loud. 'What a lucky guy.'

16

Two years ago

'It's love,' Charity glows. 'I just know it.'

I arch one eyebrow sceptically.

'For *him*, obviously,' my twin continues, stretching out on her usual side of the limo and propping her feet up next to me. 'How can a normal human boy possibly have the supernatural power necessary to resist my immense charm?'

'Shall we ask the driver to pull over so you can go get some?'

'Haha!' Tee grins and grabs her phone. 'You'll see Mer, I've come up with a long-term strategy to win Blake, and I promise you it is entirely foolproof.'

'How long term are we talking?' I ask with a wry smile. 'Because you still haven't had a conversation with him off-set. Romance in a retirement home? Woo him from beyond the grave?'

'I've already set the wheels in motion.' Tee looks inordinately smug, even for her. 'Five minutes from *now*, Blake will tell me that he loves me.'

'He barely knows you.' I raise the other eyebrow. 'Ten quid says that doesn't happen.'

'Get your purse out, sis, because you're about to owe me a *very* miserly amount of money, you total tight-wad.'

Grinning, Charity starts typing.

Curious, I scoot across the limo so I can watch her add a photograph of a tiny white rabbit. It's sitting in a teacup with its little pink tongue sticking out. She adds:

Welcome to the Fluffy Bunny Newsletter! To unsubscribe, text STOP.

Charity grins.

'Umm,' I frown as she presses SEND. 'Where did you get Blake's phone number?'

'Stole it,' my twin explains comfortably.
Beep.

Who is this? STOP.

Giggling, she attaches a photo of a hedgehog with a hat on.

Congratulations! You've been upgraded! Henrietta has just the littlest nose on the block. To unsubscribe, text STOP.

Beep.

I NEVER SUBSCRIBED I DON'T WANT PHOTOS OF RABBITS OR HEDGEHOGS PLEASE STOP

We're both snorting with laughter.

You're now added to the Happy Hamster Bulletin! This is Foo-foo. He's a real climber! To unsubscribe, text STOP.

Beep.

STOP STOP STOP HOW MUCH IS THIS COSTING ME?

We've collapsed against each other in the back of the limo, giggling so hard we're unable to breathe properly.

'And when Blake works out that this is your number?'

'He'll realise I'm going to be the most fun girlfriend on the planet.' Tee wipes her eyes. 'Now get your money out.'

Thank you for your continued support! Puppy Buddy loves his wellies! To unsubscribe, text I LOVE YOU.

Beep.

I LOVE YOU

'Tada,' my sister giggles, thrusting her hand at me. 'Gimme those riches.'

Shaking my head, I do as I'm told. The limousine

takes a corner and starts gliding serenely towards our mansion in leafy Richmond.

Charity narrows her eyes at me.

'What?' I narrow my eyes back. 'What are you planning, Mistress of Mayhem?'

'Swaps,' she says, promptly ripping off her purple hoody.

Hesitating, I take off my red jumper and hand it over. My sister smooths her hair into a tight bun at the base of her neck and scruffs my hair up so it's slightly dishevelled. Then she reaches into her bag and pulls out a razor. I lurch away.

'You're not shaving my legs,' I snap, covering my jeans protectively with my hands. 'I have many issues with the cultural management of female body hair.'

'Of course you do. Relax, nobody wants your spidery leg fluff all over nice leather seats. Stay still while I—'

A section of my eyebrow is missing.

'WHAT DID YOU JUST DO TO ME?'

'No no, look!' My twin beams and turns a mirror towards me. 'We look exactly the same now!'

I stare at my newly edited reflection. It's true, we're pretty much indistinguishable: same brown skin, prominent nose, delicate lips. Black hair with the V of a deep widow's peak that turns our face into a sharp heart; the same black eyes, set wolfishly close together.

But we're still different: our characters shining through our faces, communicating totally different energies.

Tee is warm, lively, fun, quick to laugh.

I am . . . not.

'Stop gritting your teeth, for starters,' Charity says, prodding my cheek with her finger. With effort, I loosen my facial muscles, soften my shoulders, smooth my brows.

'Better,' she approves.

Then I watch in dismay as my twin knits her face together: eyebrows furrowing, jaw tightening. She looks hard and intense. She looks like someone you wouldn't approach for directions; someone you wouldn't joke with or open up to; someone you wouldn't giggle with or tickle. This is not the face of someone you want to be close to. It's the face of someone you'd try your hardest to stay away from.

'Ready?' Charity says as heavy sadness sweeps through me.

'Yes.' I nod and swallow. 'Ready.'

17

Amethyst
You still coming out, Mercy?

Nova
LOL. What else would she be doing?

Dior
She's here, I can see her!!!

Dior
She's walking towards us!

Dior
She's looking at us! She's on her phone! She's texting!

Mercy

DIOR STOP NARRATING MY OWN ACTIONS TO ME

'Cee, they won't let us in!' Amethyst pouts as I stomp towards the east London club queue, pushing her over-lined red lips out like a painted clown. 'We showed them our fake ID but we're not on the list, so they said we're still not coming in!'

'I told them my daddy *owns*, like, half of London and some of New York,' Dior complains with wide eyes. 'But I don't think they appreciated quite *how* wealthy I am!'

Nova crosses her thin arms. 'Do something, Cee!'

I sigh inaudibly – I'm still tired from last night – then stomp towards the surprisingly tiny bouncer with my haughtiest expression: nostrils flared, cheekbones popped.

'Mercy Valentine,' I announce loftily. 'Plus three.'

The bouncer hesitates.

'Mer-cy Val-en-tine,' I repeat, making unflinching eye contact. 'You don't need your little clipboard to know who I am.'

The bouncer considers briefly, realises it's not

worth the hassle, then lifts the rope and lets me through: Dee, Mee and Vee bouncing behind like cans on the back of a wedding car. The trick is, if you believe in yourself hard enough, others will find it very hard not to.

We're in a gross hipster club: all reclaimed brick and paid-for vandalism, red leather and artfully rusted tables. Sanitised grit and grot for the discerning privileged kid.

'That was *amazing*,' Amethyst trills enthusiastically.

'We totally forgive you for being rude to us at the *Vanity Fair* party now!' Dior squeaks as I lead us on to the heaving, sweating, packed dancefloor. 'You're, like, fully redeemed!'

'Go, me,' I say drily as I squeeze into the middle.

'So are you going to take us out in your hot new ride or what?' Nova calls over the music. 'We can go on a road trip! You can wear a little cap and be our chauffeur! It'll be hilaire!'

'Just shut up and dance,' I sigh flatly.

The music pulses and the bass takes over and I let it: drilling into my soul, loosening the bad stuff and shaking it all out like a pepper pot. The sweaty crowd jostles and sways and for a moment we've finally escaped ourselves. We're nobody and we're nothing and we're nowhere.

Then Dior tugs on my arm and I reluctantly open one eye.

Her phone is over our heads. Nova and Amethyst immediately drop into an identical pose: chins down, eyes large, arms pressed together. Irritated, I glare at the screen while Dee takes the photo and immediately turns it round for my blessing.

'Approved,' I nod tiredly.

She quickly types, Living my best life with my girls! Every minute counts! #Justsayin #Truestory and posts it, as if we're sailing a yacht around the Maldives instead of making faint sucking noises with our heels every time we move.

APProved, hahaha.

With a hidden smile, I get my phone out.

From: Mercy Valentine
To: Finneas O'Connor

I'm out again tonight. Just so you know you can't control me.

I side-shuffle for a few seconds while I wait for a reply.

My phone vibrates.

From: Finneas O'Connor

Wouldn't dream of even trying. Chances of arriving tomorrow?

Still swaying, I type:

From: Mercy Valentine

100% – I'M A PROFESSIONAL. What are you up to anyway? Bet you're doing something really lame.

The reply is instant.

From: Finneas O'Connor

Still stuck to the floor. It's been a looonnnng night.

I laugh out loud.

'WHO ARE YOU TEXTING?' Nova yells over

the thumping music, leaning forward. 'IS IT A BOY?'

'IS IT THAT ELI GUY FROM YOUR LITTLE SHOW?' Amethyst leans over and I pull my phone away. 'HE'S SO SEXY. I SAW HIS PAD IN *HARPER'S BAZAAR*! I'LL HAVE HIM IF YOU DON'T WANT HIM!'

Can't hear you, I lie with my hands, pointing to my ears.

Then I impulsively write:

From: Mercy Valentine

My parents are doing my head in. I needed to get away.

My phone vibrates.

From: Finneas O'Connor

Know that feeling. Condolences.

Smiling, I put my phone back in my pocket. The Birdbrains are watching me suspiciously, so I close my eyes and focus on the pulse of the music so I can drift away into blissful nothingness again.

'MER!' One of them prods me. 'WE'RE BORED! THIS IS BORING! WHAT WE GONNA DO NOW?'

'I DUNNO,' I yell back, shrugging and shifting into an oblivious sway. 'KEEP DANCING UNTIL WE SLIP INTO AN ALL ENCOMPASSING VOID?'

'*WHAT?*'

'NOTHING.'

'Well,' Nova says sharply as the volume suddenly dips for a birthday shout-out. 'I mean, if you're just going to do *nothing* all evening, Mercy, why did you even come in the first place?'

'*Yeah,*' Amethyst agrees. 'We can do *nothing* all by ourselves, all the time, for free!'

'And we do!' Dior chirps up. 'Daddy says so!'

The desire to dance suddenly leaks out of my body, and I grind to a halt. It's no good: I can't escape, not really, not ever, not anywhere.

I open my eyes, my friends are pouting at me.

'Right,' I sigh. 'Sure. Okay.'

With a vague air of desperation, I look around the club until I spot a fire alarm over our heads.

'Follow me,' I order, grabbing a forgotten pack of candle matches off a nearby table. 'And get ready to run.'

18

This time, I don't even make it home.

'Mercy,' the costume designer says the next morning as I flinch and twist away from her tape measure for the hundredth time. 'Could I just . . . ask you to . . . move to the . . . right, so I can—'

I try to swallow a burp; my 5am burger is not sitting comfortably.

Feeling nauseous, I twist away again.

'Okay, so that's thirty-three inches,' she mumbles, writing down my statistics. 'Lovely.'

'I don't need your body value judgements,' I snarl with a mouth that tastes and no doubt smells like an old wet dog bed. 'Keep your unnecessary adjectives to yourself, thanks.'

The fitter mumbles an apology and guilt twinges.

Why didn't I just go home last night? Yet again, I hopped with the Birdbrains from club to club until daylight and now I'm exhausted, filthy and aching. I've been here hours already. As I've been told several times, I'm a 'very different size' to the previous Beatrice, so they can't just alter her costume for me. Everything has to be made from scratch, which requires a lot of prodding and poking.

I'm seconds away from grabbing the fitter's face with my teeth and shaking her like a terrier.

Also, I smell like a nightclub.

Correction: I smell like *four* nightclubs. And a McDonald's.

I burp again.

'So I'm just going to tighten—' The woman anxiously tugs on the cloth at my waist and I twist away. 'Could you just—' I twist again. 'Mercy, if you could hold still for a—'

'I'm *trying*,' I snap in frustration.

Never liked being touched, huh.

'Okay.' The woman hesitantly starts unpinning the lace on my shoulder very carefully, hovering like a butterfly near a Venus flytrap. 'I'm very nearly finished, so—'

Holding my breath, I close my eyes tightly. As always, the sensation of another human this near me makes my skin feel tight and itchy, as if it doesn't fit any more and I need to desperately peel myself out of it before I'm suffocated inside.

Breathe, Mer. It's nearly over. Breathe. Breathe.

There's a knock on the door.

'Yes?' I bark rigidly. 'What do you want?'

'Is it okay to come in?'

This experience can't get any worse, so I bark: 'Fine, the more the merrier.'

The door creaks open and there's that weird prickle again, the one from the read-through.

'Sorry to intrude,' a husky voice says. 'But Daisy has arrived for her final fitting and she's wondering if you're nearly finished or if she should pop out for a coffee?'

'TELL DAISY THAT THE SECOND WATCHMAN HAS FIVE LINES AND NOBODY GIVES A ROLLING FUDGE NUGGET IF SHE WEARS A DUSTBIN LID AS A HAT, OKAY?'

There's a long silence.

'Right.' The Irish voice sounds dry and amused. 'If you could just explain what a rolling fudge nugget is, I'll do my best.'

Curious, I open my eyes.

The boy standing in the doorway is a year or two older than me: tall, freckled, hair the colour of rust. His eyes are bright green, wide-set but narrow; there's a small gap between his front two teeth and he's wearing ripped jeans and an ancient grey jumper with holes in it. He's covered in sawdust and paint and my stomach has dropped so quickly there's a near-certain chance I'm about to puke greasy hamburger down my dress.

Well, helllllooooo, Finneas!

How do we even know it's him?

Oh, come on, it's obviously him. He is GORGEOUS.

He's all right.

Understatement of the century.

A bit grubby.

In a crazily hot, carpenter, I-can-use-a-saw kind of way.

Meh. Not my type.

So why has your entire body started flashing hot and cold?

I'm very tired. Shut your face.

You realise you're still staring at him with your mouth open, right?

'I—' I swallow. 'I . . . Wha—'

'Daisy,' Finn prompts in a lilting voice, lifting thick, incongruously dark eyebrows. 'Shall I tell her to wait or—'

Okay, I am OBSESSED.

Well, of course you are. You haven't even exchanged one full sentence – that's exactly your type of relationship.

Say something flirty!

'We are *busy*,' I snap hoarsely, finally finding my voice. 'Was that not abundantly clear from the closed door?'

'My mistake.' The boy's eyes are so fiercely green they look like they belong in a jungle and *where* did that cheesy image come from? 'When you imperiously and rudely demanded to know what I wanted, I randomly assumed you wanted me to tell you what I wanted.'

Umm, what the hell did he just call me?

You're staring again.

'So . . .' He waves a hand and I feel weirdly off-kilter: is he going to reference the emails?

I flush again and cross my arms. 'So . . .?'

'So . . . Daisy? What shall I tell her?'

For the love of—

126

The designer woman steps in helpfully. 'We're nearly done.' I'd forgotten she was still here. 'Give us five more minutes, Finn, and then go ahead and send her in.'

Finn! Aha! Told you it's him!

'Excellent.' The guy grins widely and his green eyes crumple and he has one deep dimple in the corner of his mouth and I feel myself flash hot and cold again. 'Can I get you a coffee, Nancy?'

'Who the hell is Nancy?' I bark, lifting my chin and glaring at Finn defiantly. 'My name is *Mercy*. M-E-R-C-Y.'

Silence.

'I'm Nancy,' the designer says quietly.

'I—' I cough in crippling embarrassment and rub my throat. A scrap of white lace falls on to the floor. 'Yes, well.' Panic is rapidly mounting. 'I tend to go by *surnames*, it's more *professional*.'

Finn looks at me steadily. 'And Nancy's surname is . . .?'

Silence.

'Tell Daisy we'll be five minutes,' I sigh in defeat.

Finn nods, picks the lace up from the floor, hands it to me and walks out, closing the door behind him.

19

Mercy, what did you just do?

'Nancy,' I bleat into the silence. 'I am very—'

'It's fine!' The costume designer plasters on a smile and makes a few final amendments. 'Totally fine! It's been a long morning, I get it! There! I think we're done.'

She spins me towards a long mirror and I cringe so hard I basically fold into myself like a paper fan. My hair is greasy and stiff, my foundation shiny, my eye makeup smudged, my lipstick smeared. I stink of body odour and fast food, aka standard morning-after evidence. But all of this is a drop in an ocean of humiliation, given that I'm wearing a flaming *wedding dress*. Nothing says 'stay the hell away from me' quite like a nasty cow, dressed as a *bride*.

Nancy finishes unhooking the long, white, lacy outfit and within seconds I'm dragging on last night's clothes and run-of-shaming it out of the back doors of the Globe as fast as my sticky heels will carry me.

Increasingly emotional, I march up and down the rainy pavement in steadily escalating panic.

Where is my limo?

Why isn't John where I told him to wait?

What's the *point* in being rich and famous if you can't curl up in a ball on the backseat of a limousine and scream your shame loudly into an armrest at a moment's notice?

There's a loud *BEEP*.

Relieved, I spin round, see a huge silver Bentley, spin back round and start striding away as fast as I can in the opposite direction.

'Mercy Valentine!' The car trails me closely, like some kind of not-so-secret MI5 mission. 'Get in the automobile immediately!'

I'm sorry but *that* is what I call an 'imperious' voice.

'Rather not!' I shout back.

'Young lady!' The voice goes up an octave. 'You appear to be mistaking a requirement for a request. Get. In. The. Car.'

Defeated – I don't have the energy left for any more yelling and apparently I do need a lift – I turn and click open the door handle. Dame Sylvia Valentine and her assistant, Genevieve, are sitting neatly on the white-leather backseats, with matching expressions, wearing almost identical pale blue suits: stern and creepy, like something from a well-dressed horror movie.

'What?' I snap tiredly. 'What have I done now?'

'It's more about what you are *not* doing.' My famous grandmother lowers her gold-rimmed glasses, so she can stare at me over the top of them like a cartoon posh person. 'I hear that you are already missing rehearsals, Mercy. Is this true?'

I flinch. 'Absolutely not.'

'I beg to differ.' Grandma sniffs. 'In case you have forgotten, child, the Globe Theatre and I have been on intimate terms ever since it reopened. I am kept fully aware of your attendance record.'

'She didn't go to the social after her first rehearsal either,' Genevieve chips in helpfully, looking at her clipboard. 'The cast went to dinner at a local burger restaurant without her.'

I turn to glare at the snitching rat.

'Mercy.' My grandmother's lips thin. 'What you normally do in your own time is your own business. But you do *not* treat Shakespeare as if you're an extra on *EastEnders*, do you hear me? And if the cast invite you to interact after hours, you *go.*'

'But—' I object.

'I don't want to hear excuses! I do not care if you have no interest in other people, Mercy. I do not care if you deem socialising with colleagues beneath you, or of no value to your party-girl reputation. The acting world is not a clock-in, clock-out job! Theatre is community! Connection! It's about . . .'

My grandmother has entered stately monologue mode, so I stare out of the window and watch drab, grey London glide past while I patiently wait for her to finish: something something industry something something wasting talent something Faith handing the baton something generation of Valentines, the usual jazz.

Then Genevieve rummages around in her briefcase and pulls out a familiar gold item and my attention has finally been won. I turn to stare at it.

That had *better* not be the—

'We have a scrapbook,' my grandmother confirms curtly. 'In which we will collect your newspaper and magazine cuttings, along with suitable social media updates in order to ensure that you are representing the Valentines in the best possible light.'

The lame scrapbook is opened, and you have got to be kidding: you can literally *see* the glue where Faith's articles have been peeled out and replaced with headlines about me.

'Your current trend,' Genevieve says smugly in her fake little old-lady voice even though she can't be more than twenty, 'is to take to social media to eviscerate other celebrities at random. This does not play well for the Valentines brand.'

'I'm not a *brand*,' I hiss at her. 'I'm an *actor*.'

My legendary grandmother whacks the floor near my feet with her gold-tipped walking stick so hard I jump back.

'If you think they are not the same thing,' Grandma says sharply, 'then you are both naive and childish. You *are* a brand, Mercy, just as I am a brand, just as your mother is a brand, just as your great-grandmother was a brand before all of us.

Artists are products, we are temporary and we are replaceable. You'd do well to remember that.'

'Well, maybe I'm just not a big sell-out like you,' I snap, trying the car door: it's locked.

'Then, my dear, you will never be an actress.'

Grandma's voice is clear and cold.

'At the moment,' Genevieve interjects, tapping the scrapbook, 'the world doesn't take you seriously, Mercy. You profile as a diva and it-girl, not as genuine talent. So we thought you should post some selfies in your stage costumes, with the caption *Cannot wait to knuckle down and start this new chapter of my life, hashtag Shakespeare hashtag working hard hashtag even party girls gotta focus sometimes.*'

A wave of fury sweeps over me.

'I'm a real person.' I try the door again with more vehemence. 'Not a character in a play. You can't just put words in my mouth whenever you feel like it. And that's not a *hashtag*, that's just you writing random sentences without spaces.'

Genevieve remains unresponsive for a heartbeat, then says, 'There's also a lovely aspirational quote you could use, along with this photo from the

Vanity Fair shoot, which makes you look extremely professional—'

'No,' I say fiercely, watching as we begin to approach some amber traffic lights.

'All you need to do is—'

'No.'

'We're just asking you to—'

The limo stops, and my fury condenses into something hard, cold and glittery.

'I'm going to save you both some time,' I announce, hitting the electric button that rolls down the window. 'I'm not Faith. You can't control me. I'm saying no.'

I squeeze the top half of my body out of the car window, then start trying to fit my leg out. The traffic lights turn green and there's a *beep* from behind us.

'Go *brand* someone else,' I say as I gracelessly fall out of the stationary Bentley on to the pavement. 'I belong to myself, not to anybody else and certainly not to *you*.'

Then I stand up, brush myself off and get my phone out.

'Mercy!' My grandmother shouts out of the window

as the *beeps* behind them intensify and the Bentley reluctantly starts moving again. 'This discussion will be continued later! I have arranged a civilised family dinner, and you will be in attendance!'

'Whatever!' I shout back, sticking one finger high in the air and marching through the rain.

Yeah, we'll just see about *that*.

20

Two and a bit years ago

'Girls!' Dad yells from the kitchen. 'Dinner!'

Charity and I glance at each other in amusement. Our father is between films and thus the entire family is being subjected to half-charred pies, disintegrating pasta and mushy casseroles.

'Is that what we're calling it these days?' I shout back, but Charity widens her eyes: we've swapped, remember? Quickly, I rearrange my features and swagger into the kitchen; Tee skulks behind me, glowering intensely.

'What's on the menu tonight, Daddy-o?'

'The results of culinary genius,' Dad grins at me from the Aga. 'That's what's on the menu tonight, kiddo.'

We do technically have a huge, formal dining room – carved ceiling and crystal chandelier and velvet and porcelain – but we rarely eat there: the huge kitchen dining table is where we like to bicker and kick each other to our heart's content.

Max doesn't even look up from his iPad.

'All right? How's your stupid show going? You cancelled yet? I'm still surprised your ugly faces don't break all the cameras. Especially you, Mermaid.'

I open my mouth but Tee gives me a warning glance.

'At least we don't stink like pig poop,' she snaps in my voice as we switch into each other's usual seats. 'We could smell you the whole way from the end of the drive.'

I lift an eyebrow – lame – and she mouths *sorry*.

'Guys!' Po has got her head bent over the edge of her kitchen chair, eyes shut in a blissful expression. 'Mum's making *me* look like a mermaid!'

Our mother is engrossed in Hope's curls, twinkly hairpins sticking out of her beautiful mouth. 'Nsh ab tat,' she mumbles, frowning as she sticks another one in at random. 'Ss wyeploy pr shun als.'

'Eloquent as always,' Dad says from the stove. 'There's a movie star if ever I've heard one.'

'I *said.*' Mum removes the pins and stares in disappointment at the mess she's made of Hope's head. 'I'm not sure about that. This is why we employ professionals.'

'Here,' Eff calls from the corner where she's cutting vegetables. 'I have an accessory for you.'

She pops the green frond of a carrot into Hope's hair.

'Perfect,' Po sighs, examining herself in the back of a spoon. 'I am ready to gracefully accept your condiments.'

The whole family laughs.

'Here you go,' I say, grabbing the ketchup and putting it on the table in front of her.

'Thanks, Tee,' she says easily, blowing me a kiss. 'Love you.'

Something in my stomach twists.

'How was work?' Faith continues chopping. 'Any progress with the Blake plan?'

Charity and I glance at each other.

'Oh yes,' I say just in time. 'He's going to be . . . uh . . . besotted with my beauty and charisma by the end of the week.'

Faith's shoulders stiffen – she knows we've

swapped without even looking – and I feel a wave of affection for her.

'NO BOYS,' Dad shouts automatically, incinerating some onions. 'YOU ARE TOO YOUNG FOR BOYS.'

'Boys are stupid,' Charity sighs haughtily, glaring at everyone. 'Love is a temporary chemical trick played by nature to force connections that will inevitably die. It is therefore a waste of time and effort that could be better spent elsewhere, like acting.'

Everyone – bar Faith – rolls their eyes and my throat abruptly tightens.

I don't want to play this game any more.

'The masterpiece is ready!' Dad puts down a pot of slop on the table and basks in a glow of his own triumph. 'All critical reviews, as always, will be defensively and belligerently received.'

Then he casually reaches over to affectionately scruff up my hair.

I flinch and instinctively brush him away.

He stops and frowns. '*Mercy*?'

'Hurray!' Charity bursts into loud laughter and springs up with an exaggerated bow. 'Gotcha!'

'Yeah.' I force a stiff smile, take the purple hoody off and smooth my hair back. 'Fooled you.'

Something in my chest feels tight and hot.

'Wait,' Hope says, staring in confusion at the table. 'Hang on. I don't get it. What's the ketchup for again?'

Everyone laughs and the family settles at the table to eat: dynamics restored, roles in place. I blink at my plate, my heart aching, the world temporarily blurred and watery. Faith gently taps me under the table with her toe.

Looking up, I smile faintly at her.

'Right,' Dad says, rubbing his hands together. 'Let's eat.'

21

Without any idea of where I'm going, I keep marching blindly through the rain: over Southwark Bridge, past the Imperial War Museum and down Kennington Road.

You know exactly where you're going.

Across the park, round Oval station and down a long road clogged with buses, under a railway bridge—

You've literally got Google Maps open.

Until I'm standing in soggy, grumpy exhaustion, outside a concrete tower block plopped in Brixton. Scowling, I text John to tell him where to meet me later, then check my phone again. Now I know for certain that there's something wrong with Faith: why would anybody sane exchange a multimillion-pound mansion in Richmond for what appears to be a multi-storey car park?

Completely drained, I lean my greasy forehead against a chipped grey wall and smash the entry button five or six times.

'It's Mercy,' I intone.

The door buzzes and I heave myself up so I can stomp wearily towards a rusting metal lift. Grunting, I kick the OUT OF ORDER sign over – freaking typical – and start my mushy way up a dank, smelly stairwell. It's so grubby and depressing. Why can't Faith live on the ground floor? More importantly, why can't she just stay at home and sponge off our parents forever, like the rest of us?

By the third floor, I'm stomping and groaning so loudly an old woman opens her front door and peeks out dubiously.

'*What?*' I snarl. '*What are you looking at?*'

She shuts the door quickly, as if *I'm* the problem here. Finally, I reach the right floor and lean my dripping forehead on a flaking blue door while I smash it with my fist.

'Faith?'

Nothing, so I smash it again: harder.

'FAITH? Let me in, dude. I've had the worst morning and no sleep and I need chocolate ASAP.'

The door swings open and I nearly fall into the flat.

No.

NO.

'WHAT ARE YOU DOING HERE?'

'Hello, Mercy,' Roz says, beaming at me with her chubby chipmunk cheeks. 'Faith invited me over for a cup of tea. Then she – uh – she ran out for some milk.' She laughs lightly. 'And when I say *ran*, I mean she literally put trainers on and sprinted out the door.'

My fury mounts. 'WHEN IS SHE GETTING BACK?'

'Soon.' The beam gets brighter. 'Would you like to come in and wait for her?'

'DON'T INVITE ME INTO MY OWN SISTER'S FLAT!' I scream at her. 'I WILL WAIT HERE THANK YOU VERY MUCH, YOU CHEEKY FLAMING AMERICAN.'

Exhausted, I slump onto the floor and get my phone out.

WHY IS THE PARASITE AT YOUR HOUSE

Then I add:

Bring chocolate. Twix ideally. Twirl will also do.

SEND.

Completely out of energy, I lean my head back and close my eyes for a few glorious seconds, then open them again. Roz is still standing in the doorway, watching me.

'YES, WOMAN? WHAT DO YOU WANT?'

'Do you mind if I sit with you?' The American inexplicably beams at me again. 'This seems like an unexpected yet excellent opportunity to get to know each other, doesn't it?'

I glare at her dully. 'You seem to think we are both of mutual interest, which is a huge leap of logic on your part. But sit where you want. It's your butt.'

Closing my eyes again, I sense Roz perch opposite me and carefully assess my tired, makeup-stained face.

Irritated, I grab my phone.

HURRY. She's about to make conversation.

SEND.

'So your father tells me you're acting at Shakespeare's Globe Theatre.' Her voice is calm and gentle, irritatingly genuine. 'How exciting! Have you always loved the stage, or is—'

'Stop it,' I sigh.

'I'm sorry?'

'Stop trying to *therapise* me, or whatever. Have I always loved acting, why do I enjoy being someone else, what is it I'm running away from, why don't I like myself, yada yada. Congratulations, you've landed on exactly the same page as every other therapist I've ever met.'

Grumpily, I check my inbox: nothing.

'I wasn't actually going to say that,' Roz smiles. 'And I'm on my day off, so no "therapising", I promise. Your father tells me you're an extraordinary actor, so I suppose I was wondering—'

'Here come the empty compliments,' I sigh. 'Your attempts to bond with me are pathetically transparent.'

Roz frowns. 'Why would they be empty compliments?'

'As *if* my dad has ever noticed my acting.' I snort loudly. 'He's a world-famous director and yet he's never let me audition, not even for a supporting role in any of his films.'

'Mercy . . .' She looks like she's going to say something, then pauses. 'I don't think that's the reason why.'

I laugh sharply. 'So he just doesn't want me on set with him? You're right, that's *so* much better.'

There's a silence while I check my inbox again: still nothing. Not that I expected any different. I've shown my true colours. Finn is never going to email me again.

'I think you need to talk to your dad,' Roz says finally. 'It's not really my place. But I know that you are incredibly important to your father, and your father is important to me, so . . .'

Now my laughter is genuine. 'Oh, he is, huh?'

The American frowns. 'Very.'

'You "love" him, do you?'

She nods. 'I do.'

'Then more fool you.' I make cheerful, direct eye contact with her. 'You don't have what it takes to keep my father interested. *Nobody* does. Not you, not Mum, not me, not any of his remaining, undead children. You're a blip on Dad's radar, and when he's done, he'll leave you. Just like he did us.'

Roz is assessing me carefully. 'Do you honestly think so?'

'Obviously.' I smile cruelly, aiming my poison with precision. 'You're nothing. You're nobody. At best you're a secondary character, at worst a plot device.'

The bomb fails to detonate: her infuriating chipmunk face remains calm.

'So don't bother getting attached,' I finish flatly, looking down at my phone. 'You'll only end up getting hurt.'

Where the hell did Faith run for milk, South Africa?

Come *on*, Eff. Where are you?

'I see,' Roz says, and I can feel her big cow-brown eyes fixed on me steadily. 'Mercy . . . how long have you been scared of getting attached to people?'

A pulse of cold runs through me; I glance up.

'*Excuse* me?'

'Given what you've been through, it's completely understandable.' Her eyes are full of real compassion. 'Especially with twins, when one dies, it's often a way of—'

I jump up, my heart suddenly pounding. 'Don't.'

'I can't even imagine how alone you must feel.' Roz's voice gets even softer and my hands are abruptly shaking, my eyes filling. 'But I am trained specifically in grief management, so if there's ever a time you need someone objective to talk to . . .'

'I SAID STOP TALKING,' I scream, turning quickly away.

Bewildered, I lurch towards the stairs.

'Mercy!' Roz calls after me. 'I'm sorry, I didn't mean to—'

Vision wobbling, I run down the cement stairs: smashing into a wall, knocking the scab off my hand, barely feeling the pain, staggering round the corner on weak, rubbery legs.

'Mer!' Faith slams straight into me. 'What's wro—'

'*Get out of my way,*' I hiss, pushing my sister aside. '*Traitor.*'

22

Finally, the limo is where it should be.

'Apologies for the delay,' John says kindly as I climb in, glancing at my face in the rear-view mirror. 'Your brother needed me for a last-minute event, and we were caught in traffic. This is a new pick-up spot. Is it where Faith lives?'

Scowling, I turn away and wipe a finger under my eye.

'How was the costume fitting?' John continues after a long pause. 'We drove past a poster for your new play earlier, with your name right at the top! Very impressive, I must say.'

With my throat working, I close my eyes and turn further away: none of his flaming nosy business.

After another pause, the car begins moving.

Breathing hard through my mouth, I focus every ounce of energy I have left on compressing my tears into a dense, hard block. Gathering them together, forcing them into a solid, dark shape inside my chest, as if I'm creating a black diamond. Something sharp and indestructible, that I can cut the world with.

When it's done, I open my eyes again.

Then I get my phone out of my pocket and click on my emails: my stomach still queasy. Shame is starting to loop in circles, tightening at every turn.

Forgetting someone's name isn't that bad, you know.

Except I didn't forget it. I never asked it in the first place.

Impulsively I do a little research, then type:

From: Mercy Valentine
To: Finneas O'Connor

Her name is Nancy Mitchell

Leaning back, I sit numbly as John drives us past Clapham Common, through Putney and into pretty, green, incredibly expensive Richmond. Through the dark glass, I watch people on the streets: talking to friends, holding hands, laughing, shopping, eating sandwiches. I watch them turn in curiosity to stare at my limo, wondering who's inside. It suddenly feels like there's so much more separating us than just a tinted window.

Finally, the limo slides up a tree-lined road to the Valentines' security gates, then into the driveway and up to our enormous red-brick mansion.

I wait as John gets out to open my door for me.

'I'm sorry I couldn't be at the theatre when you first called, Mercy,' he says gently. 'But whenever you need a lift, I'll always try to be there. Anywhere, at any time.'

I don't know what's worse: the empathy or the pity.

'That's your job,' I say tightly, bracing my shoulders and limping exhaustedly up the steps into our house. There's nothing inside me left to fight with.

'Darby,' Hope says as I open the front door. 'It's Darby, isn't it?'

Max laughs. 'What?'

'Daria.' Pause. 'Dariana.' Pause. 'Darla. Darleen.' Pause. 'Darlene spelt the other way. Darlyn.' Pause. 'Dasha. Is it Dasha?'

Po is standing at the bottom of the stairs with a notebook. She's examining Max's face like a dermatologist with severe boundary issues.

'Why would I date a girl named after a reindeer?'

'Love moves in misty ways.' Hope crosses the name off her list. 'Davina.' She studies his face for a reaction. 'Dawn. Dayana?'

'I don't have a secret girlfriend,' Max sighs. 'Po, will you *please* stop cross-examining me?'

'That's *exactly* what someone who has a secret girlfriend would say!' Hope says triumphantly. 'I must be getting closer!'

I narrow my eyes and my heart squeezes.

Something's different, but it takes me a few seconds to work out what it is. Hope's outfit and makeup are normally cobbled together – bright and mismatched, like a cute clown – but now she looks . . . beautiful. Her curls are swept back, her makeup is understated, her heels are high and she's wearing a long, black dress. Something in my throat tightens: my baby sister looks like such a *grown-up*.

Then I stare at the dress again.

'Mer, you're home!' Hope does a faux-modest spin. 'Don't I look *glorious*? Ben's taking me to a fancy restaurant to celebrate our monthiversary and I spent *all* day getting ready. Luckily I was born with style and grace, so it was easy.'

'It's only 3pm,' Max says fondly, as one of her heels wobbles and he catches her in time. 'Unless you're having dinner in Russia, you've got a few hours to go.'

I'm still staring at the dress.

Don't do it.

Please, Mer, just look at her happy little face and—

'Is that my dress?' I step forward, jaw rigid. 'Hope Valentine, *is that MY DRESS?*'

'What?' My sister blinks down at it. 'No.'

'LIAR!' I take another few steps, because that is *totally* my dress, it's Louis Vuitton and I bought it in the hope that I finally get a BAFTA invite this year. 'That's *my* dress. I have *told* you, over and over again, not to take my stuff!'

The numbness is gone and in its place is familiar rage: fizzing in my stomach, rising through my chest, tightening round my throat with claws and teeth bared.

'It's not your dress!' Hope looks panicked. 'I promise it's not yours, Mercy! I swear!'

Roughly, I spin her round and grab the back of the dress.

'You've cut the label out! Oh my God, you've cut the label out of a Louis Vuitton couture gown!'

'I didn't!' Hope's voice is squeaking with distress. 'I wouldn't! You told me not to take it so I—'

'As if you've *ever* listened! Why can I have nothing that's just mine? Why do none of you listen to what I'm saying? If you had asked, Hope, I would probably have said yes! But you can't just go around *taking* my stuff!'

'Except—'

'All I ask for in this family is *boundaries*! Why is that so hard for *any* of you to appreciate?'

'What's going on?' Ben appears behind me, handsome and sweet in a slightly-too-big tux. 'What's with the yelling? Wow, Po. You look like a freaking movie star.'

'I . . .' Hope's desperate eyes flicker to her boyfriend and then back to me again. 'So . . . if I had asked if I could borrow a dress, you would have said yes?'

'YES! I DON'T CARE ABOUT THE DRESS! I CARE ABOUT BEING ASKED!'

'Mercy,' Max says in a low warning voice.

'Can I wear the dress?' Hope whispers. 'Please?'

'NO!' I yell, incandescent. 'TAKE IT OFF RIGHT NOW!'

For a few seconds my sunny sister's face shifts and struggles, then she bursts into wild tears.

'Ben, I don't want to go any more!' she sobs, running up to her room. 'I think I'll just stay here please if that's okay with you!'

'Hope!' Ben gives me a look of pure disgust and chases up the stairs after her. 'Don't worry about the dress! I don't care what you wear! Wear your pyjamas, you'll still look amazing!'

Hope's bedroom door slams.

There's a long silence.

'You know,' Max says finally, looking at me. 'We all bend over backwards trying to understand what you're going through, Mercy. But sometimes you're just unforgivable.'

I open my mouth, but he turns away from me.

'Maybe,' he adds in a dry, flat voice, 'it's time to accept that we've lost you too.'

23

With my mouth still hanging open, I stand in the empty hallway.

Everyone has gone.

I'm all alone.

Slowly, I start climbing the stairs. I can't remember ever feeling this heavy: as if I'm moving through thick sludge, and every limb is filling with sand. Even from the corridor, I can hear Hope sobbing loudly. No doubt flopped on her big four-poster bed with her swollen heart-shaped face tucked under a pillow so only her nose peeks out, the way she used to hide when she was younger.

When was the last time I even saw my baby sister cry?

You know exactly when it was.

For a few seconds, I lean my forehead against Hope's door. Closing my eyes, I lift my hand to knock on it. Tears are prickling the insides of my eyelids, so I blink a few times until they clear. On the other side of the wood I can hear Ben's gentle voice, comforting my sister – full of support and understanding – and something inside me clenches and hardens again.

Swallowing, I lower my hand.

'Take the dress,' I grunt through the door. 'It'll be crumpled and ruined now anyway.'

Then I walk into my bedroom, lock the door and lean heavily against it, staring at the ceiling.

I wore black for the funeral.

And when it was over – when the other half of me was buried – I kept it on. There was no point in pretending everything hadn't changed forever, and that I wasn't different without my sister.

She took all my colours with her.

Intense grief ripples through me, the black diamond feels like it's about to explode, ripping me and everyone around me to shreds. I'm not sure I can bear this any longer. All I want to do is shout, scream, hurt, ruin, destroy, humiliate.

Anything to give this pain to someone else.

My phone *beeps*.

Amethyst
We're heading out! Meet at 7pm?

For a few seconds, I deliberate. Yet another night of dancing, of trying to lose myself, of yelling nonsense at strangers, just to feel heard.

Then exhaustion sweeps over me and I text:

Mercy
Boring family stuff tonight. :(Enjoy

Honestly, I'm not sure who is more surprised: me or them.

Weary to my bones, I slip out of my grubby nightclub dress and stagger into my en-suite shower. I scrub myself for so long, I feel like a snake crawling out of my own shrivelled skin. Finally I moisturise, condition, leave my hair damp and curly and slip into my favourite pyjamas, tucked secretly into my bottom drawer.

Eyes stinging, I crawl into bed and curl up into a tight ball.

It's only 6pm but I ache like I have flu. My eyelids are leaden, my cheeks are hot. The heaviness has grown, as if the sand is rising up my chest and into my lungs. Reaching under the mattress, I haul out my ancient teddy bear, Butter, tuck him into his familiar nook under my chin and close my eyes.

The day feels broken, like something else I've thrown at a wall.

My phone vibrates.

Nearly unconscious, I grab it and open one eye.

From: Finneas O'Connor
To: Mercy Valentine

Hurray! Another of us simple plebeians you can add to your list. Are you okay?

Both of my eyes shoot open. He's still talking to me?

Slowly, I type:

From: Mercy Valentine

I AM FINE. What the hell makes you think I wasn't feeling—

Delete.

From: Mercy Valentine

Oh, RIGHT, so because I was a bit scruffy this morning you

Delete.

You know what? Nobody seems to understand how much *energy* this level of hostility takes.

Before I can stop myself, I type:

From: Mercy Valentine

Not really. But there's nobody to blame but myself. :)

SEND.

Blinking, I curl into myself a little tighter. I suddenly feel raw and dangerously soft, like a peeled egg.

Ping.

From: Finneas O'Connor

Oh, I'm sure you can find someone. Would you like me to volunteer?

I smile faintly.

From: Mercy Valentine

Perfect. You will also be shouted at, patronised, insulted, ignored, attacked, humiliated, undermined and bullied. This will be relentless and entirely intentional. You in?

Ping.

From: Finneas O'Connor

Absolutely not. When do I start?

My face is abruptly warm.

From: Mercy Valentine

Obviously you've already started. PS How did you know I wasn't feeling okay?

I wait a few minutes.

Let's just say I recognise the symptoms. My turn to postscript – why aren't you here?

My smile abruptly drops.

Excuse me? So this is how it goes, right? A few casual messages, and suddenly they think they *own* you. I am not a flaming *conquest*. I'm not a piece of property or somebody this Finn dude can just order around. He's a random guy I'm casually flirting with to pass the time. How *dare* he treat me like somebody who *belongs* to him?

Furious, I smash out:

From: Mercy Valentine

WHY AM I NOT WHERE

Simmering, I glare at my phone.
Ping.

From: Finneas O'Connor

Bowling

Uh?

From: Mercy Valentine

Why would I be bowling? Why would anyone ever be bowling?

From: Finneas O'Connor

It's Friday night! Everyone's bowling for Piper's birthday. You probably know her as 'Hero'. ;) Why don't you come join us?

I stare at my phone, eyes prickling.

My vehement refusal to socialise with the rest of my cast has been heard, loud and clear. Which is fine, so why does it hurt so much that they didn't invite me?

Ugh, my lack of sleep must be making me weak. Defensively, I write:

From: Mercy Valentine

Yeah well bowling is for losers anyway

Sure you want to send that?
Yes.
So, you don't want to go bowling this evening?
Obviously.
You don't want to see Finn?
Nope.
Going out with the cast would get Grandma off your back.
And?
And it means you won't have to lie here.
All night.
In the dark.
And the silence.
On your own.
My shoulders collapse in defeat.

From: Mercy Valentine

Remind me which bowling alley it is again?

SEND.

24

What kind of *moron* named a bowling alley '*All Stars*'?

This isn't the Academy Awards or a table at The Ivy: it's in an underground basement somewhere in the depths of Soho.

With distaste, I pull my huge Gucci sunglasses firmly over my eyes and survey the pink-lit room. There was no time to get ready – the 'party' started early and this lot probably go to bed around 9pm – so I slammed on a long black coat, a black felt hat and knee-high pointy boots, then ringed my eyes with kohl in the limousine on the way back into town.

I assess the situation carefully from behind my dark lenses. An hour ago, I was nearly asleep: now I'm surrounded by loud *clunks*, followed by irrationally joyful screaming. After condemning Dior's personal alley so severely, I feel somewhat of a hypocrite.

I also feel . . . weird. Off-kilter.

Okay, I feel *anxious*. Apparently I can handle the attention of paparazzi, a film set or an audience of hundreds, but a dozen work colleagues and a few bowling balls and I'm a jittery mess? Man, I *really* need to get some sleep.

Tentatively, I take a step forward. Why is everyone so intent on making bowling a *thing*? Yet more exposed industrial pipes and vintage neon lighting, badly painted wooden walls and red-leather armchairs. As if throwing balls at bottles can be made cool by adding fake plumbing.

I think it looks fun.

Of course you do. Your standards of passable entertainment are incredibly low.

Clearing my throat, I scan the room once more. Eli is showing the 'Messenger' and 'First Watchman' how to 'spin' a ball, despite – I glance at the score board – not knowing how to do it himself. 'Margaret' is lurking nearby, desperately eager to get his attention again – good luck with that. The guys playing Antonio and Don Pedro are laughing at the quiz machine, 'Dogberry' and 'Balthasar' are devouring mounds of chips and hotdogs as if it's a competition. Daisy is cleaning a bowling ball with a wet wipe, deep in conversation with Verity.

With a wave of unexpected guilt, I turn quickly away before my director spots me. We haven't discussed my missed rehearsal in person yet, and a birthday party is neither the time nor the place.

I swallow and then scan again for Finn.

Where is he? Has he already left? Did he *trick* me, or did something else come up? Another girl, maybe? Ugh. This is why cute guys with dimples are to be avoided: they make you do stupid, impulsive things like come *bowling*.

In the corner, a large group of cast members are cheering as 'Hero' opens a present and squeals with apparent delight at a cheap high-street wool hat.

Holding my breath, I walk towards them.

Then I stand there in awkward silence for a few seconds, absorbing all the light and joy in the room simply by existing. Anxiety kicks up another notch, so I cough discreetly and rummage in my pocket for the hastily gift-wrapped present I brought with me. It's a dainty gold Tiffany necklace I don't wear any more that suddenly seems entirely inappropriate for a total stranger.

'Mercy!' Hero blinks and stops laughing. 'You came!'

The rest of the cast stiffens around her and I feel them tighten together to shut me out, like a wall.

Something in my chest twists painfully.

'Oh! Sorry, we just weren't sure this was your kind of *thing*?' The woman playing Ursula smirks. 'We figured you'd be doing something more *exciting*?'

I flush: in fairness, I asked for that. 'Apparently not. Happy Birthday, Piper.'

'Hero' jumps – clearly surprised I know her real name – and I promptly decide against the expensive designer necklace. I don't want to give the birthday girl a minor stroke.

'Thanks,' she smiles, suddenly looking embarrassed.

There's a tense silence, and I realise with a sinking stomach that the fun isn't going to continue until I'm gone. The laughter, the giggling, the playfulness, it all ends with me. I'm poison, and the tiniest drop of me can stop people functioning entirely.

I cannot *fathom* why nobody wanted me here.

'Size seven?'

A smelly pair of black-and-white shoes with numbers painted on the back get passed into my hands and – with a bolt of relief – my sadness promptly flashes back into rage.

'Get those monstrosities away from me,' I snarl gratefully, dropping them on the floor. 'I would rather rip my face off and stuff it in the hole that used to be my mouth than wear them, thanks.'

There's a husky laugh; I push my sunglasses on top of my head and turn to face it.

'Well, that's a powerful visual image,' Finn says drily, picking up the bowling shoes and examining them with exaggerated care. 'How many feet do you think have gone into these over the years? Fifty? A hundred? Just think of the unique concoction of bacteria I'm offering you as a free extra.'

Another bolt of warm relief sweeps through me. *Finn! He's still here! He didn't trick you!*

'Less bacteria than currently resides in your trainers.' I feel myself smile, lifting my eyebrows. 'Guaranteed.'

'How dare you?' Finn grins widely. 'For your information, I am creating a trainer colony. A *trained* trainer colony.'

'Over which you rule?'

'Like a revolting tyrant,' he confirms. 'Ready to

set them all loose on the world. One day, Mercy Valentine, you will wish you had been politer about the contents of my shoes.'

I laugh loudly and behind me I sense the group pause momentarily to stare over in shock. Quickly, I straighten my face and look for something to snark about.

'Nice party clothes, Finneas. Were you planning on redecorating while you were here?'

Everyone else is glammed up, but Finn is still wearing exactly the same grubby outfit as last time I saw him: dust-covered jeans, ripped blue T-shirt under the holey jumper, paint splotches, unbrushed hair.

Still gorgeous, though.

Sure, if you don't mind bringing a clothes brush with you any time you go anywhere near him.

'I am always prepared to do a little scaffolding, and ditto, Valentine.' He visually notes my massive coat and hat. 'I'm sorry my email interrupted your trip to the North Pole.'

We grin at each other and my stomach abruptly unsticks and flips over like a pancake.

You like him.

I do not: I'm just relieved that there's someone

here willing to talk to me, that's all. There's a loud *clunk* and a cheer. Finn glances up at the screen with a frown.

'So, you bowl, huh?' I say, suddenly needing his attention.

'Professionally,' he nods, still checking the scores with a tiny forehead crease. 'World champion. Don't tell anyone.'

'Trust me.' I look up at the screens too but it's all nonsense to me. 'I'd prefer nobody know that I'm voluntarily conversing with a human who does this kind of activity for fun.'

'Oh, bowling is not fun.' Finn looks at me again with an earnest expression. 'I'm afraid my fragile masculinity entirely depends on being able to knock things over from a distance, at speed, before eating a hotdog tucked in an inadequately sized napkin.'

I laugh again – a loud, bright bark – and this time I feel the entire cast stop what they're doing so they can goggle at what Finneas O'Connor is doing to make Mercy Valentine behave like a human.

'Aren't you hot?' Finn asks. 'Literally. Not a creepy metaphor.'

'Can't afford to be recognised by paparazzi,' I

explain, tugging on my big black coat and pulling my sunglasses back down. 'Bowling doesn't work well for my *brand*.'

'You have a brand?'

'Apparently so.'

'FIIIINNNNNNN!' Daisy calls at a leisurely pace across the room. 'It's your tuurrrrrnnnnn. Hi, Meeerrrccyyyyy! Sooo cool you're heeeeere!'

'That sucks, Mercy.' Finn sounds genuine and my stomach flips over again. Then he grins and picks up a blue ball. 'I'm afraid I have to go throw this now or nobody will respect me any more. Coming?'

He walks away and I hesitate briefly.

Finn's team appears to consist of Daiiiissssy – still waving in delighted slow motion at me – a jump-suited 'Don Pedro', and 'Friar Francis': a tiny, decrepit old man who uses his entire body to lift a bowling ball. I can think of gangs I'd rather belong to: the mafia, for instance.

On the other hand . . .

Finn turns to grin widely at me and my cheeks tingle.

'Fine,' I snap, picking up the numbered shoes and trying not to gag. 'Whatever. Wait, I'm coming.'

25

This was a horrible mistake.

'We're called *All In The Gutttttttterrrrrr*,' Daisy explains with infinite slowness, holding a yellow ball that smells of antiseptic lemon reverently out in front of me. 'It's a reffffffffference to the—'

How long have I been sitting here?

'Oscar Wilde.' I'd like to get to the end of this sentence before I'm retired, please. 'Got it.'

'Yes!' Daisy lights up with genuine joy. 'Because bowling has gutters and we're in *Allllllllll Stars* so the quote is *We are allllllllll in the guttttttttterrrrrrrrr, but some of us are looking at theeeeeeee—*'

'Stars,' I sigh, snatching the ball. 'Again, got it.'

So far, I've spent five million years with Daisy-Dork and almost no time whatsoever with Finn. I'm starting to seriously question my hormones: one hot boy with green eyes and dusty hands and my decision-making skills detach their parachute and plummet to earth in a ball of flames.

'You're so clever!' Daisy smiles, completely ignoring my death-stare. 'And your hair is *sooooo pretty* all curly and wiiiiiiiiiild, Mercy. You should wear it natural moooooooooore often!'

'DON'T TELL ME HOW TO WEAR MY HAIR!'

'Ooooooh, of course not!' She beams at me, completely unfazed. 'What a Dilbert! I'm sooooooo sorry!'

I pinch the bridge of my nose. 'Just tell me when to bowl.'

There's another loud *clonk* from the alley and we turn simultaneously to look at it. Finn is at the top of the leaderboard and is now doing a subtle triumph dance in the middle of the lane: a tiny twitch of the hips, a miniature punch of the fists, closed eyes and the smug smile of a cat in the sunshine.

He's so freaking cute.

Umm, totally without style or rhythm, is what he is.

There's a sexy little dip at the base of his spine.

Creep.

You're checking him out too or I wouldn't have seen it hahaha.

'Your go,' Finn grins as I turn fluorescent red.

Quickly looking away – his arms are freckled and toned and I suddenly don't know where to put my eyes – I stand up and try to focus on the ball. I'm not sure how this works, but I think glaring at anything aggressively is always worth a shot.

'Shoes,' Finn reminds me over my shoulder.

He's not that close but his breath hits my neck and a tingle sweeps down my arm and into my hand, like a miniature – and yet not entirely unpleasant – heart attack.

'Stand back,' I snap, moving away. 'Don't distract me.'

Reluctantly, I bend down and roll my secret pyjama-trousers up above my knees, so they're completely hidden by the coat. Then I pull my knee-high boots off, stick the disgusting bowling shoes on with a small dry-heave and turn back round. Grimacing, I take a few steps with the ball, squint in the dark through my sunglasses and hesitate.

'Can you actually see anything with those on?' Finn laughs, lightly resting one hand on my shoulder and briefly nudging me in the direction of the bowling lane.

A pulse of electricity crackles through me.

What the hell was that?

'No,' I say gruffly, recoiling away. 'In the interest of anonymity I have chosen not to.'

Then I reconsider my options – I really cannot see a thing – toss my head and take my sunglasses off. Bowling is obviously a game for losers and saddos, but that doesn't mean I want to lose to them.

'Good luck, Mercy!' the rest of my teammates call and I jump: I'd totally forgotten they were even there.

'Side-guards?' Finn calls cheekily.

'Sure!' I retort. 'Anywhere in particular you'd like me to stick them?'

Finn laughs and I hide a smug grin by dipping my head.

Swinging my arm back, I narrow my eyes and aim the ball down the centre of the polished aisle. Then I let go and hold my breath as it careers smoothly in a curve, from right to left, and smashes into the centre bottle – or whatever – with a very satisfying *clunk*.

Every single one of them totters and falls over.

'YES!' I scream, jumping around and punching the air. 'I *did it*! In your FACE, you stupid little skittles! I am the WINNER, I am TRIUMPHANT, and you are—'

I come to an abrupt, humiliated halt.

Yet again, my cast-mates have turned to stare at me, except this time they're watching me do what has apparently turned into a jubilant, hands-in-the-air, bum-swaying dance.

'Yay,' I shrug, quickly folding my arms and sitting down on the fake-leather sofa. 'Or whatever.'

'Nice hit!' the dude playing Don Pedro calls.

'Yes!' Ancient 'Friar Francis' mishears, picking up a bowling ball with an audible *oof*. 'Mercy, why don't you sit? Good job!'

'That was *so impressssssssssssive*!' Daisy claps, bouncing up. 'I can't belieeeeeeeeeve this is your first time bowling, Mer! I *knew* you were just naaaaaaaaturally good at eeeeeeeeverything!'

Flushing with unexpected pleasure, I hide behind my sunglasses again and wait patiently for the rest of my colleagues to go back to minding their own flaming businesses. With a few long steps, Finn strides across the room, picks up two hot dogs and returns. Then he sits next to me and holds one out.

Oh my goodness, he smells so good! Kind of woody and dense and sweet and sharp, like—

Bonfire Night. He smells like Bonfire Night.

'For you,' he says, nodding at the cheap, limp hot dog. 'Manly tubular mashed pig innards to celebrate your big strike.'

I eye it dubiously. 'Is it . . . organic?'

'It is literally full of organs,' Finn nods, the dimple in his cheek deepening. 'So I'm going to say . . . yes?'

Tentatively, I take a small bite, then a much larger one: it's surprisingly tasty and it turns out I'm starving. Never mind sleeping, when was the last time I actually ate? No wonder I'm falling apart.

'Umm, Mercy?' Finn shuffles towards me on the sofa. 'Can I ask you a question?'

'Mmm-hmm.' I swallow and instinctively shuffle away from him.

He moves again. 'I hope it's not awkward.'

I slide back a few more centimetres until I'm essentially perched on the edge of the sofa with nowhere to go but open space. I flip my sunglasses back onto my head. There are golden freckles on Finn's nose, his eyes have flecked stripes of gold in them like a tiger, his bottom lip is slightly dented with bite marks and if I am noticing these details he is *too close*.

'Mmmm,' I manage, holding my breath.

My stomach has clenched. It's going to be about Charity, isn't it? You think you're safe and having fun and escaping then *boom*: let's talk about your dead twin sister.

Finn takes a deep breath. 'Are you wearing penguin pyjamas?'

I stare at him. '*What?*'

'Are you wearing red-fleece penguin pyjamas under your coat, and do those penguins happen to be skiing, and are some of them wearing little bobble hats?'

Disorientated, I look down. One of my pyjama trouser legs has unrolled with all the jumping and dancing and is now hanging out from under my long black coat.

'No! Of course not!' Embarrassed and relieved, I pull the fleecy pyjama leg up.

'No they're not penguins, no they're not pyjamas, no they're not skiing or no they're not wearing bobble hats?'

My face is on fire. 'Actually, it's designer *leisure* wear.'

'Because they are penguins on their day off?'

A juicy snort of laughter pops out of my nose, and something new shoots through me: warm and calm. But also excited. And thirsty. Every cell in my body is stretching towards Finn, like he's water.

Taking a deep breath, I slide in a minuscule motion towards him.

Are you doing it?

Finn dimples and my stomach folds in half.

No way, you're going to kiss him!

I slide closer and breathe as slowly as I can. It's just a kiss, no big deal. Seventeen-year-olds do it all the time. *I* do it all the time. Kissing people I barely know is kind of a Mercy Valentine pastime.

Finn smiles and I shuffle a little closer again.

There's nothing wrong with having a bit of fun. It's the weekend. A quick make-out session with a smoking-hot guy could be good for me. Two pairs of lips, connecting because it feels nice. A pleasant diversion that means nothing; a different way to fill an evening.

My eyes close and my heart pounds.

'Smiiiiiiiiile!' I feel Daisy plonk heavily down next to me. 'Team photo! Jack? Ed? Gather roooooooound! We need to immmmmmooooooortalise the success of *Alllllll In The Guttttterrrrrr*!'

I jump away and open my eyes to a bright *flash*.

'Umm, hell no.' Cheeks flaming, I kick the bowling shoes off and pull on my sunglasses and hat. 'Daisy, you will delete that photo *immediately*. Do you hear me? *Now.*'

'Oh.' She looks at it, then brightens and erases it. 'Okaaaaaaay, though Rosie – 'Margaret' – has been taking photos alllllll night anywaaaaaay.'

I stare in alarm at 'Margaret': sure enough, she's taking a giggling selfie with her arm round Charlotte and whoever it is that plays Leonato. This is outrageous! A complete intrusion of my celebrity rights! Why was I not warned? I was so busy watching out for paparazzi, I forgot normal people record everything all the time too.

'I'm leaving,' I say quickly, grabbing my boots off the floor.

Finn nods and picks up a bowling ball, 'Laters, Valentine,' and I suddenly know that we're going to be emailing each other again tonight, even if I'm not entirely sure why.

A weird, luminescent glow starts to spread through me.

You like him!

You like him you like him you like him —

'NOBODY POST ANY PHOTOS OF ME ONLINE,' I yell at the room. 'OR I WILL DESTROY YOU ALL.'

And I stomp into the night, lit up like a Christmas tree.

26

Mercy
Hey guys! Where are you? Wanna party?

Amethyst
Thought you had 'family stuff'?

Nova
Where we're at is one in one out now. Boo! :(

Mercy
Fine, I'll find my own entertainment.

The glow just keeps spreading.

Carrying me down the pavement like a glittering, sinuous river: picking me up and sweeping me along. Disorientated, I find myself smiling at a complete stranger for no reason, at a scruffy little dog, a couple arm in arm, a tree, a signpost. Gentle music floats through the air, and I don't automatically snarl at it. The whole world suddenly looks brighter and clearer, as if I've put in contact lenses.

You like Finn.

Umm, I have obviously contracted some kind of terrible virus.

'Oh, hi, John.' As I approach, my driver clambers out of the limo and politely opens the back door for me. 'You can go home, if you want. I just feel like . . . wandering around for a bit.'

My driver lifts his eyebrows. 'It's gone ten, Mercy. I can wait for you.'

'You really don't have to.' I smile, unexpectedly touched. 'I'm not sure how long I'll be.'

'That's fine.' John smiles back. 'How about I wait until midnight and then text you? See how you feel then.'

'Thank you,' I say with a wave of gratitude.

Then I glide off again. I have literally no idea where I'm going or what I'm going to do when I get there. All I know is that I feel loose-limbed and lit up, tired but somehow giddy.

You like Finn, you idiot.

Okay, fine, maybe I like Finn a little bit. Happy now?

Yes.

He's hot and funny and interesting. In fact, maybe he's *exactly* what I need at the moment.

Yes!

We both know my life has slipped into something of a . . . rut. Doing the same things, with the same people, over and over and over again. Party, nightclub, rinse and repeat. Maybe it's time to shake things up. Indulge in some casual fun with a cute, green-eyed scruff-pot. Finn can be a new and enjoyable recreational activity: one that happens to have a little back dip and a dimple that makes my stomach dive.

YES!

I mean, everybody needs a hobby.

Spirits lifting even higher, I get my phone out:

From: Mercy Valentine
To: Finneas O'Connor

Do you perchance like coffee?

pastel nylon shirts watch girls with cheap hair extensions take selfies, duck-facing for each other in the hope of emulating dissolvable fillers.

Ugh. The things I do to preserve my reputation.

Teeth gritted, I head towards the main room, which – from what I remember – is on the other side of some heavy, silver-painted doors with zodiac signs etched into them. Truly criminal music is pounding through it, and any residual urge to dance immediately evaporates. Let's just get this done and photographed as fast as possible.

With a deep breath, I shove the door with a shoulder.

Then I freeze.

'. . . hashtag *blessed*,' a familiar voice continues at full volume. 'It's so important to remain *humble*. That's why I party with my fans on a weekly basis. They need to know that, deep down, I'm *just like them*!'

In slow motion, I turn just as a film-crew swarms in behind me.

'As you can see, though, it's not always easy blending in! Everywhere I go, I'm surrounded by people who *love me*. It's exhausting! Fame has its disadvantages too, you know.'

Amazed, I watch my brother hold his hands out like some kind of designer-clad messiah.

'It's *so hard* to find the right girl when you're a household name!' He beams at his audience. 'Guess that's why I'm still single, even though I'm such a catch! Though I'd have no problem dating a Norm, because—'

'CUT!' An irritated voice shouts from the centre of the compact huddle. 'Max, we've talked about this. Please do not call non-celebrity people *Norms*.'

'My bad!' My brother's smug, handsome face is lit neon-pink and flashing. 'What's the word? Ordinaries? Averages? I get so confused with this script. I mean, as *if* I'd date a Norm. We'd have nothing in common *at all*.'

'Fine,' the director sighs tiredly, I suspect not for the first time. 'Let's keep rolling and see what we can do with the edit, okay?'

'"Humble" my *bum*,' a cameraman mutters behind him.

Frowning, I push into the middle of the growing group of girls clustered excitedly round my monumental show-off of a brother and the cameras.

'Max?'

'How are my cheekbones looking?' He angles them at a flustered blonde. 'These bad boys could cut steel, no sweat.'

'Max.'

'Did you see my last vid? I got my teeth whitened especially.'

'*MAX VALENTINE.*'

'Mercy?' Max finally clocks me and his face drops like an overstuffed handbag on the floor. 'Wh . . . Ah. Where . . . Umm. Sugar in a bucket, I thought you were at home tonight.'

'Yes,' I say, pointedly looking at the professional camera crew. 'I'm obviously the *big* surprise.'

I watch my big brother's stupid brain sputter, grind to a halt and finally burst into flames like a faulty robot.

Defeated, he shrugs and then lobs an arm round me.

'Guys!' Max spins me towards the crew. 'Of course you already know my famous sister, Mercy! By far the best actor in the Valentine family. Don't tell her, but she's kind of hilarious, in a brutal, terrifying way. Hey, wanna cameo in my new TV show, Mer?'

I deliberately peel his arm off me.

'I'd rather eat my own nasal hairs. So this is what you've been—' I whip towards a flashing green light. 'ARE YOU FILMING? TURN THE CAMERAS OFF UNLESS YOU WANT TO IMMEDIATELY LOSE THE HANDS HOLDING THEM.'

'See?' Max says proudly as the crew do what they're told.

Irritated, I reach up, grab his wrists and drag him into a relatively private corner, lit by an alarmingly psychotic neon-yellow smiley face. Then I let him go.

'So I'm guessing there's no secret girlfriend,' I state.

He straightens his shirt sleeves. 'Umm, no.'

'Figures,' I snort as he attempts to check out his reflection in the silver door frame. 'The only person you're capable of falling in love with is yourself.'

'Hey!' My brother inflates indignantly. 'Low blow! There's nothing wrong with self-adoration, Merciless.'

'Grandma's going to kill you,' I sigh, already seeing the drama unravelling at home. 'Reality TV? *Made in Richmond*, yeah??? What the hell were you *thinking*?'

Max glances carefully at the waiting camera

crew, who are pretending not to watch us bicker.

Then he pulls me a little further into the corner and rotates us away.

'I'm *thinking*,' he whispers. 'That you have no idea what it's like to be me, Mer. I don't have a *talent*. I don't have a *dream*. And I can't just be happy with normality.'

I open my mouth, but Max holds up his hand to stop me.

'I'm a *Valentine*.' His cheeks are flashing yellow as the leering smiley face mocks over his shoulder. 'I was born into money and fame and privilege. Except . . . what the hell am I supposed to *do* with it? Just sit around and sponge off my parents for the rest of my life? Spend money I haven't earned forever? Or give it all up and walk away with nothing, when I already know what it's like to have everything?'

I stare at my big brother, genuinely shocked. It never occurred to me that Max had any hesitation about spending his entire inheritance, and then – let's be honest – moving on to mine.

'I didn't think about that,' I admit in a small voice.

'This is *my* big shot.' He grimaces with visible embarrassment. 'You've got your career, but this has to be mine. Endorsements, sponsorships, merchandise. My own independence. Please, Mer. I just need a couple more weeks, and then the trailer goes out. I'd rather ask the family for forgiveness than permission.'

I stare at my brother in amazement. His handsome face is almost unrecognisable. All his normal maverick charm has disappeared, and his eyes are wide and vulnerable: his cheeks flushed, his jaw tense. He really, really wants this. Honestly, I've never seen Max genuinely invest in *anything*.

Something in my chest abruptly softens.

'I won't say anything,' I nod. 'Promise.'

'No way! You won't?' With a mewl of gratitude, Max lobs himself at me, wrapping me in a huge, tight bear hug and kissing the top of my head before remembering I hate it and springing back. 'I won't forget this, you little stink-bag. I owe you one.'

Smiling, I shoo him away as my phone *beeps*.

I click on my inbox:

From: Finneas O'Connor

Second most traded commodity in the world? Love it. Tomorrow?

I feel myself beam.

'You wanna do something for me, bro?' I call out impulsively, grabbing my brother and holding my phone over our heads. 'Smile.'

I post the photo online: alibi achieved.

'Wanna come partying?' Max offers warmly, holding a finger up at the camera crew. 'Me and you, quality brother and sister time? Except filmed for the entire world to see at a later date, obviously.'

I laugh and glance quickly at my watch. John should still be waiting outside, like a bearded guardian angel.

'I'm going home,' I tell my brother firmly. 'I need an early night, for once in my life.'

Then, grinning widely, I type:

From: Mercy Valentine

Great. Meet me tomorrow, 9am. St Pancras International.

PS Bring your passport.

27

Finally, a *real* escape.

'What kind of time do you call this for a date?'

The next morning, Finn strides through St Pancras International station towards me, rubbing his eyes, and my stomach somersaults so hard it essentially lands on its feet with its hands in the air, like a prepubescent gymnast.

Finn looks ridiculously good, even to my bleary, early morning ravaged eyes. He's wearing a new outfit: a pair of faded black jeans and a large grey jumper under an open navy coat that looks ancient and heavy, like it's been handed down through multiple world wars. His rusty hair looks freshly washed and wavy, and there isn't any paint or sawdust on his hands. His face is clean and freckled, his jaw devastatingly square.

Clearly, the boy has made an effort to look good,

and if we're being honest, I'm wearing one of my favourite black dresses, my hair carefully styled and my red lipstick precise.

This might be the best idea I've had in years.

'It's not a date,' I clarify sharply.

'Okay.' Finn yawns and stretches sleepily. 'What kind of time do you call this for "not a date"?'

I laugh, already enjoying myself.

'Actually,' I concede, as we start walking through the cavernous station. 'Early mornings are a bit of a mystery to me too. Normally I've only just gone to bed.'

With some consternation, I stare at dozens of people milling around the concourse. Efficiently dressed men and women, holding briefcases and takeaway coffee, marching with determination, then loitering and staring at the departure boards before charging off again.

'Who knew the world was so diurnal?' I frown.

'It's madness, right? Almost as if they have jobs and places to be.' Finn glances at a sandwich shop. 'I used to work there, you know. I did not love weighing out chicken mayonnaise at five in the morning.'

'Gross.' I shiver. 'There's so much of the *day* left. I'm exhausted just thinking about it.'

On the upside, though – at least there's less of the night.

'So.' Finn looks quizzically at me and pulls his passport out of his pocket. 'We're at St Pancras International station at nine am in the morning and I've brought my ID, as requested.'

'Imperiously and rudely,' I smile.

'Naturally.' He holds it out towards me. 'I've added all the clues together and deduced that you intend to steal my identity and run away to Costa Rica to start a banana farm.'

'Busted.' I promptly go to snatch his passport.

'Oh, I don't think so, Valentine.' Finn puts it firmly back in his massive coat pocket. 'You want to find out that my middle name is *Gordon* and that in my photo I'm wearing a Batman T-shirt, you're going to have to work for it. We don't know each other that well yet.'

I laugh with another jolt of surprise.

'Finneas Gordon O'Connor,' I nod. 'Hot.'

'Finneas Gordon *Batman* O'Connor,' he corrects. 'Please respect my full title, thank you very much.

It's bad enough that the government failed to acknowledge it.'

With a wry grimace, I pull my own passport out. 'Mercy Nina Cordelia Valentine. Trust me, I feel your pain.'

We're walking together past a range of glossy and surprisingly busy shops, lit up and cosy: selling candles, scarves, handbags and suitcases.

'Why would anyone come to a train station and *buy a suitcase*?' I roll my eyes. 'What do they expect people to do? Come with all their holiday stuff in a bin liner and pack as they're going through security?'

I lead us on a left turn towards the Eurostar Departures.

'Aha!' Finn lifts his eyebrows. 'So you admit it – we're going on *holiday*? If I'd known that encouraging someone to bowl resulted in an immediate trip abroad, I'd have been forcing my skills on everyone.'

'It's not a holiday.' I guide us past the Normal Person queue to the empty First Class lane. 'It's a *day trip*.'

'Just like at school. How romantic.'

'It's not *romantic*,' I hastily correct, handing two

tickets to the inspector. 'I just happen to be extremely bored of London and desperate to escape for a few hours. With anyone, pretty much. You were just lucky to be in the right place at the right moment.'

Then I glance hastily over my shoulder, to see if I've hurt him.

His face remains serenely amused.

'Got it.' Finn grins as we pass swiftly through security: the benefit of having no suitcases and no weapons. 'Not a date, not romantic, not a holiday, but I'm clearly going to Paris with a girl called *Valentine*.'

I flush. 'Shut up.'

'The city of love.'

I scowl. 'Amsterdam is too far for a day trip. I checked.'

Another laugh. 'You know, when you suggested coffee, I had no idea it would be so dramatic.'

'Really?' I lift my eyebrows at him as we take our places in the queue onto the train. 'I'm the headline-hungry daughter of a movie star and an award-winning director, granddaughter of a thespian dame, great-granddaughter of a Hollywood icon. And an inclination for *drama* surprises you?'

'That is a valid point.' Finn nods gamely. 'Actually, I'm now blown away that you've been so restrained. Step it up, Mercy.'

Trying not to grin, I head down the train aisle.

Honestly, I've never actually been to Paris on my own before: had I known that it would be this easy, I'd have been doing this on a weekly basis. I'm starting to understand why both Hope and Faith legged it abroad so recently. A sense of excitement is starting to bubble.

'At least I didn't use the private jet,' I tell Finn drily.

'Do you have one?'

'Nope,' I laugh. 'But I could probably get hold of one if I wanted to. My dad would ground me for the rest of my life, though. He had a "normal" upbringing or whatever, so he likes to enforce it on us too.'

'Want to swap fathers? Mine won't even know I'm gone.'

I glance at Finn briefly – curious – but decide not to push: from the slight twitch in his jaw, that's all the information he's comfortable offering right now, and I'm going to respect that. I know all about keeping some truths out of the spotlight.

In a weird kind of easy silence, we take our seats. I really, really like the way Finn takes everything in his stride. Nothing seems to throw him, or shock him, or freak him out. Last-minute trip abroad? Sure. I feel like I could say anything, do anything, and he'd shrug and say, 'Why not?'

For the first time in a very long time, I can feel my guard starting to slip. Maybe I don't really need one if nobody's trying their hardest to break through.

We sit and gaze out of the window at the people walking past.

Correction: Finn is staring at me.

'What?' I snap, feeling my cheeks go bright red.

'You're not the only one capable of surprising,' he says, digging a hand in his coat pocket as the train pulls smoothly out of the station. 'I brought something terribly unromantic with me, as befits a not-first-date with a girl I don't find attractive or interesting in any way.'

Flushing, I hold my breath and wait for him to ruin everything with some kind of cheesy gesture.

He pulls out an old, tired pack of playing cards.

'You're such a nerd.' I sigh in relief as Finn puts them smugly on the table between us. 'I've made a horrible mistake and you need to get off at the next stop.'

Finn grins at me. 'Snap.'

28

We play card games all the way to France, slamming matching cards down on the table and yelling at each other like excited little kids. Except every time we slam the pile of cards at the same time, our hands land on top of each other – just for a moment – and I feel a sharp bolt of excitement: a tingle that shoots all the way up my arm and down my neck to meet at the top of my spine.

'Stop trying to hold my hand,' Finn says eventually, turning over a two of Spades. 'You're fooling nobody, Valentine.'

'And yet my hand is always underneath.' I turn my card: four of Diamonds. 'Because I'm faster.'

'You're not faster.' A Jack. 'You're just trigger-happy.'

I turn mine quickly: eight of Hearts. 'I'm winning.'

'Don't count your cards.' Finn looks up with a

wide, gap-toothed smile and now the base of my spine tingles, like a warm button being pressed and – 'SNAP! Haha! Wow, Mercy, you are *easily* distracted.'

'Cheat,' I grumble as he collects all the cards.

'*Bienvenue en France*,' a sultry voice announces over the tannoy as the train begins to slow down. '*Maintenant, nous approchons Paris. Veuillez-vous assurer que vous avez vos bagages lorsque vous quittez le train. Merci d'avoir voyagé avec Eurostar.*'

There's no way we're here already: surely we've only been playing three minutes?

'What did she say?' Finn frowns at the ceiling, putting the cards away in his pocket.

'She said Finneas O'Connor is a cheat,' I lie smoothly, grabbing my handbag from under my seat. 'She says "We've been watching him and his dorky competitiveness is deeply unattractive. We don't want him in France, thank you."'

He laughs loudly. 'I'm glad I never learnt the language.'

'Yes,' I nod, trying to hide how pleased I am with myself. Finn's laugh feels like I've just won some kind of award. 'They've discussed it as a nation and decided they're glad too.'

We stick our tongues out at each other as the train stops, hop up to queue in the aisle then step lightly onto the platform. In the bright cold air, I take a long, deep breath. Gare du Nord is always impressive. It has an aged green-and-ivory delicate elegance that immediately feels like somewhere *else*. A memory suddenly hurtles forward: five of us, racing each other to the barriers, followed by our laughing parents.

'Right.' Blinking, I clear my throat. 'France. Here we are.'

'So, where do you want to start, Mercy Valentine?' Finn prompts, watching my distant face carefully. 'The Eiffel Tower? Or is what looks like a giant telephone pylon too *romantic* for your tastes?'

I roll my eyes, snapping back to the present. 'I invited you for coffee, Finneas O'Connor.'

'You did indeed.'

'So.' I take a deep breath and push through the ghosts constantly following me. 'We are going for a coffee. Idiot.'

Shakespeare & Co. perches on the Seine: a tiny, dark green vintage bookshop, stuffed with a clutter of novels and plays, punctuated by chalkboards with curly white quotes. In front of the shop, the river glows in the sunshine, and on the other side Notre-Dame looms, damaged but undefeated. The pavements are prettily cobbled, and buildings rise around us: pale and elegant, with long windows, tiny balconies and grey turreted roofs. Red canopies poke over green lamps that look like they could be straight out of Narnia.

It's exactly how I remembered it from all those years ago.

'Fitting,' Finn acknowledges as we stand outside. 'Given that we literally work together on a Shakespeare play in the theatre that Shakespeare owned, I think this now amounts to a business trip.'

'What can I say?' I grin. 'I'm an enthusiastic colleague.'

With a nod at a waiter, I grab an outdoor seat in the sweet little Shakespearean bookshop café next door and sit down. '*Pouvons-nous avoir deux cafés et croissants s'il vous plaît?*'

Something tight across my shoulders is loosening. Escaping London – even if just for a moment – seems to have abruptly lifted a weight off my chest. Frankly, this was an idea of epic proportions.

'Hey,' Finn says, taking the seat opposite me as

I beam at him. 'You realise your name means *thank you* in French?'

'Yup.' I grimace. 'And *compassion* and *tender-heartedness* in English. Clearly my parents had no idea who I was when I was born.'

Glancing across at the bookshop, I see my family again. Dad, examining novels; Mum looking for exclusive first editions; Hope and Max playing hide-and-seek behind shelves, Effie engrossed in poetry, Charity giggling while she tries to surreptitiously edit a chalkboard quote.

'We don't get to choose them, huh?' Finn says, as croissants arrive with impressive rapidity. 'Parents, I mean.'

'Nope.' I lift my eyebrows and pick at my pastry, suddenly not so hungry. 'But I guess they don't get to choose us either.'

There's a beat while we smile at each other.

'So.' He points at the bookshop. 'Given the way you headed here like a homing pigeon on steroids, I'm assuming this is somewhere you've been before?'

'When I was a kid,' I nod. 'My mum read me her favourite passage from Chekhov over there, and I . . .'

Embarrassed, I stop and stare at the tablecloth.

Stupid memories. Stupid, dead and rotting memories. What do they matter? They're gone, irrelevant, over. But when I look up thirty seconds later, Finn is patiently waiting for me to finish.

'And you . . . ?' he prompts gently.

And the expression on his face bursts some kind of dam; the rest comes flooding out in a fierce wave.

'That's when I realised I wanted to be an actress too. It hit me that when you're acting you can be anyone. We only get one life, sometimes not even that. But if you're an actress you get to . . . hop between lives. Between people. You get to live over and over again, because each role makes you someone new and different. Each performance is a chance to change. You can be anyone. For once, you get to *choose* how the world sees you.'

The coffees are placed on our table, and I abruptly flush bright red. Where the hell did that little speech come from?

Thanks, Grandma – now I'm monologuing too.

'Also, fame and riches.' I laugh shortly as I pick up a cup with both hands and start blowing on it. 'I'm terribly thirsty for attention from strangers.'

'Sure.' Finn smiles thoughtfully, sticking his finger

in the milky foam. 'Although if I were you, I'd be stoked that I get to be Mercy Valentine every single day. Nobody else does.'

My throat suddenly tightens.

In silence, I take it out on my poor croissant, then awkwardly cough.

'So, what about you?' I start spreading the pastry flakes around the plate. 'Do you like your job, Finn? Are you similarly obsessed with sawing things?'

'And glueing things.' He lifts one eyebrow. 'Please don't forget glueing things.'

'Sorry. I didn't mean it to sound like that.'

'I know.' Finn smiles, then his nose wrinkles. 'I need the money, but I do also genuinely like . . . *making things*. There's nothing there and then there's *something* there, something you can touch with your hands, something that won't go anywhere, and there's a comfort in solidity, you know? A joy in permanence.'

'We're literally the opposite,' I find myself wryly grinning. 'I'm trying to undo myself and you're making yourself three-dimensional.'

Finn grins back, his eyes bright green. 'Yeah, I can see that.'

My stomach abruptly cartwheels and I quickly
look down. Flustered, I get my phone out. It's barely
lunchtime but the Birdbrains are already frantic:
five missed calls.

Amethyst
MERCY PICK UP YOUR PHONE WE ARE
GOING TO HARRODS ARE YOU COMING
OR WHAT

Quickly, I text back:

Mercy
Sorry guys! I'm really sick. Can't get out of
bed. Go without me!

There's an immediate *beep*.

Nova
'Sick' yeah sure saw the photo of you and Max
clubbing last night.

Ugh, I'm going to pay for this later.
'So,' Finn says, sipping his coffee as I put my

phone back in my handbag. 'Mercy, what's your problem with dates?'

'What?' I glance up. 'Nothing.'

He grins. 'So it's just a date with me that's the issue?'

'No!' I flinch. 'It's *dates* in general. I mean, it's all a bit stupid, right? You can hang out and have fun with someone without, you know, *labelling* it.'

'Labels.' Finn rolls his eyes very delicately. 'Famously dangerous. Like a bottle of bleach that doesn't have anything written on it.'

I laugh and relax slightly. He doesn't seem offended.

'Romance is a decoy, that's all.' Hitting a familiar stride, I hold my hands out in a cup shape. 'It's like the red nectar inside a Venus flytrap. It's literally designed to trick you, draw you in, and you're so busy sucking it up you don't notice when the plant slams shut on you and—' I clap my hands together. '*Snap.* You're bickering about cutlery in Ikea and crying in the bath.'

'Snap, indeed.' A tiny snort. 'So love is the equivalent of being eaten alive?'

'Sure.' I scowl at Finn and pick at the scab on

my knuckle. 'Why not? One minute you're a fly thinking "Hey, that looks pretty sweet", and the next minute you're being digested and absorbed until you've completely—*What?* What the hell are you *laughing* at?'

'Your contrariness,' Finn grins. 'You love acting because you get to disappear, and you hate love because ditto.'

I open my mouth and shut it again.

Our hands are both on the table, and all at once I'm very conscious of the space between them. Scowling, I stick mine under my butt and sit on them.

'Hey, I'm not disagreeing with you.' Finn moves his hands away as well. 'Too many people are in relationships because they're bored or empty or lonely. I'm just suggesting that your ideology could do with some streamlining.'

With a loud laugh, all my irritation vanishes.

How does he do that? How does he flip some kind of switch inside me that feels like a light turning on?

Impulsively, I pick up a napkin and throw it at him.

In the sun, I see the flecks of gold in Finn's hair, and – I notice in surprise – a few strands of white. My stomach twists again and with an abrupt bolt of longing, all I want to do is reach over the table, grab him by the coat collar and kiss him.

Except now I can't.

I've boxed myself into a corner.

You can't talk about hating *love and romance* and then kiss someone in Paris: they'll get the wrong message, even if you've just told them exactly how you feel.

'This is on me,' I say quickly, reaching for my card instead.

'It's not a date,' he laughs, reaching for his wallet too. 'Remember? And you paid for the train.'

'Today was my idea,' I insist, overwhelmed by a sudden urge to make sure I stay in control, that I don't owe him anything, that nothing is expected from me. 'And I'm very, very wealthy.'

'Yes, thanks for reminding me.' Finn pops his bank card on the table. 'But I am an employed adult, so I think I can manage two coffees and . . . are you going to eat that, or have you satisfactorily destroyed it now?'

We look down simultaneously at my croissant, lying in crumbs on the table.

'Yeah,' I admit sheepishly. 'I'm done.'

'Great,' Finn says, picking the remnants up, shoving them in his beautiful mouth and grinning. 'Waste not want not. For the record, Mercy, it's just as lovely, even when it's in pieces.'

29

I regret everything about this day trip.

Finn and I bicker all the way to Gare du Nord, through security, onto the train and back through whizzing countryside: mocking, arguing, lobbing insults at each other like miniature grenades. But at one point, when I make a snide comment about another commuter's high-street dress, he tells me to go and sit somewhere else if I'm going to be a judgemental cow for no apparent reason. I sulk in the vestibule for a few minutes, then shuffle back and mumble, 'Sorry.'

And – when I search my soul – I realise I mean it.

So, yeah, I regret this day trip because it should have been longer and it should have started earlier. It should finish in four or five weeks' time. Or months. Honestly, I cannot conceive of a day when

I would not want to hang out with this funny green-eyed boy.

Way too fast, we reach London.

I'm now prevaricating like a total loser: rustling through my handbag, pointing out stupid things, making vague noises about maybe needing some kind of dinner. Then I see Finn glance subtly up at the huge St Pancras clock, and the black diamond in my chest hardens. He wants to go. He's not having as much fun as I am. He's clearly got other, better plans, and this is exactly why it's not a date: 'dates' make you feel like *this*.

'Well,' I snap quickly, before he can come up with some paltry excuse to leave. 'I'm afraid I've got a celebrity party to go to, so . . .'

'Stop it.' Finn looks down at me.

I immediately bridle. 'Stop what, precisely?'

'Stop trying to reject me before I can reject you.' He grins. 'You can't control everything, you know.'

'Watch me,' I grumble, my nostrils flaring.

Finn smiles and hesitates. 'I had a fun day today, Mercy. A really fun, if considerably unexpected Saturday.'

He seems genuine, and I soften. 'I had fun too.'

And there it is again: a desperate, surging need to stand on my tiptoes, grab him and kiss him. Or not even *kiss* him. Just . . . be nearer to him, somehow.

Oh, who am I kidding?

It's a need that's been pretty much constant for the last eight hours: at this point I'm so desperate for physical contact with him I'd settle for rubbing ears or bumping thumbs.

'I've really got to go,' Finn says after another hesitation, glancing at the clock again. 'There's somewhere I . . . need to be before it closes.'

'Mysterious,' I observe without pushing. 'Me too, obviously. Busy, busy.'

He laughs. 'But I'll see you on Monday? At the theatre?'

'Yup.' I clear my throat. 'Monday.'

Finn smiles and turns to leave and it's not a date, I don't believe in romance, I don't believe in love, but now we're standing under a clock in a train station and he's walking away and I need to kiss him but I *can't* kiss him, except I can't just leave it like *that*.

Impulsively, I reach out and grab his arm.

'Thank you,' I whisper as Finn turns back, and before I know it all willpower has gone out of the window and I'm grabbing his coat collar and kissing him with a force and passion that surprises even me. That bonfire smell is still there: sweet and dense and drenched in cold and my cheeks are suddenly rosy.

'Mercy—' he says hesitantly.

Amazed by myself, I walk away fast before Finn can finish his sentence.

Before he can see the smile on my face.

An hour later, I kick my boots off and flop onto my bed, still beaming all over.

So . . . how was it? Tell me EVERYTHING.

Weren't you there?

Don't be weird, dude. Why would I come on a date with you?

Not a date.

Totally a date.

It was just two friends, trying not to make out.

That's a date.

Getting to know each other.

Literally the definition of 'a date'.

Kissing a little bit.

No way! Tell me EVERYTHING.

Absolutely not. Anyway, it was a successful distraction: I barely thought about you all day.

Charming.

Grinning, I get my phone out.

Amethyst
Mercy it's Sketch for dinner.

Nova
You still 'ill'?

Dior
Wanna drive us in your hot wheels? ;)

Nova
Dior, that's what you call a car that's been stolen, you total idiot.

My inner beam falters.

The Beast is waiting outside, you know.

I do know, yes: I had to walk past its aggressively oversized bulk on my way into the house yet again.

You'd think Dad would have noticed it hasn't been moved since he dumped it there and got the message by now.

You haven't even looked at it.

'I don't need to look at it,' I say sharply. 'It's the size of a tractor.'

Impulsively, I reply to the Birdbrains:

Mercy
Still sick. Go without me.

I don't want them to wreck my happy buzz.
Then I switch to email.

From: Mercy Valentine
To: Finneas O'Connor

I don't have your phone number?

There's an immediate *ping.*

From: Finneas O'Connor

One step at a time, Valentine. Next we swap fax.

With another laugh, I throw my phone on my bed.

It's only 7pm, but the night is already starting to loom, heavy and dark. Standing up quickly, I venture into the rest of the house before my mood can dampen.

'Hello?' I say in the corridor: nothing.

'Hey, thief.' I rap hard on Hope's bedroom door. 'I forgive you. Want to watch a film?'

Nothing.

'Is anyone here?' I try Max with increasing frustration, then Faith: nothing, nothing. 'Oh, come on, guys. Since when do you losers have something interesting to do on a Saturday night?'

Briefly, I lurk outside Mum's room. The small gap under the door is silent and dark, but that doesn't mean anything: she could be asleep, she could be hovering vacantly by the window like a ghost, she could have wandered out into the public in her nightgown again like a wayward Ophelia.

I feel a sudden, unexpected wave of compassion for my mother.

I guess we all break in different ways.

Giving up, I head down the achingly silent, dark

stairs and push softly into the cinema room. It's red, velvety, warm, lined with thousands of old films. It feels like what was once the beating heart of my family has grown still and quiet, as if it's been patiently waiting. I breathe in deeply: that familiar, leathery, dusty smell.

When was the last time we came in here?

'Our birthday,' I whisper, locking the door firmly behind me. Without needing to look, I go straight to one particular shelf and pick out Mum's breakthrough movie, *The Heart of Us*.

I curl up in a huddle on the comfiest sofa.

And I start watching.

Two and a bit years ago

'Roll up! Roll up! Come celebrate the big one-five!'

Tee stands outside the cinema room with Dad's black top hat perched on top of her wild curls, grinning and using Grandma's beloved gold-tipped walking stick as a ringmaster's cane.

She points the end of the stick at Max as he ambles past.

'Fifteen today!' Charity beckons him in. 'Welcome, brother! Enter! Witness the Valentine twins reach the middle of their teens in true style, glory and comedy value!'

Max rolls his eyes affectionately. 'Your party isn't for another hour and a half, dumbo, and you do realise that *thirteen* is the start of your teens, not ten?'

'Details!' Tee laughs. 'And it's a party *all day*, right Mer?'

I look up from the middle of the cinema-room floor, where I'm fiddling with a pile of DVDs, trying to decide which film we should kick the event off with. It's our birthday, and that's my only request: an epic film-fest, which Charity has given me full control of as part of her gift to me.

'Uh?' I look down again. 'Yeah. I guess. I'm not that fussed.'

'Then I'll be fussed for you.' My sister begins to sashay up and down the hallway, swinging the walking stick around like an umbrella in *Singin' in the Rain*. 'Knock knock.'

Max shrugs dutifully. 'Who's there?'

Tee swings round again, stick in the air. 'Control freak.'

'Cont—'

'Now you say *Control Freak Who,*' my sister laughs, landing with a jump in front of the hallway mirror. 'Get it?'

'Charity Valentine!' Grandma's voice projects along the hall. 'Young lady, I have been looking for my walking apparatus *everywhere*. How am I expected to punctuate my words sufficiently without something to bang on the floor?'

Charity hands the cane back to Grandma. 'Oops.'

'Max?' Our grandmother smiles and lifts amused eyebrows at him. 'A quick word. Kitchen. Now, if you'd be so kind.'

With the air of two conspirators, Max and Grandma disappear.

'They're talking about our birthday gift,' Tee observes, taking Dad's hat off and throwing it like a Frisbee into the cinema room. 'What do you think we'll get from her this year, Cee?'

I continue shuffling through films for the right birthday *tone*. Comedy? Horror? Something amazing with Mum in it? No: everyone will laugh at me for being a butt-kisser.

'Don't mind,' I say distractedly, pulling out a black-and-white film featuring a close-up of Great-Grandma's strong, striking face.

'I really want a voice transformer.' Tee flops onto one of the red-velvet seats. 'One of those swanky ones that makes you sound unrecognisable. My pranks would be *off the charts.*'

I smile. 'I fear for all of mankind.'

Charity chortles, pleased with herself, then there's a pause.

'Mer, do you think we'll get two separate gifts?' My sister chews on her lip and faux-casually nudges the DVD pile with her toe. 'Grandma is super generous, I know that, but she has a bit of a tendency to . . . lump us together.'

'Mmm.' Now I look up properly. 'Does it bother you?'

'Sometimes,' she confesses with a guilty grimace. 'Does it bother you?'

'Yes,' I admit. 'Sometimes. But whatever it is, let's take it back and find a voice thingy for you, okay? Although I may regret this when I'm the pranking victim.'

Charity's face lights up, and my heart goes squishy.

'Really?' Leaping up, she crosses the room and lobs herself on the floor next to me and pokes me with a finger, which is our version of a hug. 'You'd do that for me?'

Grinning, I poke her back. 'Of course I would.'

'You know,' my sister says in satisfaction, stretching out and picking up one of the Valentine DVDs I've chosen: this time, directed by Dad, 'twins are kind of magic, aren't we? Me and you, we got really lucky.'

Fondly, I take the DVD out of her hands. 'We did.'

'I'm glad I get to share today with you,' Charity says easily, lying down and staring at the ceiling. 'No, actually – that's not quite right. I'm glad I get to share *all* the days.'

I cough, a sudden lump in my throat. 'Gross.'

'You know it,' Tee grins, jumping back up and clapping. 'And I'm a minute older than you, so I know what's what. Now, which boring old film of Mum's are you making us sit through this time?'

31

I watch films for the rest of the weekend.

Still glowing from Paris, I plough through Mum's greatest works: *The Hurtful Ones* (she actually learnt to sword fight!); the heartbreaking, recently award-nominated *Pinnacle;* the blisteringly raw *A Thousand Years* (she was gone for months filming that time). My favourite, Hardy's *A Pair of Blue Eyes*: she was only eighteen when she filmed that one, barely older than me now, and so luminous.

Rapt, I binge on movies for twenty-four hours: emerging only for toilet breaks and food. Outside the locked door, I hear the rest of my family bustle around, chatter, argue – completely unaware that I'm even here, assuming I'm creating noisy havoc elsewhere.

But with every movie, I can feel myself getting more inspired, more hopeful, more encouraged.

With every film, my future opens up a little more.

Wake up.

Yawning, I roll over.

Wake up.

I pull a pillow over my head.

Wake up and look!

Opening one eye, I sit up with a jolt of panic.

Where am I? The room's a different colour. There are unfamiliar noises outside. Why am I not fully dressed and wearing shoes? Why don't I have a headache? Why can I open my eyes without my lids sticking together? Where's Faith?

It's the morning! You slept properly! In your own bedroom!

That's the DAWN CHORUS!

'I know what the *dawn chorus* sounds like,' I lie, staring out of the window in amazement. Huh. With a quick twitch of my hand, I open my curtain and blink in astonishment at a blaze of pure, direct sunshine. Why is the sun in that weird position? Why do I feel such an air of positivity and . . . *anticipation?*

It's MONDAY! YOU GET TO SEE FINN!

Lunging, I grab my phone from the bedside table. There's an email from last night:

From: Finneas O'Connor

To: Mercy Valentine

Not gonna lie, kind of excited about seeing you.

Heart hopping, I type:

From: Mercy Valentine

Calm down, keen-bean.

But another flush of brightness swoops over me: a warm, light sensation that feels like . . .

Happiness.

More like sleep-induced endorphins.

Swinging my legs out of bed, I stretch in surprise. My body feels like everything's in the right place. My mouth isn't stuck together, my tongue isn't covered in beige felt like a Sylvanian Families bunny.

Ew, am I . . . *humming?*

Glancing at my watch – not even 7 am yet – I bounce up and warble some lame, chirpy nonsense as I skip to the shower. You know, I actually feel like making an effort today. Using my favourite coconut body wash, picking a lipstick I actually like, as opposed to one that makes me look like I chewed the head off a bat. My brain feels weird, giddy, awake.

What do you think Finn's doing right now?

Probably still fast asleep, rusty waves messy, green eyes shut, dark eyebrows furrowed, maybe snoring gently, arms sprawled out—

Ugh. Okay, I might have a tiny crush.

Umm, you don't say.

Rolling my eyes, I grab my script and spring down the stairs like an overexcited gazelle. I'm going to head into the theatre early, see if I can get a little extra practice in before I see him.

Pausing in the hallway, I impulsively check my reflection in the bureau mirror. Clear skin, bright eyes, no scowl-line between my eyebrows. Sleep, man, who knew?

'Ben!' a tinkly voice calls out of the library. 'Is that you already? How much money do you think an old painting is? Because I was thinking maybe we could pool our allowances and . . .'

Hope's face appears from round the door.

'Oh!' She ducks back awkwardly and looks at my left ear. 'Sorry, Mercy, you're not usually up this early.'

I smile at my little sister, then frown. Why is she being so—

The stolen dress.

I'd totally forgotten about it. My stomach twists, and I decide to be the bigger person for once.

'Hey,' I start, but she's disappeared into the library. What the—

'Hello?' I knock on the door. 'Hope?'

It opens and her face peeks out nervously. 'Hi.'

'I was just going to *say*,' I try again, holding out my hands in a generous, understanding and philanthropic gesture. 'That I have decided to accept your apology. For stealing my belongings.' Adding, before I can stop myself: '*Again.*'

'Okay.' Po looks at the floor. 'Thanks. I genuinely didn't mean to cause you any inconvenience or offence.'

Then she quietly closes the door in my face.

Umm, how am I supposed to be the bigger person if my sister is not going to accept my acceptance of her apology? She was in the wrong. I'm just trying to do the right thing here.

'Hope?' I rap on the door, harder this time, and wait impatiently until it opens once more. 'I *forgive* you. That's what I'm trying to say. I know I got a bit . . .'

The scene suddenly flashes in my head, in full technicolour: me, centimetres away from her terrified face, screeching like a banshee about my stolen couture. Purple, with the veins in my face pulsing in rage.

'Dramatic,' I finish lamely.

Hope nods in silence.

'*Okay*,' I admit with another, even fiercer flush of guilt. 'I went totally bonkers about a black dress when I own literally twenty others, and I appreciate it was perhaps a *little* extreme but maybe *now* you'll stop stealing my stuff?'

That's not an apology.

'I will never steal your stuff again,' my youngest sibling says in an empty voice, still not looking at me. She shuffles on the spot, visibly uncomfortable. 'Can I go now?'

My stomach drops and I nod. 'Of course.'

'Sorry,' she whispers, vanishing back into the library, and I stand for a few seconds, staring in bewilderment at the closed door. I yell at Hope all the time. I'm horrible to her, pretty much constantly. Why is she being so weird about it now? She normally bounces back immediately. She's Hope Valentine, the human equivalent of a rubber ball.

Just apologise!

'I *am* sorry,' I call quickly through the door. 'For getting so mad. Let's forget about it, okay?' A wave of inspiration. 'You can borrow another outfit if you want, I don't mind.'

'No thanks,' the little voice says from the other side.

Grimacing – what else can I do? – I turn to leave and immediately jump: how long has Ben been standing there?

'Ugh,' I say quickly, crossing to the other side of the hallway to cover up my embarrassment. 'You don't actually live here, you do appreciate that, right? When are you going back to Scotland? Or have you failed college already?'

Ben looks at me steadily through his dark-rimmed glasses – he's never been scared of me, even when we were kids – and it suddenly hits me all over again how much he's changed in the last year. The faint moustache has totally gone, he's broadened out, his hair is no longer crispy, cheekbones have somehow emerged from nowhere.

Okay, I'll admit it: the housekeeper's son is a solid hottie.

'She adores you, you know that?' Ben frowns at me, folding his (alarmingly toned) arms. 'Your sister. She thinks that you're the coolest, most glamorous person on the planet.'

I feel my cheeks flush hot. 'Pfff, well—'

'All she wants is to be like you,' he continues smoothly, as if I haven't said anything. 'Just a *little* bit of your ferocity and strength, Mercy. But you don't give her the time of day any more. Maybe dressing up like you is the closest she can get.'

My cheeks get hotter. 'Ha . . .'

'So remember that,' Ben snaps, 'next time you're screaming at Hope, or calling her names or laughing at her, just remember that your little sister loves you unconditionally. She always has done.'

My eyes fill with abrupt tears, and I glance back at the library door with a knife-stab of intense guilt, my happy Paris glow starting to wobble, fall apart.

'Ben—' I start, but our childhood friend walks straight past me, then turns back to give me one last, sad smile.

'I'm just sorry you can't see it.'

32

Now I *really* need to be someone else.

By the time I reach the South Bank, it's nearly 8am. A quick glance at the darkened windows of the Globe confirms that nobody else has arrived for rehearsals yet, which means I've got roughly an hour.

An hour for me to fully disappear.

With a fake haughty swagger and flash of my official pass, I manage to convince one of the early-morning cleaners to let me in a side door, then I wind my way through to the main stage.

No matter how many times I have been here, I remain in awe of this theatre. Shakespeare himself helped pay for it in 1599 so that his actors would have somewhere decent to perform. It was burnt down shortly after, then rebuilt, then closed, but they rebuilt it last century, almost exactly as it would have been, with the same architectural layout and the same materials.

Heart pounding, I push open a heavy door.

It's so beautiful.

Constructed in a huge oak circle, the wide auditorium and two layers of thatched wooden balconies curve round to face a simple roofed stage. There is no ceiling, so above my head is bright blue early-morning sky, punctuated with small white clouds. The theatre was designed like this to mimic the gathering of crowds round actors in marketplaces, with the upper galleries built to echo the way people would hang out of windows to watch bearbaiting or cockfighting. More than anything, this theatre was built for immersion in the sheer *joy* of stories.

With my breath held, I take a few tentative steps forward and push Hope to the back of my mind, my throat tightening, my heart full.

I've never actually stood on the stage until now.

All these years, I've watched from the gallery, leant over the edge with my eyes on fire, mesmerised by the stories of people I longed to be.

Sitting just over there, I watched my grandmother

become Lady Macbeth, forever washing guilty blood from her hands.

I watched my mother laugh, skittish as Viola.

And I ached with everything I had to be just like them: to walk these boards, transformed into somebody else, adored by everyone.

Taking another deep breath, I wipe my hands on my black jeans.

Finally, it's my turn.

Quietly, I walk up the stairs and stand with the sunshine blinding me like spotlights, wiping the whole world out. I already know who I want to be today. There's only one part I really want to play.

'I am a seagull,' I say into the silence.

The empty theatre listens, waiting for me to continue.

'No,' I continue, more loudly. 'I am an actress.'

I walk across the stage, as Chekhov's Nina: a young ingenue trapped on a farm in the Russian countryside, desperate to act, hopeful, full of dreams. Ripped apart and destroyed because she fell in love with the wrong person.

No. Because she fell in love at all.

'*He* does not believe in the theatre,' I whisper as

tears spring to my eyes. 'He used to laugh at my dreams, so that little by little I became down-hearted and ceased to believe in it too.'

As I talk, the wooden auditorium begins to melt.

With a deep roar, enormous trees erupt from the stage and shoot upwards, gnarled and opening with earth-shattering creaks into a canopy of deep forest green. When I look down, my feet are bare and damp, covered in broken, wet grass strands. Tiny white and blue flowers push through the mud, delicately dotting the ground like confetti; birds I don't recognise sing overhead.

In the distance, I see the large, shimmering lake where I fell in love, where everything changed; just behind me, the elegant house I don't belong to, and never will.

A Russian boy looms in front of me, pale and lovesick.

'Do you remember how you shot a seagull once?' I ask Constantine in a broken voice. 'A man chanced to pass that way and destroyed it out of idleness.'

Now I hear the storm starting: a rumble of thunder, a darkening sky, the rain shuddering through the leaves with a loud crack, a sudden burst.

I feel myself getting abruptly wet, cold, desperate. I see the ghost of my past self, and it overwhelms me: the naivety of my hopes, the loss of my dreams.

'I have changed now,' I tell the boy defiantly, lifting my chin. 'Now I am a real actress. I act with joy, with exaltation, I am intoxicated by it, and feel that I am superb.'

The rain pours and my voice wobbles: I am lost.

'I have been walking and walking,' I whisper, wandering vaguely through the wood. 'And thinking and thinking, ever since I have been here, and I feel the strength of my spirit growing in me every day.'

My cheeks flush and my eyes begin to fill.

'I understand at last Constantine, that for us,' I whisper, 'whether we write or act, it is not the honour and glory of which I have dreamt that is important, it is the strength to endure.'

And something in Nina's words hits me like a train, pulling me out of her, tugged in half.

The strength to endure.

A warm tear trickles down my cheek.

Does anyone really love *unconditionally?* How can they, when they don't know everything we keep hidden inside?

Because I am so tired, Charity.

I'm so tired of feeling guilty all the time. I'm so tired of being angry, and of grabbing for fleeting moments of happiness that never last. I'm so tired of waking up every day without the only person who has ever known me completely.

Because Nina's right. All that's left now that you are gone is *endurance*.

I don't think I have the strength any more.

'And when I think of my calling,' I manage in a broken voice, something inside me shattering. 'I do not fear life.'

Except, my darling . . . you do.

I feel myself totter, caught in the space between myself and someone else: unable to return, unwilling to leave. Stuck as nobody, as nothing, as nowhere.

With an overwhelmed sob, I crumple to the floor.

'I don't want to do this any more,' I cry into my hands, finally breaking character as Nina drifts away. 'Please, come back.'

And that's when the applause starts.

33

For a second, I think it's in my head.

The clapping of an imaginary audience, a besotted crowd, blown away by my performance.

Bewildered, I blink and look up.

All the trees have vanished, the rain has stopped and the storm is quiet, the sky blue. Beneath my feet are solid wooden floorboards and I feel a tipping sense of vertigo, the disorientated nausea of a sleepwalker abruptly woken up.

Yet the clapping continues.

With shaking hands, I wipe my eyes and follow the noise to the upper left gallery.

'Bravo!' A voice calls. 'Amazing! Encore!'

As the floor tilts, I try to stand up. 'Wh . . . who's there?' I stutter. 'Where are you?'

And as the cheering continues, I watch with a

sickening lurch as Finn's head appears over the balcony: scruffy hair standing on end.

'That was *fantastic*,' he beams, still clapping as hard as he can. 'It's true, Mercy Valentine. You have real, rare talent. This is your calling.'

Everything inside me plummets.

'My only feedback,' Finn continues, grinning and propping his elbows on the edge of the balcony. 'Is that you *say* you are a seagull, and yet I saw very little to support that claim.'

I stiffen in horror, my blood turning cold.

'Perhaps you could try waggling your arms?' He points his elbows and moves them about. 'Maybe run up and down the stage a few times, shrieking? You could always try stealing someone's chips and then pooping on their heads.'

Reeling, I take a nauseous step backwards.

Finn just saw everything.

He saw me vanish into Nina; saw me crumple up on to the floor, sobbing; saw me in my darkest, most vulnerable state.

It feels like he's been watching me without my skin on.

And now he's . . . *laughing?*

A bubbling, twisting sensation starts in my brain. Why didn't he tell me he was there? Why didn't he *stop* me? How could he just sit there and witness me fall apart? That was *private.* Why is he even here? Is he following me? The theatre is supposed to be *closed.*

'Five stars, though,' he continues jubilantly as I stare at him. 'The part of the seagull is yours. We just need to find you a nice, feathery costume and—'

The bubble pops, evaporating into steam.

I want to *kill* him.

'Mercy?' Finn calls as I grab my handbag, jump off the stage and start running towards the exit. 'Wait, where are you going?'

Blindly, I make it to the door.

Struggling, I heave it open and run towards the locked, dark entrance. It's not open, so I kick the door a few times and peg it towards another door to try that instead.

'Mercy!' Finn emerges from the balcony stairs as I desperately shake the next door. 'Hang on! What's happening? What's wrong?'

Panicked, I try another door; he grabs my hand.

'Don't touch me,' I snarl at him, ripping it away. 'Don't you *dare* touch me.'

'Are you . . .' He pulls back and stares at my swollen, tear-stained face. 'Mercy, are you actually upset? Oh my God, I thought you were *acting*.'

Furious, I run to another locked door and start shoving at it.

'Mercy!' He follows. 'I'm sorry! I was only joking.'

Breathing hard, I kick the door as hard as I can, just as the cleaner squeaks into the entrance with his supplies cart and stares at me with his mouth open.

'OPEN IT,' I scream at him. 'OPEN THE DOOR.'

Blinking, the cleaner fumbles for a key and quickly unlocks the entrance. I burst out into the sunshine, Finn following close behind me. I have never been this angry in my entire life. I want to bite him, scratch him, rip him, fight him, crush him.

He has ruined *everything*.

'Leave me *alone*,' I hiss, desperately searching the road for John.

'But, Mercy—'

'I said LEAVE ME ALONE.'

'I . . .' Finn reaches for my arm and I twist away with a growl. A couple of passers-by have already paused, curious. 'I don't understand, Mer. You were amazing. I was just teasing you about the seagull – I know it's a metaphor. I assumed you'd snap back, and I'd tease, and you'd snap back again. That's what we *do*, isn't it?'

And with a splintering sound that only I can hear, the black diamond inside me explodes.

I whip round to face him.

'*We* don't do *anything*, Finn, because there is *no* "*we*". You do not know me. I do not know you. We are *strangers.*'

'But we're not.' His face is pale, strained. 'I mean, maybe we are, right now, but there's a connection, you know there is, and I thought maybe we were at the beginning of . . . something.'

'THEN YOU WEREN'T LISTENING,' I scream, all semblance of control long gone. 'I TOLD YOU I DO NOT *DO* LOVE, I DO NOT *DO* RELATIONSHIPS, I DO NOT *DO* ROMANCE AND I SURE AS HELL DO NOT DO WHATEVER YOU THINK *THIS* IS.'

People on the South Bank are stopping to stare – recognising me, starting to whisper and take photographs – and I still won't stop, I can't stop.

Finn blinks. 'But I really like—'

'I DON'T CARE. I DON'T CARE HOW YOU FEEL, FINN. THIS IS NOT GOING TO HAPPEN, DO YOU UNDERSTAND ME? I DO NOT FANCY YOU. I WILL NEVER DATE YOU. I WAS ONLY USING YOU TO KEEP MYSELF ENTERTAINED. YOU ARE GRUBBY STAGE CREW AND I AM *MERCY VALENTINE*, SO GET BACK IN YOUR BOX BECAUSE NOTHING IS EVER, EVER, *EVER* GOING TO HAPPEN BETWEEN US!'

My breathing is hard, ragged, broken.

Just to my right, I spot a ratty girl with blonde hair extensions holding her phone up, filming my entire rampage with an expression of pure glee.

Scarlet with fury, I whip towards her.

'YOU WANT SOME? COME GET SOME, YOU TACKY PARASITE, BEFORE I RAM THAT SECOND-HAND PHONE DOWN YOUR CHEAP FAKE-TANNED THROAT AND SEE WHAT IT FILMS THEN!'

Flinching, she puts her phone down and shuffles away.

I turn back to Finn.

He stares at me, searching my face for something that he clearly doesn't find, and good luck to anyone who wants to try.

Then his expression shuts down like a door slamming.

'Right,' he says crisply. 'Got it. Loud and abundantly clear. Thank you for the clarification. It has saved us both a lot of time.'

Straightening his shoulders, Finn walks back into the theatre.

I stare after him, breathing hard.

Mercy—

'Oh, shut up,' I hiss. 'You're dead, Charity. Nobody gives a flying fox what you think any more.'

34

Still seething, I stomp along the South Bank.

I can't return to the theatre like this, so instead I charge up and down for half an hour, hitting trees, kicking bins, snarling at passers-by. Throwing random stuff out of my handbag into the Thames: a Chanel lipstick, club flyers, some coins, whatever I can lob hard into the distance.

At some point a fluffy black-and-white dog approaches me, tail wagging, and I immediately turn on it: 'GET OUT OF MY FACE, YOU STUPID LITTLE MUTT.'

The owner drags it away, muttering about crazy girls.

And I continue stomping, kicking and hitting, the fire inside me burning as if it's never going to stop. I *knew* this weekend was too sweet to be true. I knew things weren't getting better. I knew I couldn't be different. I knew that there was nothing out there – *nobody* out there – who would be able to make me good.

Mercy, please—

'I *said*,' I hiss under my breath. 'I don't want to *hear you*.'

Slowly, my brain starts to quieten and settle again.

The rage is still there, but as the minutes pass, I feel it darkening and tightening: condensing into a hard black lump in the middle of my chest once more.

Exhausted, I get my phone out:

Mercy
I really really need to party tonight – who's in?

There's an immediate *beep*.

Nova
Oh right, so now you're fighting with SECRET LOVER BOY you're not sick any more?

Dior

We're supposed to be FRIENDS. You don't tell us ANYTHING. :(

Mercy

What are you talking about

There's another *beep*.

This time it's a link, and even I didn't realise it would happen *this* fast. It's been less than an hour, but already the video of me screaming at Finn has been shared online thousands of times. It's even worse than I thought. My screeching voice carries clearly, my face is puce, my fists clenched, little flecks of spit are shooting out of my mouth and landing on Finn's appalled face.

Then – just to cap it off – the video includes me turning on the blonde girl and threatening her with physical violence.

Judging from the comments, the general public has never been happier:

She's legit PSYCHO. LOL

Who is he? Hot. He can do waaayyyy better than HER

OMG never date Mercy Valentine she's even worse than Faith #bunnyboiler #cantbuysanity #diva

My phone *beeps* again.

Mercy, what did I tell you about creating scenes in public? I'm coming home this evening and we're going to have a long talk about how your behavior is going to improve going forward. Love Dad x

I grit my teeth as my phone goes off again: it's Faith.

Mer just saw the video – are you ok? Who's the guy? I'll be back tonight so we can talk. Eff xxx

Now Max:

Dude. Stop distracting from my mega launch.
You're not the only deserving attention-seeker
in this family, you know. ;)

And again: Grandma.

Mercy Valentine that is NOT the kind of
'socialising' I was talking about.

Scowling, I kick another bin as hard as I can. A
grubby pigeon flies away in abrupt panic, which
reminds me—
Quickly, I text the Birdbrains:

Mercy
He's nobody. Just some guy at work who's into
me. Pathetic. WE ARE GOING OUT TO
TONIGHT IT IS NOT A QUESTION

No way in *hell* am I sitting at home tonight.
What, waiting for my entire family to descend so
they can try to *talk* to me and *pity* me and *understand*
me and tell me how to sort my life out and become
a nicer, kinder, better person?

It is way, way too late for that.

Jaw tight, I check the time. My rehearsal started five minutes ago, and I'm not going to miss it.

Not for 'locked doors'.

Not for Finn.

As of this minute, acting is all I have left.

Still simmering, I shove my phone back in my pocket and head into the Globe.

35

'What the hell are you all looking at?'

Dropping my bag on the floor, I slump heavily into a spare chair, fold my arms tightly and scowl at the rest of the cast. They immediately glance down at their feet, embarrassed by their own curiosity.

Clearly, they've seen the video too.

'Mercy is here!' Verity frowns and looks around her with a tight, confused smile. 'And yet I locked the doors on the dot, as promised, so how she got in is a mystery!'

It's not: the cleaner is terrified of me.

'That's a no-show and a lateness.' My director makes a little mark on her script. 'It means a verbal warning, I'm afraid. We are fast approaching opening night, and we need *every minute.*'

With an exaggerated eyeroll, I glance around the theatre, my eyes lingering briefly on the balconies. All the magic has leaked out of it. There's no transformation, no revelation, no connection with history or art: it's just a load of old wood, built in a circle.

At least this time, Finn isn't watching me like a total creep.

'Elijah also appears to have missed our cut-off point,' the director continues, a muscle flickering in her jaw. 'So, would anyone like to fill in today?'

I snort: please. As if anyone's going to—

'IIIIIIIIII'll do it!' Daisy wanders forward in slow motion, as if she's taking a leisurely stroll through a cornfield. '*Much Ado* is the most rrrrrromaaaaaaaantic story ever told. It's my absolute *faaaaaavourrrrrite*. I know the whooooooooollllle play, back to front!'

Of course she does: what a total muppet.

'Lovely!' Verity beams at her, her face completely transformed. 'What a star! Act Four, positions please, everyone!'

It's the big wedding scene, so practically the entire cast is on stage to create a suitable sense of festive *occasion*. The nutbag Claudio is about to falsely accuse dullsville Hero of cheating on him before ditching her at the altar, and she's going to faint in shock, presumed dead.

Nothing says *romance* like public cruelty and manipulation, huh?

Scowling, I climb up onto the stage. 'Ursula' smirks at me as she takes her position at the back, so I curl my top lip and she flushes and looks away again. Ancient 'Friar Francis' ambles past me on his way to the officiate at the front.

He nods at me. 'Still celebrating, Darcy?'

I stare at him. 'Excuse me?'

'Still out celebrating your big bowling win from Friday?' The friar straightens out his little white dog collar. 'I understand. I've been bowling for sixty years now and I never got a single strike!'

Apparently this man is not only too old to have social media but he also has no idea what my name is.

'*Mercy*,' I snap tiredly.

'Why, thank you,' he chuckles, shaking his head. 'Don't worry, I'll keep trying.'

Hero/Piper, whatever her name is, takes her place at my side and smiles tentatively. 'Hey. You all right?'

'Yup,' I snap shortly.

'It's just we, uh, saw the video. Ursula had it on

her phone so a . . . group of us . . . umm, watched it just before you arrived.'

I clench my jaw. 'I bet you did.'

'So, I just want to say . . .' She frowns, searching for the right words. 'It's not really very fair. I mean . . . nobody really knows what goes on in a relationship, right? I argue with my boyfriend *all* the time, but I would just *die* if it got posted by a stranger on the internet and everyone saw it. So . . . it sucks. That's all. We're not judging you.'

She glances quickly to the side at 'Ursula'.

'Okay, Candice is judging you, but that's just because she's got a crush on Finn, so don't take it personally.'

With infinite precision, I eye Candice up and down, then turn to look directly at 'Hero'.

'I don't take it personally,' I say calmly and loudly. 'Because I don't give a flying monkey's armpit what you talentless losers think of me. This play is just a stepping stone. And you lot are a bunch of squelchy little frogs, getting in my way.'

'Hero' flinches as if I've slapped her. 'Okay.'

'And Finn,' I say with even more volume, 'is *not* my boyfriend. So *Candy* can knock herself out.'

'Right!' Verity calls from the front as my colleagues' eyes widen. 'Beatrice? Hero? Can we stop the chat now? It's time to start.'

Sullenly, I watch the scene develop: a load of amateur screaming, shouting, fainting and histrionics. Piper swoons to the floor with such conviction she literally lands on my foot. As her best friend and kinswoman, I'm supposed to have some kind of reaction to this, but I just cannot be bothered. Gotta leave something for opening night, right?

Finally, the stage clears and Daisy steps towards me as Benedict, looking so flaming chuffed with her new role that I immediately want to jab her in the stomach with my elbow.

'Laaaaaaady Beatrice,' she says gently, reaching for me. 'Have you wept all this while?'

My face is quite clearly calm and dry.

'Yep,' I intone. 'And I will weep a while longer.'

'Ahem!' Verity leans forward. 'Mercy, could we get a *little* more emotion from you, please? Beatrice is distraught about the unjust way Hero has been treated, but I'm just not seeing much *empathy* yet? Also, it's *yea*, not *yep*. Quite a different sound.'

'*Yeah*,' I say, knowing exactly how it's pronounced.

'Not quite. *Yea*. You hear both the *e* and the *a*.'

'Yay.'

'*Yea*.' My director looks about ready to throw something at me. 'Tell you what, Daisy filled in for you the other day, when you didn't show up on your first day of rehearsals. Remember that? Day, could you show Mercy how you do it?'

Daisy beams at me. 'I'd beeeee honoured to!'

With a flicker of waking anger, I spin back towards Little Miss Slow-Moving Toffee Face, feeling something in my chest start to unravel again.

'Oh, I'm *sorry*. Which one of us has a celebrated television show under their belt?'

'Youuuuuuuu!' Daisy answers instantly.

'And *which* one of us is from a line of internationally famous actresses stretching back four generations, with so many Oscars in our family home that we use one to prop open the bathroom window?'

'You,' Daisy says in a smaller voice, finally grasping my tone.

'That's right,' I conclude sharply. 'Me. And I don't need your little community college acting tips, so pipe the hell down and be lucky you even get to stand on the same stage as a Valentine.'

They want emotion? I'll give them emotion. Closing my eyes, I consciously unleash the anger that's always inside me: letting it out like a roaring lion.

Then, I cross the stage until I'm right in Daisy's face.

'Kill Claudio,' I snarl.

'Ha!' She immediately works out which line I've jumped to. 'Not for the wiiiiiiide world.'

'You kill me to deny it,' I hiss. 'Farewell.'

She reaches for me. 'Tarry, sweeeeeeet Beatrice.'

'I am gone, though I am here.' Ripping away with a small growl, I look her up and down from across the stage, examining her with distaste, with disappointment. 'There is no love in you. Nay, I pray you, let me go.'

Her eyes widen. 'Beeeeatrice—'

'In faith,' I sneer angrily, 'I will go.'

She tries to appease me. 'We'll be friends first.'

I laugh bitterly. 'You dare easier be friends with me than fight with mine enemy.'

Daisy looks confused. 'Is Claudio thine enemy?'

I glance up to the top-right balcony and with a

painful flash of red my anger reaches boiling point. It's not mine any more, and it's not Beatrice's either; it's just a raging poison with somewhere to finally go.

'Is he not approved in the height a villain that hath slandered, scorned, dishonoured my kinswoman?' Blindly, I run across the stage towards her. 'O, that I were a man!'

With a slam, I shove Daisy backward: her eyes widen.

'What, bear her in hand until they come to take hands?' Shaking with emotion, I push her again, harder. Daisy staggers back. 'And then, with public accusation –' another push – 'uncovered slander –' push – 'unmitigated rancour . . .'

Mercy! What are you doing? Stop!

With a final, furious push, I shove Daisy to the ground.

She lands heavily, with a bump.

'O GOD, THAT I WERE A MAN,' I scream from the bottom of my stomach, bending over her with my fists clenched. 'I WOULD *EAT HIS HEART IN THE MARKET-PLACE*!'

Then I stand, shaking, eyes blurred, breathing hard.

There's a silence.

A long, dense silence that sinks into my skin as the rest of the room starts to slowly come back into focus: the bewildered cast, my open-mouthed director, Daisy's huge brown eyes staring up at me.

I stand up and lurch abruptly backwards, away from everyone.

No no, no no no – *what did I just do?*

'Daisy,' I whisper. 'I—'

'Wow,' she says from the floor, eyes widening a little more. 'Just . . . *wow*. That . . . was *iiiiiiincredible*. You're so right, Mercy. There is *nothing* I could possibly teach you.'

I blink at her.

'Impressive,' Verity nods, stepping between us. 'At last we get to see some of this raw talent we're paying for! But let's work on channelling the physical aggression – health and safety violations aren't welcome. Shall we start the scene again?'

Slowly, the rest of the cast begin to take their positions. From the wary way they edge round me, glancing sidewise, they are clearly not convinced that I was purely acting.

With a bang, the theatre door swings open.

'All right chapsters! I made it!' Eli saunters down the aisle. 'What did I miss? Thanks for holding the fort again, Day!'

I turn just in time to see Daisy's shoulders collapse.

'Suuuuuure,' she says, standing up slowly and brushing herself down. 'No problem. Any time.'

She shuffles off the stage and my stomach abruptly hurts for her.

'For the love of—' Our director turns to stare again at the swinging doors. 'Eli, how did *you* get in? Is there *any* security around here?'

'When you've got the right money, babe,' Eli grins at her, '*everywhere* is open.'

'What a horrifying thought.' Verity looks up to the balconies, shields her eyes and frowns. 'By the way, has anybody seen Finneas today?'

Everyone immediately turns to look at me.

'Disappointing,' my director continues. 'He was supposed to come in early to fix one of the squeaking gallery seats. That boy is normally so reliable.'

All the blood just dropped out of my body.

'Finn's not here?' 'Ursula' says tightly. 'Well, maybe you should ask *Mercy*.'

36

Mercy
Rehearsal is over, I need to go out NOW.

Mercy
Hello?

Mercy
CAN ANYBODY HEAR ME?

I'm starting to spiral again.

Sitting in the back of John's limo, I play the video over and over again, picking at my knuckle scab.

And with every line, I spiral a little further.

There is no 'we'.

I do not fancy you. I will never date you.

You are grubby stage crew and I am Mercy Valentine, so get back in your box because nothing is ever

Ever

Ever

Going to happen between us.

With a tiny whimper, I put my head in my hands. Never, in my entire life, have I ever been more ashamed.

Finn was doing his *job*.

He was doing what he is *paid* to do, what he had been *told* to do, and *I* broke into his workplace, commandeered the stage and ripped him apart for accidentally witnessing it. Because that's what I do, isn't it? I destroy everyone that comes near me.

'Where are we going?' John says carefully, glancing at me in the mirror. 'Home or . . .?'

Desperately, I send another text:

Mercy
Please guys, I'll tell you everything just
ANSWER ME.

There's a *beep*.

Nova
Sleepover at mine. Come if you want.

Relief floods my brain: I'll go anywhere, do anything, as long as I'm not on my own.

'St John's Wood,' I tell him. 'Nova's house. Please.'

Then I lean back and close my eyes in exhaustion. I'm completely spent: a barely functioning shell.

I was only using you to keep myself entertained.

Oh God.

From: Mercy Valentine
To: Finneas O'Connor

I need to say

Delete.

From: Mercy Valentine

I'm so sorry that

Delete.

From: Mercy Valentine

There are no words that I can

Delete.

Because there *are* no words. I cannot undo what I said to Finn, or how I said it. No matter how hard I apologise, it will stay on the internet: an eternal reminder of exactly who I am.

Putting my phone in my pocket, I stare numbly out of the window while we slowly weave through tree-lined streets into pretty Primrose Hill. For years, sleepovers at Nova's were all we did, and, as we turn into the driveway, I can feel something inside of me start to soften.

The Valentine mansion is red brick, stone pillars, gleaming mahogany staircases and antique grandfather clocks. Dior's elaborately classless house – as we've already seen – lies predominantly underground, like a war bunker for neurotics. Amethyst's parents went for faux-Tudor, attempting to buy 'history' with chintz plates and elaborate curtains. But Vee's mum is an award-winning architect and her house is incredible.

It's a large block of pure glass and steel, and – as

268

the gates swing shut behind us – I suddenly feel twelve and completely in awe again. The setting sun is turning the huge windows violet and pink and there are bright marshmallowy clouds reflected across the glass.

Shame her dad likes to hang ten-foot portraits of himself on the walls: you can literally see him for miles.

Sliding out of the limo, I walk towards the house.

'Hey.' Nova's sharp, angular face appears out of an open window. 'Looks like you're *well* again.'

I glance away. 'Yup.'

'Hurray for us.' She rolls her eyes and applies some lip gloss. 'Mee and Dee are in the garden, setting up in the tent. I'll meet you guys out there.'

A small wave of disbelief: we're still sleeping in a *tent?* We're not little kids any more, and this isn't Glastonbury. If they think I'm curling up in a sleeping bag again like a—

Sharply, I catch myself. It might be time to exercise some gratitude. Something tells me going home now will be even less comfortable than sleeping on the ground.

Forcing a bright smile, I wave at Nova's achingly

cool mother – wearing a structured navy dress and lying on a white block sofa on the ground floor, reading *Architectural Digest* – and reluctantly acknowledge Nova's father: cooking yet another vegan stir-fry while blasting out his own music.

Vee is with her younger sister in the study, helping with her homework, and something twists in my chest.

Swallowing, I head round to the back of the house.

The garden is impressive too. It's neat and zen with cement planters of rustling grasses, huge sculptural flowers and well-positioned trees. From here, you can see the entire house in its full glory, with every room exposed and open, like a doll's house with the front taken off.

Oh my gosh, do you remember the time when we—
No.

You totally do! We were sleeping over there and I had that genius idea and I woke you up and we—

'Dior!' I call, jogging across the lawn. 'Amethyst!'

Glossy heads appear out of what is definitely, one hundred per cent, in no way whatsoever a 'tent'. It's a *yurt* lined with tasselled rugs, climbing ivy, fairy lights, faux-fur beanbags and four mattresses arranged with crisp white bedding in a neat circle. Pastel bunting hangs from the ceiling, dreamcatchers are dangling over every bed and pink and white roses are coordinated in matching vases. There's a gel nail station, a bubbling chocolate fondue set, a projection screen and a temporary pop-up library, even though I've literally never seen any of these girls read.

Ah MAN. They upgraded! This is so UNFAIR.

It looks like a fairy designed her dream home and then a unicorn came in and puked all over it.

'Cee!' Dior flaps her hands like she's trying to take off. 'Isn't this amazing? It's called *glamping*, which I think is short for *Glad I'm Camping!* I'm *so* going to ask Daddy if we can get one, only mine will have to be inside because the garden totally fell into the basement.'

'Mummy says it's tacky,' Nova says proudly, appearing behind me. 'But Daddy said what his princess wants his princess gets so Check. It. Ouuuuut!'

There's a sizable hedge that has obviously just been planted between the sparkly yurt and the house. My respect for Nova's stylish mother grows exponentially.

Frowning, I stick my head in and get hit by a thick wall of burning incense. I'm no scientist, but it doesn't seem smart to combine sleeping girls and flammable fabric with *actual fire*.

'I would rather –' I start – *lick a bus window* – then swallow – 'have this bed by the entrance, if that's okay?'

'Sure! Don't you just *love* it?' Nova is taking selfies and prancing around with unbearable smugness, distributing small bcribboned packets on the beds. Green for Amethyst. Red for Dior. Blue for Nova. They've each been given their own colour, like they're the fairies in *Sleeping Beauty*. 'New jim-jams for us! They're *pure* silk and French lace, obviously. We got them from America.'

She takes another photo and posts it on Instagram.

'Then how the hell are they Fren—' I chew the inside of my mouth. 'Amazing, Vee! So thoughtful!' Then I stare in confusion at the baby pink pile I've just been handed. 'I . . . don't really wear pink, guys.'

'You don't?' Nova frowns. 'Are you sure?'

'Umm.' I look down at my black T-shirt, black jeans and black boots and fight an intense urge to rip her face off. 'Yes.'

'But *sometimes* you wear pink,' Amethyst objects. 'I'm *sure* I've seen you wear pink, Cee.'

'I have literally never worn pink,' I say. 'Ever.'

'Huh.' The girls I have known since I was five years old shrug at each other in amazement. 'Crazy!'

'Yes, madness.' I clear my throat and attempt to smile. 'But it's fine. I'll just sleep in my clothes. So . . . what's our first activity?'

Please let it be something distracting. Something that doesn't allow me to think about today for a single, solitary second.

The girls look at each other, throw their hands in the air and *meeeeeeeeeep* loudly.

Something tells me I'm going to regret asking.

'We're going to talk about *boys*,' Nova says, gesturing to the fluffy beanbags. 'Which boys we like, which boys we don't, which boys we are *secretly dating* and – Mercy, where are you going?'

37

Five years ago

'Poo-bum.' *Poke.* 'Chicken-brain.' *Poke.* 'Cabbage-stink.' *Poke.* 'Farter-McCarter.' *Poke.* 'Big-Nose-McGrue.'

I open my eyes. Charity is hovering centimetres away from me, her face so close to mine I can smell strawberry jelly sweets, and feel her fringe tickling my forehead.

She pokes me again, even though I'm clearly awake.

'What is it?' I sit up groggily, trying to work out where we are. It's dark, the air is damp and musty, my legs are trapped together and it smells of cheese crisps and girl farts, so I'm guessing we're in a tent in Nova's garden. 'Also, if I've got a big nose you've got a big nose because they're the same nose, idiot.'

'I know.' My twin leans forward and kisses the tip of mine. 'We're so cute. I love us so much.'

'Gross.' I smile and nudge her away. 'I'm sorry, did my sleeping bore you? Have you run out of snacks?'

'Yes and yes. Dee is a greedy little munchkin and I think she's fallen asleep on top of a secret packet of biscuits because every time she snores it rustles and gives her away.'

We look in the same direction.

In the dim light, you can just see shapes where the three other girls have passed out together on the other side of the tent. Dior is snoring and rustling, as predicted. Amethyst is making kiss-y sounds: already practising, even in her sleep. Without warning, Nova rolls over, sighs and farts so loudly the entire tent vibrates like a washing machine on spin-cycle.

Charity and I immediately start giggling.

'*No*,' I whisper, as we snuffle incoherently into each other's shoulders. 'I'm not *marinating* in Vee's bum gas.'

'Agreed,' Tee sniggers back. 'We have to get out of here before the fumes casserole us. Go go *go*.'

Scrambling over each other in the dark, we manage to free ourselves from the caterpillar-like sleeping bags and tumble out of the front tent flap: falling onto the grass and laughing so hard I have to cross my legs at the ankles so I don't pee myself.

'*Sssssshhhh.*' Tee pokes me again, this time in the bladder. 'I've had an idea for something fun.'

Of course she has. I roll over and look at her in moonlight. Her face is lit with an animated, ghostly glow. It's very slightly drizzling now, but Charity's pranks know no weather limitations.

'It's *three in the morning*,' I yawn, wiping rain off my forehead. 'Can't we just save the fun for daytime?'

'Beep beep,' she grins, holding a hand up to her face like a walkie-talkie. 'This is mission control for Mermaid Valentine. Fun incoming regardless. Over.'

'You're so lame,' I laugh.

'Beep beep, you're so lame. *Over*,' she corrects. 'Copy.'

I give up. 'Roger, wilco.'

'Who's Roger Wilco? He sounds hot. We'll come back to that later.' Charity begins to crawl around the side of the garden on all fours. 'Stay low!'

With an unseen eyeroll I shuffle after my twin,

getting increasingly confused and covered in grass stains.

Then she stands up. 'Ready?'

'No,' I whisper. 'Because not for the first time you haven't told me what we're doing.'

'You'll pick it up,' she grins. 'You're the smart one.'

I glow with pleasure as my sister reaches into her hoody pocket and pulls out a bluetooth speaker. She must have grabbed it from the tent while I wasn't looking. Hooking it up to her phone, Tee places it on a tree stump and blasts out ridiculously loud pop music.

With a wink, Charity runs into the middle of the grass.

At once, the garden lights up.

She begins to do a ridiculous dance, swinging her arms over her head and wiggling her bottom. Then she stops, frozen in position. After a brief pause, the security lights go back out again. Then Tee starts dancing again and the garden lights up.

Darkness. Light.

Darkness. Light.

Darkness. Light.

Darkness. Light.

And every time she freezes in an increasingly ridiculous pose: climbing the stairs, swimming like a shark, puffing her biceps out, until finally – unable to bear it any longer – I laugh and run onto the lawn to dance with her.

Darkness. Light.

A few seconds later, three yawning, bleary-eyed girls poke their heads out of the tent. Then the gang starts giggling, running out in their fleece pyjamas to join us. As the rain falls harder, the dancing becomes looser, more haphazard and messy. We're spinning and jumping and flailing and giggling, until we're sliding around in a happy, muddy heap.

The lights in the house go on.

'Girls!' Nova's mother is standing at the back door in a silk dressing gown, smiling but attempting to look mad. 'What in the name of my precious beauty sleep do you think you're doing?'

Without hesitation, our friends turn to point. 'Charity!'

'It was Charity!'

'Charity started it!'

'I did not!' Soaking and triumphant, my sister

grabs my hand, squeezes it tightly and holds it in the air. '*We* did.'

And I feel a rush of pride so fierce and loud my insides bellow like a dragon because I suddenly realise that I love my sister more than I will ever love anything or anyone.

More than I will ever love myself.

'Bedtime, girls.' Nova's mum laughs. 'Get back in your tent before I call your parents.'

38

'*AAAAAAAAAAAAAAAAAARGGGGGHHH-HHH.*'

I punch the tree as hard as I can.

'OH, MOTHER—' I scream as my knuckle splits and abruptly starts bleeding again. 'OWW.'

Dude, stop starting on the foliage!

Out of breath, I shake my injured hand and stare at the twilight garden. The past feels like it's alive and waiting for me. Right over there is where the old tent was pitched; there's the path we crawled along; there's the bush Charity used to pee behind when she was too lazy to go into the house.

I can't believe you just told them that.

Nothing has changed and yet everything is different.

Still one of my best-ever nights, you know.

I know.

Mer . . . It's so unfair.

I know.

I was great at being a teenager, wasn't I? I was such an awesome thirteen-year-old. A legendary fourteen-year-old.

You were the best.

But fifteen was just starting. Sixteen. Seventeen.

My chest hurts.

I reckon I'd have totally nailed being an adult too. We could have moved out, got a flat, played so many tricks—

I know.

I would always have woken you up so we could have fun.

I know.

I still want to do that.

'I know,' I whisper. 'I'm so sorry.'

Aching with guilt, I turn round and head reluctantly back into the yurt.

'I'm here,' I state flatly as I sit on the end of my designated bed. 'I was just so . . . uh. Excited . . . I had to go outside and scream.'

Dior nods – sounds reasonable – and hands me a chocolate-dipped marshmallow. 'I was *just* telling

I clear my throat and clench my aching fist under the duvet. 'He's nobody. Like I said, he's just this random stage-crew guy who keeps, umm, following me. So I told him to leave me alone.'

Another hot wave of guilt: *I'm sorry, Finn. Again.*

'Oh.' Nova accepts this immediately. 'Well, obviously you wouldn't date *stage crew*. What would you even have in common? Haha! Can you imagine? He probably goes to, like, Nando's or something.'

'I mean, he *could* always pick us up when we go out?' Amethyst tries hopefully. 'Does he drive?'

'Unlike *you*.' Dior pouts pointedly, applying bright pink lip gloss. 'You've had that brand-new Land Rover *days* now and you've not driven us anywhere. You can be so selfish sometimes, Cee.'

'As I said,' I state firmly, hating myself, hating them. 'He's production staff. He saws wood and sticks things together with glue.'

And he's lovely and now I'm incredibly sad.

'So, what about that Eli guy?' Nova tries with more optimism. 'He's hot, *and* rich. His hair is very blond. Is it natural? If you go out with him, can you find out who does his highlights?'

'I'm not dating Eli.' I laugh awkwardly. 'You know my rule about actors. Relationships can only handle one ego-maniac and ideally I'd prefer it to be me.'

I try for a smile but nobody joins me.

'You never date anyone,' Amethyst objects, painting her nails pale sickly green. 'Eli Bickford-Boggins is a *total* match for you, Cee.'

'Yeah,' Dior nods then laughs. 'Tell you what, if Tee was here, she would *totally* have gone for it already.'

Excuse me? I would never have gone for Mr Mickey Mouse.

'She'd have won him over in like thirty seconds!' Nova giggles. 'She was *so* charming and funny and sweet. Oh my goodness, what was the name of that boy she liked . . .'

'Benson.'

'No, Jake.'

'Blake,' I say through my teeth. 'His name was Blake.'

'Blake!' All three girls start giggling. 'Whatever happened to him when the show was cancelled?'

Hey, what did happen?

I don't know, Charity, I was too busy grieving the

unexpected death of my identical twin sister to look on IMBD for Blake's career progression.

'Not sure,' I grunt, desperate to change the subject. 'Hey! Why don't we . . . uh.' I fumble for a distracting sleepover activity. 'Braid each other's hair?'

The three girls ignore me.

'I miss her, you know?' Amethyst blows on her nails. 'Like, sometimes I'll be like, that was funny, I should text Tee! And then I'm like, oh, I can't. And it's, like, *so* sad. You know?'

'Right?' Nova dips another marshmallow in the melted chocolate and nibbles at it delicately. 'Sometimes, when we're all hanging out, I'll just look around and be, like, something's missing, and I forget what it is, and then I remember and it's totally *tragic*.'

Wow. Please tell me they didn't speak at my funeral.

'Tee was the best,' Dior agrees, pouting. 'Sometimes I just wish she hadn't died.'

Swallowing, I get my phone out.

'Ooooooh, do you remember those messages Tee sent that guy about the kittens and bunny rabbits? That was just—'

From: Mercy Valentine
To: Finneas O'Connor

I am so sorry.

I know it's not enough. I know it can't make anything
I did or said to you better. But the truth is, I am so
sad it physically hurts, like someone is breaking my
bones, all of the time. I am so lonely, and so full of
anger and pain I can't contain it. It shoots out of
me the way water from a tap will spurt when you
put a finger over the end of it: hitting everyone,
destroying everything. It's exhausting and
uncontrollable, and sometimes the only way to find
a moment of relief is by hurting someone else.

But I'm sorry. You don't deserve to be treated like
that.

You deserve better than me.

Mercy

SEND.

Amethyst is unsubtly attempting to lean over my shoulder without messing up her nails so she can read my email. With a wave of horror, I quickly lock the screen and shove my phone in my pocket.

'Work,' I say quickly. 'New script amendments.'

'You know, I really miss Charity,' Nova continues, sighing and lying gracefully back on her bed. 'She was always so much *fun*.'

Followed by a pointed look at me.

'Oh-Em-Gee,' Amethyst squeaks with wide eyes, 'we should *so* post a throwback to honour her memory!'

With a tight throat, I watch her scroll carefully through her phone until she finds a photo of us as twelve-year-olds, huddled in sleeping bags and high on sugar. A shiny Amethyst with metallic braces has one cheerful arm round a pre-blonde Dior. Her sunburnt cheek is on Nova's skinny little shoulder. Charity is lying on the floor, grinning with a double chin and her head resting in my lap, and I'm kneeling on the edge, trying hard to smile and look comfortable.

'Oh, I *love* that!' Dior is already applying magnetic eyelashes. 'We should totally do a *now* and *then* shot. Show our glow-up!'

After half an hour of solid preparation, the girls huddle into a tight group. Holding the camera up high and dropping into poses that arrived in our lives over the last couple of years: pouty lips, one hand on hip, clavicles popped, eyes large.

Okay, I have to ask, do you actually still like hanging out with them?

It doesn't matter. They're all I've got.

'Mercy!' Fingers are clicked at me. 'Come on!'

Reluctantly, I crawl into the frame and stare blankly at the screen as my friends take a trillion photographs.

'*Remembering Charity Valentine,*' Dior chants out loud as she face-tunes a photo, narrows her waist, filters it with Valencia and begins typing. '*Gone but never forgotten. We love you, beautiful. Always with us. xxxx PS French silk and chocolate marshmallows! Living our best lives!* And . . . three, two, one post!'

'Share!'

'Share!'

I swear I can hear Charity laughing.

'Right,' Nova says, smoothing her hair and clicking on LIVE STORIES. '*Pillow fight!*'

39

My friends are fast asleep by midnight.

Staring blankly at the twinkly yurt ceiling, I listen to the girls snuffle and mutter, sprawled under satin duvets with hair extensions flung on bedside tables. No longer hiding biscuits, farting, giggling or trying to stay up till dawn. Charity is right: we've all changed so much. When did we lose ourselves? When did we become so dry and grown-up and *joyless*?

My stomach twists sharply; maybe when they lost her too.

Impulsively, I jump up, unzip the yurt door flap and slip outside.

Oooh, what are we doing?

'It's not too late,' I whisper. 'Let's do this.'

Quietly, I zip the tent back up again, edge round the garden, find a bouncy track on my phone and turn the music up as loud as it'll go. Then I stare at the lawn for a few seconds, hesitating – something's missing, it's not raining – and then in a wave of ingenuity I jog towards the wall and hit the sprinkler switch.

Then I flex my shoulders.

Ready. Steady.

Go.

I run awkwardly onto the lawn as the security lights flash, just as they did before.

Light, dark.

Light, dark.

With a hiss, the sprinklers fizz into action: covering the lawn in fake rain. Throwing my arms high in the air, I stick out my bottom, take a deep breath and *woooooooooo-woooooooo-wooooooo-wooooooooooo-woooooooooooo-wooooooooooooo-wooooo-woooooo-woooooooooo-woooooooooooo-wooooooooo.*

'WHAT THE HELL!' Indignant screams come from inside the yurt. 'WHAT IS GOING ON?!!'

'THERE'S WATER EVERYWHERE!'

'MY FRENCH SILK IS DRY CLEAN ONLY!!!! NOOO!'

Still yelling, the others struggle with the door zip,

smashing against the walls of the yurt, then burst through, falling over each other in their haste to get out. In horror, I watch as my drenched friends charge across the lawn towards me, shrieking and slipping and sliding on the wet grass. Water is running down my face, shooting into the air, spraying onto the yurt, spiralling out from *inside* it.

And the sirens just keep going: *wooooooooo-wooooooooo-wooooooooo-wooooooooo-woooo.*

Oh God, this isn't what I—

'I'm sorry!' Nobody can hear me over the alarms. 'I'm so sorry, I didn't mean to—'

'WHAT DID YOU *DO, MERCY*?!!' Amethyst shrieks, water dripping off her nose. 'Why would you turn on the freaking *sprinklers*?'

Woooooo-wooooooooo-wooooooo.

'The garden is alarmed!' Nova runs to switch off the sprinkler system, her face puce. 'Daddy has a stalker! Everybody knows that!'

'I—'

Wooooooo-wooooooo-wooooooo-wooooooooo.

'Somebody help me!' Dior has slipped in the mud and is trying furiously in vain to get up. 'I can't—'

Amethyst reaches down for her, and in one sharp

tug gets pulled onto the ground as well. As they scrabble around in the dirt, I hear Dior beginning to sob.

Even Charity seems temporarily stunned into silence.

Bewildered, I open my mouth. 'But this isn't what I—'

My breath vanishes: reflected in the huge glass window next to me is a girl with dark, solemn eyes.

Maybe you should have run that one by me first.

Blinking, I turn back to face my so-called friends. 'Guys, I—'

'What is *wrong* with you?!' Dior screams as – one by one – all the lights in the house go on and the sirens finally switch off. 'My parents are right about you, Mercy! You are just *bad.*'

 40

I am bad.

Alone in Nova's spare room, in the dark and the silence, I hear that word all night: bad, bad, bad, bad.

Because I am, and I've always known it.

Charity balanced me out, made my darkness less obvious, but without her it's all too clear.

I am a black hole, sucking the light out of everything around me. Even when I don't want to. *Especially* when I don't want to. I just don't seem to have whatever quality it is that makes people smile, warm to you, gravitate in your direction. I'm the opposite, and I can feel the people around me, growing cold and spinning away.

So I hate them for it.

I hate them for leaving me, even before they start to.

I hate them to save myself time, so I'm ready when they go.

Finally, it gets light.

Shivering in my damp clothes, I text John:

Amethyst isn't giving me a lift home any more, can you pick me up from Nova's?

Then I creep quietly down the stairs.

Everybody's still asleep but there's mud and water everywhere: smeared footprints on the glossy floors, dirty handprints on the white sofa. I've managed to ruin two of my friends' houses in the space of a week – something tells me a third invitation will not be forthcoming.

Beep.

Max has the car this morning. I can get to you in an hour and a half? John.

With a wave of sharp panic, I glance at my watch. It's an early-start rehearsal today. I've already had a verbal warning for lateness. Verity is blatantly hanging on to the end of her tether by her passive-aggressive fingertips.

Quickly, I type:

An hour and a half is too late!

Beep.

Oi, I saw that message you cheeky little monkey, we're on the motorway RN – get a taxi

Beep.

PS Still v grateful Mermaid, please don't be mad with me xxx

A second, more intense wave of panic.

I'm beginning to regret making such a fuss about The Beast now: having my own transport would have been kind of handy.

FINE HOW DO YOU GET A 'TAXI'.

Beep.

You don't need to bunny-ear 'taxi', Mercy. It's a legit form of transport. I'll make a call and get one sent to you now. Xx

Relieved, I type:

OK thank you xxx

Then I collapse on the doorstep and do my best to calm down.

They'll forgive you eventually, you know.

I know: they always do. For old times' sake, for your sake, for the sake of my queue-jumping skills and connections. It'll be okay. I just need to focus on getting to the theatre ASAP, and yes, I'll be muddy and damp, but at least I won't get screamed at by—

My stomach abruptly spasms.

Finn.

Holding my breath, I open my inbox.

Nothing.

Just in case, I refresh again: nothing.

And again.

Nothing.

Humiliated, I tuck my head under my arms and

try very hard to fold myself inwards, like human origami. Finn is not going to forgive me, and I know that. He'll never talk to me again. But he could at least *acknowledge* my apology, right? Just a proof of receipt? So I know he definitely read it?

A flash of familiar anger flickers.

You know what? That was a very magnanimous expression of regret. I deserve a response.

A brighter flicker now.

You know what? Finn is a very harsh, obstinate and judgemental boy with zero empathy and that's not the kind of person I want to spend time—

Mer, you're doing it again.

My anger abruptly flattens. I suppose attacking someone because they made me feel vulnerable and then attacking them again because they didn't respond to my apology and thus made me feel vulnerable again could be considered ironic, even for me.

'Mercy Valentine?'

More than half an hour later, I look up from my knees at a black cab with the motor still purring. With effort, I stagger to my feet and attempt to smooth my now frizzy hair. The driver peers out of the window, looks me up and down and widens his eyes, visibly startled.

'Yes,' I bristle tiredly. 'I'm *that* Mercy Valentine. Yes, you've read everything about me. Yes, I'm exactly as horrible as you have no doubt seen online. Please, I will pay you extra if we can just leave the small talk at the door.'

'Right.' He frowns. 'You going to leave the muddy shoes at the door too? Because there's a fee for getting my seats dirty.'

I look down at the state of me and cringe. I am literally coated all over in mud and grass stains. Okay, maybe this taxi driver wasn't totally mesmerised by my notoriety.

'I'll pay for that too,' I say in a subdued voice.

'Fine.' A sharp nod. 'Get in.'

I climb meekly into the cab and glance at my watch once more. There's no time to go home and get changed now but, traffic depending, I should still make the rehearsal. I may even have time for a swift clean-up in the bathroom. And who knows? Maybe Finn won't even be there. He didn't turn up after our fight yesterday; maybe he won't turn up today.

Oh God, I hope he turns up today. If all else fails,

at least I can grovel in person: down on my knees, sobbing into his trainers.

Because that'll make me look *much* more sane and desirable.

With my eyes shut, I lean back tiredly.

Something *beeps*.

Heart leaping, I scramble to pull my phone out of my bag with such urgency I drop it on the floor of the car and have to unclip my seatbelt to reach for it under the driver's seat.

Finn! He's forgiven you! I knew it!

Swallowing, I stare at the screen.

COME OVER. FAITH

Followed by the emergency running-girl emoji.

This time my heart drops to the floor.

'Change of plan,' I say quickly, leaning forward and tapping the glass. 'Brixton. As fast as you can.'

41

Effie are you okay?

I *knew* there was something wrong with her.

EFFIE TALK TO ME

I should have listened to my instincts.

**FAITH HOLD ON DON'T WORRY I AM ON
MY WAY xxx**

This is my fault.

After what I did to Faith a month ago, I should
have *been making sure* I was there for her. But no,
I was too self-important. Too preoccupied with me.
What kind of selfish, empty monster *am* I?

Biting my lip, I text:

EFF I LOVE YOU DON'T BE SAD JUST WAIT FOR ME

Verity can lock me out of the play forever – I don't care.

This time, I am getting my sister.

'Please,' I beg, leaning forward. 'Can you go faster? My sister, I think she's had another breakdown.'

The driver glances at my wild-eyed panic, then nods and begins to steadily up the speed. It still takes forever to get there. By the time we screech up to the tower block, I'm convinced that Faith has already smashed up her grotty studio flat to pieces.

Grabbing all the cash I have out of my handbag, I lob it at the taxi driver with a terse *thanks*. Then I leg it towards the front doors, hit all the buttons until somebody in the building lets me in and peg it up the stairs, jaw clenched.

'Faith!' I smash my fists on her peeling door. 'FAITH!'

Spinning in a panic, I spot a fire extinguisher on the wall, wrench it off with a grunt and hold it in my arms like a badly behaved toddler. Then I back up so I can gather some speed.

'FAITH!' Three . . . Two . . . . 'FAITH, I'M COMING! DON'T MOVE!'

One . . . I sprint forward.

'What the—' Faith says as the door swings open and I sprint straight past her into the flat. 'Crikey, Mercy! Why are you trying to smash our front door down?'

Swearing loudly, I hit a sofa and bounce off it.

'Are you okay?' Breathless, I drop the extinguisher and roll over. 'Eff, what happened?'

Leaping up, I assess Effie in a panicked micro-second. Shapeless grey tracksuit bottoms, a huge black LES MISÉRABLES T-shirt, odd socks: green and yellow. Her hair is beginning to grow back in a halo of black fluff, and she has toothpaste on her left boob. Nonetheless, Faith Valentine is still the most beautiful human I have ever seen.

She also seems – physically, at least – *fine*.

A gigantic bolt of relief.

'Look at the state of you!' Eff takes a bite of toast and frowns at me. Grease drips on her chin; she wipes it with the back of a hand. 'Even I'm impressed. Some kind of secret rave in the woods?'

Feeling faintly suspicious now, I glance around

the tiny, grubby flat. It's all still in one piece (thankfully), but roughly the size of our larder and considerably less well stocked. The shower is practically touching the microwave, the television is on top of a cardboard box and there are several empty pizza boxes stacked on the crate that passes for a coffee table. If this place isn't a cry for help, I don't know what is.

'My texts! You didn't answer any of my texts!'

'Oh!' Faith looks bewildered. 'Sorry, my phone was on silent. I didn't see them.'

'Is it Noah?' I start pacing the room, which takes all of three seconds. 'Has he upset you? You don't have to go through it on your own again. Let me help you.'

'Noah?' Effie is watching me curiously. 'What are you talking about? He has a new girlfriend, I think. She seems nice. Why *are* you so muddy? Do you want to borrow some clothes?'

I pause and stare hard at my sister. Nope, she's not fobbing me off this time: there's definitely something wrong with her. I can see it in her flushed cheeks, the floppy way she's standing, the brightness in her eyes.

'Faith,' I say sharply, glancing at my watch. Yup. Next time I see her, Verity is going to string me up by my own intestines. 'I was led to believe that you were in crisis. If this conversation could have waited until this evening, I'd have appreciated a heads-up.'

'Oh!' She giggles. 'No, we can chat anytime.'

'IN WHICH CASE DO NOT EMERGENCY TEXT ME LIKE THAT WHAT IS WRONG WITH YOU I NEARLY HAD A FREAKING HEART ATTACK.'

'I didn't send you an emergency text!' With round eyes, Eff reaches for her phone. 'Look! It just says *come over*!'

'No, it doesn't!' I grab her phone back. 'It says COME OVER in capitals, Faith! That means shouting! And there's a *running girl emoji*! Everybody knows that means *Emergency!*'

'No, no!' Eff's horrified. 'That's me! *I'm* the running girl!'

I'm going to literally bite her. 'Who casually signs off with an emoji of themselves doing sports?'

There's faint, tinny laughter behind me.

'What was that?' I spin round with my fists up. 'Who else is in here?'

'Well,' Faith says, turning a darker shade of neon-pink. 'That's kind of what I was inviting you over for, Mer. There's someone I want you to officially meet.'

Frowning, I follow the laughter to a laptop open on the windowsill. There's a pretty girl grinning at me from the screen: blonde, freckled, green eyes, elfin. I faintly recognise her. I feel like at some point in the past I may have threatened her with physical violence, although obviously that doesn't narrow it down much.

'Mercy Valentine!' The pixie girl is waving at me. 'It's an honour! I'm a *big* fan. I watched *My Boo* all the time when I was a kid. You're, like, the Juliet Valentine of our generation and, yes, I appreciate the irony.'

I turn back to Faith. 'Who the hell is that?'

'Letty,' Faith smiles at the girl, her eyes softening, 'meet my big sister, Mercy. Mercy, meet my . . . umm, Scarlett.'

I lift my eyebrows at the girl, then at my radiant sister.

At my sister, then at My Umm Scarlett.

Scarlett. My sister.

This is why Faith has been so quiet and preoccupied? This is why she's not talking to me? This is why she's spending every day in a disgusting hovel?

Hope was right: Effie is in *love*.

'I cannot wait to meet you properly,' Scarlett says warmly as the news sinks in. 'I'm an actor too actually, out in New York, but I'm heading back in a fortnight, hopefully for good. I miss your sister too much, and, hey – who doesn't want to play a cat? Furballs, here I come.'

'No!' Faith jumps up and down and claps her hands. 'You *didn't* hear back already!'

'I did.' the girl beams. 'I got the job.'

'Aaaghh!' Eff squeaks. 'Why didn't you tell me?'

'I was saving the news for maximum impact,' Scarlett chuckles. 'Faith Rivers, turn on the toaster and prepare the peanut butter, I'm coming home!'

Fascinated, I watch my sister's exquisite face grow tearful, happy and overwhelmed in equal measure, and something in my chest abruptly floats, then drops: both warm and cold at the same time, the way a plane plummets over a coastline.

Swallowing, I glance at my watch again. Looks

like Daiiissssyy is going to be playing Beatrice today too, and there's not a single thing I can do about it.

'Cool.' I smile wanly. 'I'm very happy for both of you.'

Grabbing my handbag off the floor, I take one more look at the glowing couple and make a move to leave. Surprised, Faith quickly mumbles 'I'll call you back, Letty,' closes the laptop and runs in front of me with her hands held out.

'Mercy?' Her hazel eyes widen. 'Are you okay? I know this is a bit of a surprise but . . .'

'It's actually not,' I admit honestly. 'It makes perfect sense. If anything, I'm surprised it took me this long to work it out.'

No wonder she never really gave a monkey's butt about beautiful, boring Noah.

'So what is it?' Eff asks gently.

'I'm just . . .'

Worried you're building your happiness on somebody who might leave. Scared of how much they could hurt you. Overcome by the strength and bravery it takes to give yourself to someone else. So jealous I could scream my heart out.

'Stressed because I'm late. I was supposed to be at a rehearsal and I've already had a verbal warning.'

'Oh, Mer, I'm so sorry.' My lovely sister instinctively moves to grab my hand, then hesitates and pulls away again. 'It means *so* much to me that you dropped everything to be here because you thought I was in trouble. You've got the biggest, fiercest, most loyal heart in the world and I love you for it.'

I snort lightly – 'Sure.' – and turn to leave.

'And I'm really happy,' Faith blurts behind me. 'I mean it, Mercy. You don't need to worry about me any more. If anything, it's my turn to worry about you. You're the one who seems like you're . . . still lost. And I know how hard it is. It took me a long time, but I finally found what I was looking for.'

This time my snort is louder; I turn back to face her. 'Love?'

My sister beams and tilts her head to the side, her beautiful eyes soft and full of light.

'No, Mer. The freedom to be *me*.'

42

So, there you have it.

Everyone in my life has officially healed and moved on. Dad has the American khaki-witch and his new movie; Max has his reality-TV narcissistic love-fest. Hope has Mr Glow-Up; Grandma is shouting orders from her grand dame pedestal with renewed zeal; Faith is living independently, madly in love with the pixie actress; and even Mum has emerged from hiding and is slowly piecing herself back together with varying levels of success.

The Valentines are putting the past behind them, and I know I should be happy for them.

But I'm not.

Because I just feel left behind, all over again.

It does briefly occur to me that I could break into today's rehearsal, late for the second time, but rocking up in this state – filthy, damp, dejected and sleepless – feels like rubbing salt in the wound. So I decide to taxi it straight home. Might as well let Daisy have the stage all day: she's earned it.

Limping up the driveway, I check my inbox again.

Still nothing from Finn (obviously), but there *is* now an irate email from the Valentine family agent:

Mercy,

I have just received a phone call from Human Resources at the Globe. You have apparently missed two rehearsals now. As you are aware, this is a high-profile opportunity with considerable financial compensation. Roles like this do not come up often, and will not come up again if you continue this behaviour. You have not acted in the last two years – for understandable reasons – but this is not an auspicious way to break back into the industry.

While you have great and unquestionable talent, it does not outweigh a reputation for unreliability, arrogance or 'being a diva'.

I suggest you seriously consider what you want for your future.

Persephone

My stomach tightens into a hard ball. I want to defend myself, but she's completely right: my one big chance to do the thing I love most in the world, and I'm screwing it up.

I have to do better, try harder.

Feeling hollow, I edge carefully round The Beast – still squatting in the driveway – and consider telling Persephone the truth: that I missed the rehearsal because I thought my sister was in trouble.

Then I realise I've already used that excuse.

Bat-bum.

Hi Persephone.

I've been up the whole night, vomiting. I think I'm allergic to prawns.

I'll sort my behaviour out, I promise.

Mercy

SEND.

With a *click*, I open the front door and jump. Mum is hovering right by the security intercom, holding my script again. With a flush of faint irritation – where did she get it from this time? – I stride forward and pull it out of her pale hands.

'Mum,' I admonish tiredly. 'If you want to help me with a scene so badly, you need to—'

Oh, hang on. This isn't actually mine.

'I've just been offered a new part,' my mother explains, her eyes aglow. 'Irina in *The Seagull*. The older, fading actress – if you remember, I once played Nina – it's my favourite play . . . and I thought . . . maybe it's time for me to start . . .'

'Moving forward,' I whisper numbly. 'Yes. I've realised.'

Then I stare in amazement at her luminous face. Her skin is clean, glowing and she's wearing makeup again. Her hair has been subtly highlighted blonde, her nails painted a delicate peach. When I look down, I realise with a bolt of emotion that she's wearing her beautiful ice-blue Givenchy suit and a pair of sweet Prada flats. The expression on her face is alive, almost present. She's taken another small step towards reality.

'My mother,' I quote with a sad smile, handing the scripts back to her, 'is a psychological curiosity.'

'You remember!' She beams. 'Chekhov! I read it to you in—'

'Paris.' I nod. 'I know.'

My mum gazes carefully at my face – studying my features with her grey eyes – and I look quickly away. It feels like she's actually seeing me for the first time in two years.

'You look exhausted, sweetheart.' Her hand goes up to wipe the dirt from my cheek, then freezes and flutters to her side again. 'The stylist has only just left – shall I get her back?'

'No thank you,' I say stiffly. 'This is exactly the look I was going for. I took my inspiration from you.'

Mer, come on.

I don't even know how to stop now.

'Mum!' Hope bounces down the stairs in a gaudy dress and pink lipstick, looking like a teenage My Little Pony. 'Now that we've been spruced up together, we should totally try out that new day spa with a cream tea and—'

She sees me and abruptly stops bouncing.

'Oh.' She tucks an elaborately curled and hair-sprayed ringlet behind an ear and looks somewhere below my right elbow. 'Hello again, Mercy. I didn't see you there.'

My little sister can't even make eye contact with me any more; that's how much I scare her.

Something in my chest starts to ache.

'You look very pretty, Po,' I say carefully, suddenly needing to reach out to her, to make it all better. 'Completely gorgeous.'

'Thanks.' Hope kicks her toe against the stairs. 'None of it's yours, I promise. Look, there's no black *anywhere*.'

'I can see that,' I say gently, feeling sick.

It's one thing smashing vases and mugs – quite another to have broken this too.

I open my mouth to apologise, but nothing comes out.

'Well,' Mum says, clearing her throat and glancing between us. 'Since you're home, darling, why don't we *all* go to a spa? Have a girls' day out? I could call Faith, see if she'd like to meet us there?'

Go with them, Mer. It'll be fun. I never got to do that.

My eyes abruptly sting. Why is everybody so willing to forget there's still one of us missing?

There's a knock on the front door.

'Coming!' I call with a sharp wave of relief, running towards it. 'Hang on! Just a minute!'

Hopefully it's Max: he can inject some much-needed stupidity into this dynamic, and give me a feasible opt-out. Nobody wants to see my brother in a towel. Actually, quite a few people do, but let's just conclude that they're all insane.

Determinedly, I swing the door wide open.

Then I shut it again.

'Who was that?' Hope cocks her head to the side. 'Mercy? Why have you gone bright red and why are you hiding behind that massive vase?'

In a panic, I hold my finger up to my mouth.

'Now why are you *shhhhing* me?'

Oh my days, if she doesn't shut up right now I'm going to have *two* dead sisters.

'I did actually see you the first time, Mercy,' Finn says calmly through the letterbox, as my heart starts to pound so hard it feels like my face is going to melt right off. 'I don't think that invisibility spell has taken quite yet.'

Cheeks burning, I try to recalibrate as fast as I can.

Finn.

Finneas O'Connor is at my house.

316

Why is Finn at my house?

Okay.

Time to be a grown-up.

Heart jumping, I smooth my hair out, lift my chin and come out from behind the Ming vase. Clearly, Finn is even more mature, sensitive and compassionate than I gave him credit for. He took the time to consider my apology and realised that it was heartfelt. Now obviously he forgives me, because I am – contrary to evidence – absolutely capable of being vulnerable, open, affectionate and—

'What?' I snap, swinging the door open sharply again. 'What do you want?'

Honestly, now even *I* want to punch myself in the head.

'You missed a second rehearsal,' Finn says gruffly from the doorstep. 'So I've been sent to give this to you.'

I stare at him. 'Uh?'

'It's a written warning.' He holds out a piece of paper. 'Verity would like you to sign it and give it back to me so she knows it's definitely been received.'

I look down at the paper in his hand. 'Uh?'

'It's not really my job,' he continues. 'I'm supposed

to be stage crew, but I have access to a van, so here we are.' And his voice is so professional and completely without any kind of warmth I have to turn away quickly so he can't see my eyes well up.

Finn's not here for me. He's here for Verity.

He doesn't forgive me.

I ruined it all.

'No,' I say thickly, dropping the paper and running up the stairs in a panic before he sees me start crying. 'Unacceptable. My agent should have told her that I'm *sick*.'

'A written warning?' My mother turns towards Finn. 'I'm afraid that doesn't sound right. Mercy is an incredibly conscientious actress. Some kind of mistake has clearly been made.'

'It hasn't,' Finn corrects gently. 'If it's okay, Mrs Valentine, I'll wait. I think it's probably in Mercy's best interests to sign it today if she can, and I can confirm in person she's . . . unwell.'

'I'm not signing it!' I scream, doubling down.

'Okay,' Finn says calmly, taking the love-seat in the hallway. 'I'll wait here for you to think it over. Don't worry about performing today – they've got quite used to replacing you.'

Breathing hard, I make it to my bedroom, slam the door behind me and lean my head against it with my eyes shut: breathing slowly and trying to push my incoming tears down as far as they will go.

But it's not working. The tears won't compress and instead they start to rise from my chest, burning my eyes. Panic is swallowing me like hot sand: everything is collapsing on top of me at once.

I'm screwing up my beloved career.

Finn hates me.

Hope's scared of me.

Faith's worried about me.

The Birdbrains are tired of me.

Grandma's angry with me.

Dad's frustrated with me.

Mum's oblivious about me.

My family is moving on without me.

Mercy.

My dead twin sister won't shut up.

Mercy.

For pity's sake, Charity, have I not got enough to deal with right now?

Mercy, turn round.

43

Eight years ago

'How do I look?'

With a dramatic swish, Hope throws a red silk scarf over her neck and slings herself against the bookcase.

'Very glamorous,' I say, trying not to smile.

'One day,' Po declares with another little swish, 'I am going to be savage, iconic and in-domino-able.'

'Yup.' Nostrils twitching, I take a sip of water. 'Although the word is indomi*table*.'

'Are you sure?' My seven-year-old sister pauses thoughtfully, considering this information. 'I always thought it was like *dominoes*. If you're *indominoable*, it means nobody can push you over. Tables are much more solid so does your one really make sense?'

'I'll push *you* over,' I laugh. 'Sit down, Little Miss Procrastinator, we're in the middle of a class.'

Defeated, Hope sits with an extended groan.

'But it's all so *boring*,' she complains. 'Do I really need to know how rainbows are made? Why aren't we studying poetry with Mr Gilbert and the others?'

'Because,' I explain patiently for the umpteenth time this morning. 'You're behind in Science and I'm ahead, so I'm giving you an extra lesson to try to catch you up.'

'*Ugggghhhh.*' My little sister flops onto the library table, her fluffy hair spreading onto her arms. 'My *life* is *wasting away.*'

I roll my eyes and smile, then lob an eraser at her and tap the textbook with my nail.

'Hope Valentine, *focus.*'

'Hey – Camera, Action!' She suddenly says, jumping up and squaring her fingers like a lens at me. 'Maybe we could do something *fun* instead? You know, we *never* hang out just the two of us, Mer. Eff is always swanning off on her own, Max says he doesn't want to play with a *little girl*, and it's always you and Charity together.'

I open my mouth, but she pokes me winningly.

'Go on, Mer. Play with me? Please?'

Her face is so sweet and adoring, her brown eyes so big and hopeful, I feel a fluffy warmth settle inside my stomach, like a tiny kitten purring and curling up.

'*Fine*,' I say with way more reluctance than I feel. 'Come on then, boss.'

With Hope clapping and chasing after me, I lead my sister up into the huge attic at the top of our house. It's a dusty, warm place of mystery and mess and magic. There are long-forgotten boxes everywhere, filled with candlesticks and books that have never been read; chipped antique vases; creepy dolls from fifty years ago, dressed in frilly little dresses. Enormous framed film posters of Valentines are propped against the rafters: unflattering, unfashionable, banished in embarrassment.

Hope and I look at each other excitedly, both making a mental note to steal them and take them downstairs as soon as we're done. We're the only Valentine kids who seem to care about the movie empire we've been born into.

'So,' Po says, drifting around the attic, picking

pretty, albeit very dusty, things up and wafting them around. 'What shall we do?'

I look again at one of the posters: Mum in *The Hurtful Ones*.

'We'll make a play,' I say in a sudden burst of inspiration, picking up a tarnished candlestick and examining it carefully. 'We'll perform it at Mum and Dad's anniversary party next week.'

Hope's eyes immediately light up.

'Oh, *perfectomondolia*.' Then she frowns and tips her head to one side. 'Can Ben be in it too, do you think?'

'Of course,' I smile. 'Murder mysteries are better with six anyway.'

'Coooool!' Po picks up a peacock feather and sticks it in her hair. 'Who's going to die, do you think? And who does the murdering stuff? This is so exciting! But first we're going to need *costumes*.'

Humming happily, we trawl through boxes and boxes of Christmas decorations and old photos, until we find a solid oak chest full of clothes: faded designer dresses, Grandma's ancient moth-eaten velvets, cheap accessories my parents bought for parties and used once. Then we divide them all up into piles for each character.

Inside an old blank birthday card, I start writing ideas.

'Remember,' Hope says, swishing up and down with an azure feather boa trailing from one hand, 'you have to give yourself the *biggest* role, Mercy, because you're the best actor.'

My cheeks flush and I snort. 'Pfff.'

'You are,' my little sister asserts stoutly, still wafting around. 'You're probably the most talented person I've ever met, as it just so happens. Obviously, I'll never be as good as you, but I've made my peas with that.'

Grinning, I stand up, pick a deep magenta boa off the floor and drape it round my neck. 'Your peas, huh?'

'Yes.' She nods. 'We've all got our special gifts, you see. Faith is kind, Max is easygoing, Charity is fun, I'm probably the cutest and most adorable person in the whole wide world.'

Now I laugh. 'Obviously.'

'But you're the real deal.' Hope beams at me. 'You're like a magnet, Mer. It's amazing. People are either pulled towards you or they're pushed away, but it doesn't really matter because you have that *thing*.'

My throat is feeling tight, full. 'What thing?'

With a swish, my little sister carefully wraps her boa round her neck exactly the way I have wrapped mine.

'That thing,' she says, 'that makes you a *star*.'

And I'm not sure what is more overwhelming: the love I suddenly feel for my baby sister, or the gratitude.

'Oi!' Max raps on the attic door, as I quickly turn to wipe my eyes with a red-gloved finger. 'Are you losers in there? We've checked the whole house except here.'

'I hate this manky old attic,' Charity's voice objects loudly. 'It's *so* creepy. There's probably ghosts haunting it.'

Glancing at me with a faint air of disappointment, Hope scampers over and unlocks the door and our siblings tumble in.

'I *told* you they weren't studying up here,' Max grumbles, surveying our gaudy costumes. 'Looks like they're getting ready for some kind of wacky-themed sports day.'

'We're making a murder mystery play,' I smile, as they instinctively move towards the piles and start tugging accessories on. 'For the party this weekend. I'm going to write it and then play the leader and the villain.'

Charity laughs huskily, plopping a giant lavender hat on. 'Of course you are.'

'And Hope's going to direct us,' I say, looking with tenderness at the littlest one of our group as her face lights up proudly. 'There's nobody I'd rather listen to.'

44

'No.'

Two long black dresses hang on the back of my door.

'Please, no.'

I rip the plastic dry-cleaning sleeves from them.

'No no no no—'

One is Louis Vuitton, couture, floor-length, cut to perfection, worth thousands and very much mine; the other is a high-street copy with the label cut out.

With a grunt of shame, I cover my face with my hands.

I screamed at my little sister for wearing *her own dress*.

I called her a liar and a thief and humiliated her in front of her boyfriend.

I made her take it off.

I destroyed her very first anniversary with a boy she's loved for over half a decade.

I made Hope Valentine cry. Then – just to cap it all off – I forced *her* to apologise to *me*.

Except . . . why did she then ask to borrow it?

Another wave of shame: because in my sister's sweet head it was easier to get permission for something she hadn't done than convince me she hadn't done anything wrong in the first place.

That's how terrified she is of me.

That's how brutal and unforgiving I've become.

I groan loudly into my hands.

Suddenly I remember Ben, frowning at me outside the library, telling me that my little sister loves me unconditionally, that she always has, even if I can't see it.

But I *can* see it; I just don't know what to *do* with it.

Because Hope's love isn't like mine. It's not hard and sticky; it's not difficult to give and easy to take back. It's not fierce and clawed, like a beast inside her. It's sunshine, just like she is. It shines on everyone, without limits, without demands, without expectation of return.

It's bright and boundless, generous and glowing.

And when I saw my sister in the dress – *my* dress – all I could think was: *I do not want her to be like me.*

With a tiny sob, I lift my chin and wipe my eyes roughly.

Enough.

I need to grow the hell up and start taking responsibility for my actions. I need to stop blaming everyone else, stop breaking everything when it's me that's the mess.

I don't know how to fix myself, but maybe I can start fixing some of the damage I've caused to the people I love.

Blinking, I open my door.

'Finn!' I call down the stairs. 'Could you wait for me for ten more minutes . . . Please?'

A pause, then he yells back: 'Okay!'

Before I spiral into a vortex of angry self-pity again, I pull my phone out and send a brief text to Genevieve:

Can you find an address for me?

I wait for her to reply and give her as many details as I remember.

Then I send the address to John.

Wiping my eyes, I go straight to my bathroom: quickly shower, scrub myself clean, get dressed in a cashmere black jumper and leggings. I tie my hair tightly in a bun and hesitate in front of the mirror. It's still turned to the ceiling: I'm not quite ready to face myself in it yet.

Instead, I run back down the stairs.

Hope and Mum have already left for the spa. The hallway is empty except for Finn who is flopped on the red-velvet seat, busy perusing the latest issue of *Vogue* from a huge stack on the side table.

'Hey,' Finn says without looking up. 'Did you know that curtain fringes are in this season? I wish somebody had given me a heads-up. Now I just feel stupid.'

I smile a tiny bit, at least he's still talking to me.

'Do you have the paper I need to sign?' I grab a pen out of a pot by the door. 'Let's get that done.'

He hands the papers over and I scribble my name on them.

'Thanks,' he says as I hand them to him. 'This should at least temporarily calm down the pulsating vein in the middle of Verity's forehead. It's taking on a life of its own.'

'How mad is she?' I ask, grabbing keys off the side table.

'Mad mad,' Finn says, picking his big coat off the armchair. 'Her passive aggression is about to teeter into aggressive aggression, and nobody wants to be there when that happens.'

Something tugs sharply in the centre of my chest. I appreciate him responding to me so politely, as if the last time we spoke I wasn't shrieking personal abuse into his face at point-blank range. I'm not foolish enough to think that just because I'm not being ignored means that I'm forgiven; he's a professional, and a good person. But I appreciate the kindness nonetheless.

'Can you drive?' I ask, opening the front door.

'Umm.' Finn pushes his arms into his navy coat, shrugs it over his shoulders and points at a shabby red vehicle in the driveway. 'Yes. Obviously. I drove here.'

I blink at it, then unexpectedly laugh. 'Is that—'

'A retired Post Office van?' He frowns at me. 'How dare you, Mercy. Just because it is red and a van and has the fading words "Post Office" written on the side. What an incredibly imperious and rude assumption.'

I laugh again, my chest tugging. I've always considered myself a snob of the highest order – been proud of it, in fact – but it turns out that a rusty old post van is the sexiest vehicle in the world when it belongs to Finn O'Connor. Feeling suddenly hot, I try to push the thought away. It's way too late for realisations like that.

'But,' he says, heading towards it. 'I guess if you need a lift—'

'No,' I say quickly. 'I need you to . . .'

And I almost can't do it. It's too unfamiliar, too hard, like pulling a deeply embedded splinter out of a thumb: I almost can't find the grip. I almost can't bear to.

'I need you to help me,' I finish without looking at him. 'Please.'

Then I turn towards The Beast.

My reaction to it is instinctive and immediate: my stomach knots, my hands sweat, my throat begins to work. I know it's all in my head; it's just a stupid giant lump of steel and rubber but—

'I'd like you to show me how to drive my new car,' I say, gritting my teeth and ripping the bow off the glossy bonnet. On the upside, at least it's black: Dad got that right, unlike my friends.

'Drive?' Finn says in surprise. 'You've got a brand-new, box-fresh Land Rover and you can't drive?'

'The joy of being a Valentine,' I manage hoarsely, unlocking the front door and sliding onto the cream-leather driving seat. 'They don't need me at the rehearsal today, right? They've replaced me with Daisy? And you can take another hour off?'

Finn shrugs and slides into the car next to me. 'I guess. Aren't you *sick*, though?'

He looks at me with one eyebrow raised.

'We both know I was lying.' I stare with a dry throat at all the dumb gadgets and sticks and pedals – is this a flaming *spaceship*? 'I just . . . something else came up. My sister was in trouble. Or . . . I thought she was.'

There's a pause and out of the corner of my eye I can see Finn examine my damp face, the tightness of my mouth, the shakiness of my fingers, then his face softens because—

45

I can do this. I know I can.

More importantly, it's time.

Closing my eyes briefly, I hit the GO pedal and start lurching in staccato down the driveway.

'Hands at ten to two,' Finn says calmly as I open my eyes again: oh, no way, we're *moving*. 'And loosen your grip a touch. You're holding on to the steering wheel like this car is a rampaging horse in a Victorian romance novel.'

Smiling faintly, I slide my sticky clenched fists down.

'Remember to breathe normally,' he says in a low voice, as I realise I'm starting to hyperventilate. 'You've got this, Mercy.'

He says my name, and another soft layer of calm lands on me like a fluffy blanket. Breathing slower, I manage to get the car to the end of the driveway, only smashing a small pot of pink flowers and a statue of Pan over in the process. We pause briefly at the electric gates, and I hop out to tap in the code and check my phone. Genevieve has sent the address I asked her for, so I plug it into Maps.

Then I get back in the car, hit the indicator and turn left down a quiet, empty and tree-lined street.

And, as I drive, the weirdest thing happens.

A weight starts to lift from my chest, as if somebody has been sitting on me for years and they've finally stood back up again. My lungs start to open, my heart begins to decompress, my ribcage feels free and loose.

Breathing deeply, I feel my cheeks grow hot, my head weightless.

I'm doing it, I'm *driving*!

Speeding up a notch, I feel power beginning to course through me: finally – *finally* – I am taking a tiny step towards freedom . . .

'Brilliant!' Finn grins. 'Although you might want to—'

Slamming my foot on the accelerator, I open a window and feel The Beast shoot forward, the wind lifting my hair.

'Umm,' he says in a higher voice, 'slow down?'

Grinning, I take a sharp left turn and he swings into the passenger door. Another wide, empty road opens up in front of me, and I hit the accelerator a little harder. The Beast and I are beginning to find our own private groove.

I am weak, flighty, *giddy* with relief.

'Ah.' Finn swallows as I take another corner and I feel the touch of his shoulder as he swings abruptly into me. 'As your driving instructor, I do feel I should kind of – INDICATE!'

'Chill, Grandad O'Connor,' I laugh, indicating right. 'Happy now?'

'Not really, because you've already gone round the corner.'

Chuckling, I glance to the side. Finn's bright green eyes are marginally wider than normal, there's a frown line across his forehead and his fingers are gripping his knees. With a bolt of guilt, I hit the brakes and slow down until we're at the speed limit.

'Sorry,' I say softly. 'I just didn't think I could do—'

'BRAKE!'

With a jolt, I slam the brakes on just before I ram

the nose of The Beast up the bottom of a little red Mini. Slightly shaken, I focus on driving in silence down a back road until my shoulders loosen again.

Then I swallow.

Right, time to rip the plaster off.

'So I assume you got the email I sent you last night,' I say briskly, tapping my fingers on the steering wheel like an inept manager in a televised business meeting.

Finn nods. 'I did, yes. Turn right here.'

Silence.

Embarrassment tightens my throat, so instead I concentrate on the small suburban road I'm driving on and its tiny red-brick houses. They're sweet, like children's drawings of houses. Four windows, a neat little chimney on top, a garden with a path running straight down the middle.

I pull to a stop outside one with a dark green door.

Then Finn and I sit, staring straight ahead.

I can hear him breathing quietly next to me: every rise and fall of his chest, the soft sound as he exhales. He still smells like Bonfire Night, and he's so tall the top of his bronze waves very nearly brush the ceiling of the Land Rover.

With an aching chest, I suddenly realise I desperately need Finn to forgive me. I just don't think he's going to.

'And?' I prompt gruffly. 'What do you think?'

'I think,' he says slowly, 'that you will do whatever it takes to be on your own.'

I flush hot. 'That's not what I—'

'Because if you're on your own, you're safe.'

Something collapses inside me.

He's right.

I desperately want to be alone and can't be alone at the same time, pushing and pulling and screaming and going nowhere, like a door tugged from both sides. And I *know* the people around me are hurting too. I know my family need me just as much as I need them. I know I can't shut myself away forever but—

'I don't have room for other people's pain,' I whisper. 'I have too much of my own.'

We're still not looking at each other.

'Which is funny,' Finn says gently. 'Because other people's pain might be just what you need.'

My eyes abruptly fill with tears.

Overwhelmed, I lower my head and fiddle with

the gearstick for a few seconds until I can force the tears away again. I've got so good at doing that, so good at pulling my sadness back inside myself, as if it's on a string.

Turning towards the window, I wipe my eyes with two fingers.

Then I turn back and open the glove box.

'Cool,' I say hoarsely, pulling out a bunch of documents in a transparent plastic folder and opening my door. 'I've got something I need to do now. Wait for me in the car. I shouldn't be long.'

'No,' Finn says, opening his door too.

Nobody says *no* to me. 'Excuse me?'

'You could have asked anyone to give you a driving lesson,' he says calmly, assessing the house we've parked outside of. 'But you asked me. So I'm coming with you, because you clearly want me here, whether you can admit it to yourself or not.'

I stare at Finn; Finn stares back.

He's right again.

'Okay,' I say with a small smile. 'But keep your mouth shut.'

46

Technically, this should be fairly simple.

But as I stand on the doorstep with Finn next to me, I can feel my barriers automatically flying back up again: spikes and gates and guards, shields up, pots of hot tar hanging from my turrets ready to tip, the drawbridge pulled tightly into my impenetrable fortress.

The door opens and I clear my throat sharply.

'Hello?' An old man with white hair peers at us through smudged, wire-rimmed glasses. 'Can I help you?'

'You've got my painting,' I snap, folding my arms tightly in front of me. 'I want it back.'

Then I flinch: nope, not how I intended to say that.

'Of course you do.' He sighs, unsurprised. 'I figured it was just a matter of time really.'

Embarrassed, I try again.

'You are Clarence Williams?' I check the details of the text I got from Genevieve. 'You're a waiter for the catering company "Waitressing for Godot"?'

Clarence rubs his nose. 'Unfortunately so.'

'I'm Mercy Valentine,' I explain, but from the serene expression on his face he has no idea what this means. 'You were working at a celebrity auction a month ago, and my sister Faith sold you a family heirloom by accident. I'm going to need that back.'

Finn coughs and I flinch again.

'I would *like* that back,' I correct, biting my lip. 'Please.'

'No thanks,' Clarence says smoothly. 'But I appreciate you coming all this way. Bye now.'

He goes to close the door; I feel a bolt of panic.

'Wait!' I say quickly, shoving my hand against it. 'I don't think I made the situation clear. That painting belongs to the Valentine family and has done for over a century. It has great emotional value. There was a mistake.'

'That's too bad,' Clarence says with a smile. 'Because I've already consulted a lawyer, and the painting is mine. I like it. It really pulls the living room together. Sorry you've wasted a journey.'

The door clicks shut and panic shoots through me again. This can't happen: I can't fail at this too. I need to make amends. Hope loves that painting, and I am going to get it for her.

With my fist raised, I go to smash the door.

'What's the plan?' Finn says easily. 'Have you considered getting *right up* into his face and shrieking incredibly pointed insults at him? I've got a phone. I can always film the whole thing and put it on the internet. People just *love* that I've heard.'

I go bright red. 'Look, I said *sorry*, okay?'

'No, Mercy.' He grins at me. 'You haven't.'

'Excuse me,' I bridle crossly, going to knock on the door again. 'I absolutely have said—'

I pause with my fist still in mid-air.

Hang on, he's not talking about Clarence, is he?

And though I've *emailed* an apology – kind of, although mostly a series of elaborate excuses and a weird metaphor about a tap – I haven't actually said sorry to Finn's face yet.

Ugh, what the hell is *wrong* with me?

'Finn.' I turn to face him, trying to make eye contact but not quite managing it. 'I am so incredibly sorry. You didn't do anything wrong, and I was a heinous nightmare witch.'

'Forgiven.' He nods simply.

And just like that – with a flush of warmth – anything seems abundantly possible.

I beam at him.

Then, with renewed vigour, I take one more, slightly reluctant look at the Beast and knock calmly on the front door again.

'Have my car,' I say as soon as it opens. 'It's valuable, barely driven, brand new. I will swap you my Land Rover for that painting.'

Clarence hesitates.

'I don't really need another car,' he says slowly, gesturing at a rusty grey Fiat Uno to our left. 'I've already got one.'

I begin to panic, then I glance at the multiple photo frames standing on the windowsill and make a wild guess. 'Please, hear me out. That's, umm . . . quite a *small* car. The Land Rover would mean you could maybe take all the grandchildren out at once. Wouldn't that be nice? Treat them to some nice family time with their grandfather? Please?'

His eyes sweep back and forth between the two

vehicles, still unsure, and I suddenly realise what it is he needs from me.

I realise what it is that I find so hard to give.

'I'll be open with you,' I say in a hot, painful rush. 'My little sister needs the painting back. She doesn't have any friends, has never really had any, and some of that is my parents' fault, but some of it is mine. I didn't spend time with her when I should have done – I was too busy with my . . . Anyway, she was on her own for a long time, and this painting became . . . a friend to her instead.'

My throat has a huge lump in it.

'I'm a bad sister, Clarence,' I continue, closing my eyes briefly. 'I'm selfish and nasty and aggressive, a lot of the time. But my baby sister, Hope . . . she's . . . just . . . lovely.'

Her sweet little face pops into my head, gazing at me with complete adoration.

I hesitate, then feel Finn's hand slip softly into mine.

'Please, Clarence,' I manage with a wobble, this time without pulling my hand away, 'help me. For once in my life, I want to make somebody I love happy, instead of thinking about myself.'

And I'm suddenly exhausted: the drawbridge is down.

It feels . . . like I've set something free.

There's a short pause, then – without another word – the old man turns round, heads into the house and comes out moments later with the painting under his arm.

'Here you go, Macy,' he says with a smile, and I feel Finn chuckle next to me. 'I hope she likes having it back. Friends are too important to lose without a fight, I think. So are sisters.'

I nod, my eyes welling up.

Then I stare at the piece of incredibly expensive art. It's tiny, brown, oily, and smaller than an A4 sheet of paper. There's a pale blonde woman lying in a boat surrounded with flowers, her eyes shut, and underneath it, engraved in delicate, curly writing, is: *Elaine, The Lady of Shallot*. And I almost laugh out loud. I remember studying this poem: it's about a young girl, trapped and lonely, prepared to give everything she has for love.

Who knew Hope had such a keen sense of irony?

'Thank you,' I say with genuine warmth.

Then I hand the forms and the keys for The Beast

over, and – with the painting held close to my chest – turn to leave. Already I can see the silver Valentine limousine slowly approaching us.

'Hey, Macy,' Finn grins, jogging after me. 'You're called Macy, right?'

With one hand out, he gently touches my shoulder and I feel something caged in my chest strain and break as my heart bounces up with a sharp *crack*, like a gate opening. And suddenly it's too much, it's too hard and I can't, I can't, I *can't*.

Swallowing, I firmly clang it shut again.

'Thank you for today,' I say formally, shrugging Finn's hand off. 'You're a good *friend*.'

He frowns, totally thrown by my change of tone.

'You're welcome?' he says slowly, studying my face for an explanation and finding none. 'I, uh, guess I'd better get back to the theatre. They're going to wonder where I've gone.'

John pulls the limo up to the kerb behind us.

The cage starts to rattle again, like something furious is trapped inside it, desperately trying to get out.

'Yes. You should go,' I agree crisply. 'I'd offer you a lift, but Richmond and South Bank are in opposite directions. So . . . there's a bus stop over there.'

'What?' Finn says in amazement as I open the limo door. 'You're going to *leave* me here?'

'Appreciate your help,' I snap. Unable to look at him, I slide into the backseat. 'Very generous of you. Let me know if I can repay the favour sometime.'

I sound just like my mother: clinging on to a half-remembered internal script by my fingertips.

I close the car door and lean back as the cage shakes and the thing inside starts screaming, scratching, gripping the bars and trying to rip them apart. On the other side of the blacked-out window, I can still see Finn, standing on the pavement, staring at me with his mouth hanging open.

Turning away, I get my headphones out and stick them on.

Then I hold the cage closed and fumble for the key.

'Mercy?'

'John,' I say, closing my eyes. 'Take me home.'

47

MERCY!

I close my eyes.

Mercy, listen to me!

I grit my teeth as my insides clank and shake.

Don't you dare shut me out.

Frowning, I turn my music up.

Doesn't work, you know. You can still hear me.

Obviously. What do you want, Charity?

I want you to stop doing this.

I want you to stop destroying yourself.

I want you to admit that you're falling for Finn.

No.

Admit that your heart hops every time you see him.

Admit that he makes you laugh.

Admit that you're scared.

A flush of hot rage.

Of course I'm flaming *scared*, Charity. I am

terrified. I'm so terrified it feels like I'm on the edge of a huge cliff, looking down at jagged, pointed rocks and being told to jump.

No, not to jump, to fall.

I laugh brutally. How is that better? Everyone always goes on about 'falling in love', but we fall as children and we cry. We fall and it hurts, and we decide not to do it again.

We learn to stay upright, to not hold on to anything that might give way.

Or anyone?

I learnt my lesson. Why didn't anyone else? Why do people just *keep* falling, and crying, and hurting? And then getting up and choosing to fall all over again?

How does love not terrify *everyone*?

Scowling, I open my eyes and turn my head to look out of the dark window. In the reflection of the glass is the girl who looks like me again: dark close-set eyes, widow's peak. A lump shoots into my throat and the bars give another desperate rattle.

Maybe it does.

'I'm not destroying myself,' I whisper to her

desperately. 'Charity, I am trying my very hardest *not* to.'

But suddenly I can't do it any more: can't keep pulling away, can't keep fighting, can't keep using all my energy to keep everyone at arm's length.

I'm so tired of locking my heart up.

'Turn round,' I say, sitting forward. 'Please, John, turn round and go back, as fast as you can.'

My chauffeur makes a three-point turn and I sit very still as my breathing becomes ragged and my cheeks hot.

Then I open the limo door.

'What the *hell*?' Finn says furiously, spinning towards me as I climb out of the limo. 'You do *not* get to treat me like this, Mercy. This isn't a game. You can't just scream at me and use me because you're bored and there's nothing else to—'

With one hand, I grab Finn's head and I kiss him.

I kiss him and kiss him and kiss him and the cage swings open and the thing inside me flies out and it's not screaming any more, it's not angry, it doesn't feel like a fight, it doesn't feel difficult. It feels like a release, like I've finally let go.

I kiss Finn and suddenly I'm not scared any more: I've jumped and I'm falling and it's okay.

Eventually, he pulls back for a second.

We stare at each other, cheeks burning, lips tingling, every single atom inside my body on fire.

'Mercy,' Finn says finally, his gaze holding mine. 'You are doing my head in.'

With a nod, I turn back towards the limo.

'Me too. So get in.'

We kiss all the way into central London: tugging and pulling at each other, surfacing and diving and resurfacing again like deep-sea divers. We kiss until I know exactly how Finn tastes and what his tongue feels like and the texture of the skin on his cheeks and the heat of his breath.

And it feels . . .

It feels . . .

I don't care, because it finally *feels*.

Eventually – after what might be a minute or an hour or a thousand years – it dawns on me that the limousine hasn't moved for quite some time.

'We're here,' John confirms, as I pull away and

take all my missed oxygen in one, sharp inhale. Then I look out of the window at the Globe Theatre, brain still spinning.

'Wait.' I look at my watch with a small frown. 'There's no point in dropping you here this late, Finn. Everyone will have gone home by now.'

'Here's good,' Finn says with cute smile. 'Thank you.'

He gives me another lingering kiss on the lips and then climbs out of the car.

'Why don't we take you home?' I shuffle over and call after him. 'It's completely fine. All part of the Making-Out-With-Mercy-Valentine Taxi Service.'

Honestly, I don't want him to go just yet.

Or ever.

I want to drive him all over London, finding out every single thing about him: what he's scared of, what makes him laugh, whether he gets sleepy at lunchtime or grumpy in the mornings. I want to know what his house looks like and which of his parents has green eyes and what his reoccurring nightmares are and what food he craves when he's poorly. I want to know his different laughs, his favourite colour, and where he got that awesome navy coat from.

I don't want to let him go until I know *everything*.

Finn smiles and my stomach dances.

'I've got a bit of extra work to do,' he says, glancing at the theatre and rubbing his beautiful left eye. 'Some sawing, glueing, sticking things together. You know the drill, pun intended.'

'Sure,' I say, trying to hide my disappointment. 'Okay.'

Finn looks at my face, then abruptly walks back to the car, leans in, gives me a harder, longer kiss and, oh my *days*, my entire stomach just started rotating like a fidget spinner.

He pulls away until our noses are just touching and whispers, 'You'll be at rehearsals tomorrow?'

'It depends,' I whisper back, nudging his nose gently with mine. 'Are you asking me as stage crew who just handed me a written warning, or as my brand-new boyfriend?'

It's a bit of a risk, but what the hell: I'm Mercy Valentine.

Taking risks is what I *do*.

'Oh, the latter,' Finn grins, kissing me again. 'Very, very much the latter.'

My heart is suddenly so big and so loud I'm not

sure it would fit in that cage again, even if I wanted it to.

'Then yes.' I beam at him. 'I'll be there.'

48

Guys, I have something to tell you . . .

It's about Stage Crew Boy. ;)

Beaming, I leap out of the limo.

With the painting of Elaine gripped under one arm, I bounce towards the Valentine house. My brother is sitting on the front doorstep with his laptop balanced on his knees, and as he looks up at me I realise – with some alarm – that the giddy glow on his face is probably not a billion miles away from the giddy glow on mine.

'Max!' I say, attempting to frown. 'What are you doing out here?'

'Shhhhhh!' My brother puts a finger over his lips and points at his computer. 'Mer, they've sent me the finalised trailer for my show! It goes out next week! I am *amazeballs*. A true performative genius. Do you want to see it?'

'Later.' Smiling, I glance past him. 'Is Hope in?'

'Bedroom.' Max nods distractedly, looking back down. 'Directing her teddy bears or whatever. Jeez, have you noticed how handsome I am, Mermaid? Like, I'm a *solid* eleven.'

Laughing, I pat the top of his head affectionately. 'Of course you are, idiot.'

Ping.

From: Finneas O'Connor
To: Mercy Valentine

You've done something weird to my brain, new girlfriend. I just nearly glued my phone to my own fingers.

From: Mercy Valentine

I'm not complaining, new boyfriend. Now there's no excuse not to call me later.

From: Finneas O'Connor

Apart from the fact that I don't have your number yet.
PS I AM CRAZY ABOUT YOU

From: Mercy Valentine

Gross. Lame. Pathetic.
PS I AM CRAZY ABOUT YOU TOO.

'Details?' Max demands, pointing at my face as I glance back up. 'Tell me which hot boy you're texting, *immediately*.'

Grinning, I power towards the library. 'I'm not texting.'

'Messaging then. Technicality. Tell me.'

'Nope.'

'Tell me, Mermaid.'

'Nuh-uh.'

Oh, I will tell him – trust me, at some point I'm going to tell *everyone* – but right now, he can just wait.

'You're the worst,' Max sulks. 'I tell you all *my* secrets.'

'No, you don't,' I laugh, pulling the painting out of the bag and studying the library walls. 'You get caught. That's a very different thing, Max Valentine.'

There's an empty nail over a faded rectangle that fits Elaine perfectly, so I hang her carefully up and stand back to study her with a flush of triumph.

She looks at home; she looks like she was missed.

With my brother still watching me with narrow eyes, I spring towards the kitchen, grab a tablecloth, porcelain, crystal: carry it all in to the library and set up a little restaurant table on the desk. Then I return, steal whatever food I can find (cold lasagne, sandwiches, a quiche, some fizzy drink) and lay it out. I'll ring The Ivy this evening and arrange a proper monthiversary do-over. I'll make sure my most expensive dress has been laundered so that Hope can wear it, lend her the black Gucci bag she took with her to Los Angeles.

Hell – I'll just *give* it to her.

'Call Po,' I order a still lurking Max. 'Tell her somebody's waiting for her in the library.'

Before he can ask any questions, I dive behind a packed bookshelf.

A few minutes later I hear:

'It's that guy from my new school. I just *know* it. The mystery one who sent me all the flowers and balloons last month? He's *obsessed* with me, poor thing.'

'Sure,' Ben laughs. 'And now he's breaking into your library to woo you in the creepiest way known to man.'

'Don't be sexist,' my sister says with a dramatic sigh. 'Known to man *or woman*. Anyway, you're just jealous because it took you *fifteen years* to realise you liked me, Benjamin, and I had to woo you before you would. Just accept the feet.'

There's another burst of laughter; I stifle my own.

'I'm sorry,' Ben says. 'Accept the *what*?'

'The feet. Do keep up.' A click of the library door and Hope swans in with epic dignity. 'I'm very sorry, secret admirer,' she says serenely, 'but as you can see, I already have a very handsome boyf—'

A sharp intake of breath.

'Elaine!!! You're home! How did you get back? Are you okay? Did they look after you?' My adorable little sister runs towards the picture, tries to hug it, fails and then lobs herself around Ben with a bounce of sheer joy. 'This is the best day of my *life*!'

Glowing, I slip out of the library, but not before Ben spots me over Hope's shoulder.

'*Thank you,*' he mouths at me.

I dip my head slightly – you're welcome – and escape into the hallway with a wide smile. I haven't felt this good in *years*.

'Oi,' Max says as I start climbing the stairs. 'Careful, Mer. If someone saw what you just did they might think there's a beating heart where that big empty cavern pretends to be.'

I shrug. 'Good thing you won't tell anyone, huh?'

Still beaming, I climb to the top of the stairs, feeling lighter and happier with every step.

'Mercy.' Max hesitates as I lean over the top banister to stare at his upturned face. 'I'm so sorry about what I said the other day. About you being unforgivable, I mean. It's not true.'

'It is,' I admit honestly. 'Most of the time.'

'Maybe.' He thinks about it for a few seconds. 'But if you weren't a good person, Mer, I think being horrible would probably make you much happier than it does.'

I flush and nod. 'I hope so.'

Then I turn back to the landing and get my phone out:

From: Mercy Valentine

She loved it. :)

From: Mercy Valentine

PS Time to swap numbers. I'm ready to move to the next level. ;)

Nothing from the gang yet – they're probably still angry with me about the sleepover – but it'll blow over, and once they meet Finn they'll love him, just like I do.

Wait – I didn't say that.

They'll like him *a lot,* just like I do. Although hopefully not *exactly* like I do, or I'll have to fight them all.

Laughing, I go to push open my bedroom door. Then I hesitate. There's a soft noise coming out of Mum's room, and when I turn round it's ajar. On tiptoes, I inch softly towards the gap, finally ready to have *that* conversation, the one I've been avoiding for years.

It's time to take another step in the right direction.

I am tired of pretending I don't need my mum.

'Hello?' I whisper. 'Mum, are you—'

My mother is sitting on the edge of her four-poster bed with a chunky family photo album perched on her lap. Her fingertips are touching the pages delicately, as if the photos are butterflies and she's scared they're going to fly away. She's crying quietly but hard, her face a mask of rigid, incoherent grief.

Maybe other people's pain is exactly what you need.

My heart tugs; I take a step forward. 'Mum?'

She looks up, her eyes both full and empty.

'Charity?'

49

Two years ago

'Charity?' Mum asks. 'Does anybody know where Charity is?'

Max stands up in a black tux.

'Hang on, let me try.' My brother clears his throat dramatically, then yells: 'TEEEEEE! TEE, YOU SMELLY LITTLE CHICKEN-FART, GET IN HERE RIGHT NOW OR WE WILL START WITHOUT YOU!'

Dad laughs loudly. 'That should do it.'

'Thank you, Max,' Mum says archly, glistening and glorious in silver sequins. 'Hadn't thought of bellowing the tiles off the roof.'

Frustrated, I glance at my watch again: Tee's *very* late.

We've all gathered in the dining room, as per Maggie's instructions, and it looks so beautiful. The candles are lit, the crystal sparkles, the cutlery shines, Grandma's blue-silk bird wallpaper glows and seems almost alive. Spread across the mahogany table – now getting cold – is a feast on porcelain and gold plates: garlic-roasted chicken and red wine beef, rosemary potatoes, butter asparagus, honey parsnips. We're dressed in our finest black tie, as befits an occasion as special as this, the air full of anticipation.

I've been excited about this event for literally months.

So where the hell is my twin sister?

'Ooh, can I try too?' Hope stands up in a floaty yellow-chiffon dress and cups hands round her mouth. 'CHARITEEE! Will we hear the tiles falling from in here, or shall I go outside and check?'

This time Mum and Dad laugh at the same time.

'Hope Valentine!' Grandma reproves, luminous in blue velvet and – unfortunately – matching the wallpaper exactly. 'Manners, please! We do not live in a football stadium!'

'I don't see why we can't just eat on our laps in

the cinema room like normal,' my big brother complains, glancing at the overhead projector and struggling uncomfortably with his bow tie. 'Such unnecessary *drama.*'

'Don't be petty, Max,' Maggie says sharply in a tailored grey dress. 'This is an important day, and it required a sense of occasion. You should be happy for your sisters.'

I smile at her gratefully; she winks back.

Suddenly, there's a loud *bang*, and the dining-room door smashes open. Charity flourishes a hand and gives an exaggerated bow. 'I'm here!' She unwraps a tinfoil-covered tray, plonks it on the dining table in front of us and sits down in the empty seat next to me. 'Sorry about that! I was just making some brownies!'

The tray is covered in pieces of brown cardboard, cut into 'E's.

'Very funny,' Mum says tersely. 'But, Charity, there's a time and a place for pranks, darling, and it is pretty clear that's neither here nor now. You're extremely late.'

My twin rolls her eyes at me. 'Sorr-EEE. Get it?'

I give her a tight smile back, still slightly annoyed

at how long she's made us all wait. A shimmering Faith nudges me gently under the table with her foot and I feel myself start to relax.

'Ahem.' Grandma rises from her chair and taps a silver fork against her champagne glass. 'Now we are all *finally* gathered –' a quick glance at my twin – 'I believe it is time to make a toast. Stand up, Mercy and Charity.'

Beaming so hard I can barely breathe, I get to my feet.

Charity props herself up next to me.

'Congratulations, my darlings.' My grandmother smiles at us, her eyes slightly wet. '*My Boo* has become the most-watched debut series of a teenage television show ever made.'

I glow at her, feeling like I'm about to burst.

'This family is my pride and joy,' she continues with a wobble in her voice, holding her glass up high in the air. 'But I have never been prouder than I am today. The Valentine baton is in the right hands, and I look forward to many more years of watching my talented granddaughters shine.'

'Hear, hear!' Dad calls, clapping loudly.

'To Mercy and Charity,' Grandma finishes

triumphantly. 'May your success be great, and your happiness greater.'

'Cheers!' Mum smiles, lifting her glass towards us.

'Cheers!'

'Cheers!'

'Cheers!'

'Cheers!'

'Ah, man,' Max complains. 'Who gave me *Fanta*?'

'Now,' Dad says with a wide grin. 'Let's watch the trailer for the second season, shall we? I need to know what that naughty ghost is going to do next.'

The overhead projector clicks to life.

On the pull-down screen, an image shines with the opening title sequence to *My Boo*. A deep voice announces: *'Dot has been dead a hundred years, and then she meets the handsome George. Has she finally found something to live for? Or will she have to kill him too?'*

Suddenly, my face is on the screen: bright and up close.

'That's Mercy!' Max calls in genuine excitement, pointing at it.

'Mercy!' Hope identifies as there's a shot of me running down a street, away from a fire.

'Mercy,' Maggie says confidently as the scene changes.

'Mercy again,' Faith says in a soft voice.

'Mercy?' Ben attempts shyly, glancing at Hope.

'That's Mercy too,' Max says in confusion as the screen cuts to my face again. 'Charity, dude, did you show up on set *at all*?'

'Yeah, well,' Tee says grumpily, crossing her arms. 'Maybe I just had better things to do, all right? Not *everyone* thinks acting is the be-all and end-all.'

Hurt, I glance at my sister, but she glares at the table in a sulk.

'Well,' Mum says in a firm, peace-making voice. 'I think it's *wonderful*, and you deserve *all* the awards heading your way this season. Frankly, I can't wait to be your plus-one at the big ceremonies. I have a dress picked out already.'

Flushed, I feel my eyes fill: she's smiling directly at me.

'Now,' Dad says as we take our seats again and everyone reaches hungrily for the food. 'Let's get some of Maggie's wonderful feast down us before it goes stone—'

BANG.

'*AAAAAGGGGHHHHHH!!!!*'

'Oh my goodness—'

'What the—'

FART.

Squeal.

POP.

Bright glitter bombs and streamers are exploding in rainbow torrents across the room; plastic cockroaches and spiders are falling out of every beautiful dish; chattering false teeth are jumping across the table; a whoopee cushion is being pulled out from under my grandmother's bottom.

In seconds, the beautifully arranged dinner has disintegrated into total chaos. When the bangs and pops finally stop, we all turn slowly to face a jubilant, grinning Charity. Like a smug cat, my twin preens then begins to take a dramatic bow.

'Charity Valentine,' Mum says quietly, 'go to your bedroom.'

My twin halts, her eyes widening. 'But—'

'Now,' our mother says, even more dangerously calm.

'*Fine*,' my twin grunts crossly, throwing her napkin on the ruined table and stomping out of the room.

'Clearly *some of you* need to work on your sense of humour.'

Stomach falling, I flinch as she slams the door.

'Congratulations, *Mercy*,' Mum says firmly, holding her glass up high. 'This is *your* day, my talented darling. I want you to enjoy every single second of it.'

I try to smile back, to feel happy.

But all I feel is empty.

50

I stumble backwards.

Across the dim hallway, fumbling for my door handle, falling into my bedroom with my eyes blind and stinging. For a few seconds, I stand still and breathe hard.

Then I lurch towards my mirror and flip it towards me with a *crack*.

A girl with wet, dark eyes stares back.

I'm here.

But you're not, Charity.

You're not here, and I'm not really either. I'm half of a whole that doesn't exist any more.

That's not true.

It is. When people look at me, they want to see you. They look for everything you were and see everything I am not.

No.

Without you, I don't make sense.

I'm not enough on my own, Tee. You were the light and I am the dark, and I needed you to make me brighter.

Sobbing, I reach my hand towards the girl's face. She reaches towards me too.

I didn't mean it, Mer. That day in the dining room when we were supposed to be celebrating our show. I was jealous.

I know how that feels.

This isn't your fault.

'It is,' I say out loud, forcing myself to stare directly at her blurry face. 'It was. I'm so sorry.'

I should have just gone.

Shocked, I stagger a tiny step back as if I've just been slapped.

'Charity.' I feel myself inhale with a hiss, feeling suddenly nauseous. 'What are you saying?'

The girl in the mirror stares at me with such love, I cry out in pain, wrap my arms round my stomach and fold myself in half.

You need to let me go.

'No,' I manage to say in a hot wave of panic. 'Don't leave me on my own. Please.'

There's a silence, and then—

Cee, you have never been on your own.

Then I blink and it's just me. My own dark eyes and my own lost face, distorted and soaking wet with tears.

'Charity?' I take another step back. 'CHARITY.' But my sister is gone.

She's gone and it's silent and there's nothing, and it finally hits me that I'll never hear her again, never see her again, because Charity is gone, she's gone she's gone she's—

'*AAAAARRRGHHHH!*' I scream, picking up a heavy glass and flinging it at the mirror. '*CHARITY! GET BACK HERE!*'

Breathing hard, I sweep an arm across my dresser, sending my makeup clattering on to the floorboards, breaking, spilling everything in dark piles of dust.

'CHARITY!' I bellow again at the top of my voice.

Silence.

Emptiness.

So I lie on my bed and wait for the darkness to swallow me, like a shadow creeping up a wall.

'Darling,' my grandmother says, gently reaching a pale, veined hand out to try to touch mine. 'Talk to me. Tell me what it is you need, Mercy, and I can *help* you. Are you not enjoying theatre work? I can find you something else. You want a lead role in films, or maybe television again? Say the word and I will help you *get* one. You only need to ask.'

With infinite coldness, I pull away.

My phone starts *beeping* incessantly.

Dad
Hahaha

Dad
Good joke

Dad
MERCY PLEASE TELL ME YOU ARE JOKING

The Bentley stops outside the Globe Theatre.

I look blankly at its white, round, thatched majesty, and – with no surprise – feel absolutely nothing.

I text:

380

Mercy
The Beast is gone.

Dad
COME STRAIGHT HOME TONIGHT
BECAUSE YOU ARE GROUNDED.

'Mercy—'
'Maybe I'm done with acting,' I say tightly, my
voice monotone. 'Have you ever considered that?'
Ping.

From: Finneas O'Connor
To: Mercy Valentine

Are you running late?! I've left a side door unlocked
for you. Take the one to the right of the stage. X

Delete.
We sit in silence for a few seconds, then I reach
for the car door.
My grandmother makes a guttural sobbing sound.
'You think I don't see what you're doing, Mercy?'
She grabs for my shoulder. 'You think I don't see

you punishing yourself? I've already lost one precious granddaughter – I *refuse* to lose another. You have a bright future ahead of you, my darling, and I'll be *damned* if you think I'm just going to sit here and watch you throw the rest of your life away!'

I turn towards her with – finally – a flicker of emotion.

All my grandmother's legendary icy reserve has gone. She's flushed, emotional, her eyes watering and glassy. Her chin wobbles, her mouth tugs at the corners as she tries not to cry. I look down at her pale, old beloved hands, holding on to me as tightly as she can.

And it's nearly enough to pull me back, to stop me doing what it is I'm about to do.

Nearly.

'Okay,' I say quietly, climbing out of the car. 'So don't watch.'

52

'Mercy Valentine! Are you *joking*?'

From the open side door, I stomp into the auditorium just as Verity looks up from her script.

'No,' I tell her flatly. 'I don't joke.'

'We are a full *hour* into today's rehearsal!' My director stands up, a violent red rash appearing on her cheeks. 'Yesterday I gave you a written warning, which you *signed* might I add, and yet today you are late again! Would you like to explain yourself?'

I shrug. 'Not particularly.'

From the other side of the stage, Finn pauses painting a tree on a side panel and looks up with a curious, smitten face. He cocks his head to the side – *are you okay?* – and I look smoothly away as if I haven't even seen him.

I'm alone in the dark now. Where I belong.

Just watch me burn my life down to the ground.

'Do not you love me?' I ask loudly, dropping my handbag on the floor, climbing onto the stage and elbowing the frozen cast out of the way. It looks like we're in full dress rehearsal: frilly shirts, ugly gowns and buttoned coats. I feel my anger curled up inside me, just waiting to unravel.

'*Pardonnez-moi?*' Eli blinks at me with round possum eyes, then at the rest of the cast who look similarly bewildered. 'Say what, old bean? Have we changed page? What scene are we on now?'

'Act Five, Scene Foooour,' Daisy whispers behind me.

'I *said*—' My anger begins to stir, so I prod it: grabbing Eli by the stiff collar. '*Do. Not. You. Love. Me?*'

He blinks at me again with his stupid zebra face.

Glancing over his shoulder, I see Finn put away his paintbrush and watch me, a frown between his dark eyebrows. With both hands, I move Eli so that Finn can see every single detail of what it is I'm about to do.

Then I grab Eli's face and kiss him, hard.

'Mercy!' Verity shouts. 'What on earth are you doing?'

I keep kissing him.

'*Mercy!* That is not in the script!'

And kissing.

'MERCY, PUT OUR LEAD ACTOR DOWN, THIS IS ENTIRELY INAPPROPRIATE!'

'Gosh,' Eli Bingo-Wings says cheerfully as I finally pull away, wiping his mouth. 'I had not a single sausage of an idea you felt this way about me, old girl! Not one! Well played!'

I look into the wings. Finn's frown has deepened.

'I mean,' Eli continues, grinning at me. 'Sure, you want a *soupçon* of the old Bicky. A taster plate of the Bicks, if you will. Can't blame you! But – bit awks – you're not really my type. Bit aggressive for my tastes.'

'Oh, Elijah,' I say in monotone. 'I cannot resist you any longer. Please, dissolve my identity by becoming my boyfriend. Conquer me. Destroy me. You can't deny our incredible chemistry.'

Eli pats me. 'I think it might just be you, babe.'

Finn gives me a long look, then his face hardens and he abruptly walks away.

I close my eyes: *smash.*

'Right,' Verity snaps, taking her glasses off and

rubbing them on her sleeve. 'Unless Eli wants to make a formal complaint, which he is well within his rights to do, we're actually on Act Two, Mercy, and you've relinquished this morning's rehearsal through tardiness so take a seat.'

I take a seat.

'Not on the floor of the stage.'

I shuffle on my bottom until I slip off the edge of it.

'Not there either.'

On all fours, I crawl over to one of the seats at the front, flop into it and glare at the cast ensemble, standing silently on the stage in their stupid, frilled period dress. 'Friar Francis' smiles at me tentatively, and Piper lifts her eyebrows sympathetically. I pull a mocking face – copying her expression exactly – and she flushes in embarrassment and looks away.

Then I look at Daisy, waiting with tangible happiness for her turn on stage.

Correction: *my* turn.

'Boy!' Eli calls, waving a hand at an extra.

'Signior—'

'What is *she* wearing?' I interrupt loudly, pointing at Daisy. 'Is that *my* costume?'

'Yes,' Verity grunts through gritted teeth. 'You weren't here, Mercy. Remember? Continue.'

Eli nods. 'In my chamber-window lies a book – bring it hither to me in the orch—'

'Take it off,' I say abruptly, standing up.

'What?' Daisy blinks. 'Right now?'

'*OFF!*' I scream as my anger blazes into an inferno. '*Take my flaming dress off right now, you talentless nobody. It was not made for you!*'

Daisy looks down, bursts into tears and runs off stage.

Smash.

'*Mercy*,' my director starts furiously. 'How dare you? I will absolutely *not* allow you to—'

Sitting down, I wave my arm at the cast: continue.

'Uh.' Eli scratches his head. 'Gosh. Okay. Where was I?' He clears his throat. 'I do much wonder that one man – seeing how much another man is a fool when he dedicates his behaviours to love—'

I snort loudly.

'Will, after he hath laughed at such shallow follies in others . . .'

'Hear, hear!' I shout.

'. . . become the argument of his own scorn by falling in love.'

I clap, slowly. *Clap, clap, clap.*

'Mercy,' Verity hisses, 'I swear to God, if you don't—'

'This is a terrible play.' Standing up again, I hold my arms out. 'Romantic love is a trick, a temporary madness to make us *feel* less alone. But guess what? It's just a placebo. We *are* alone. Even if we're not born alone, we die alone. So freaking *deal with it* and stop telling these moronic made-up *stories.*'

With a nasty laugh, I turn to the irritated cast.

'Also, you think you can *act*? I've seen better acting in my own front room, performed by children.'

Their mouths drop open and Verity takes a few quick steps forward, as if she's going to tackle me like a rugby ball.

'My baby sister is fifteen years old.' I spin viciously towards her. 'And she can *still* direct a play with more imagination than I've seen thus far from you, Verity Ramirez.'

I feel a rush of giddiness, a loosening, a darkness untethering.

Burn it *all* down.

'How long do we have until opening night?' I finish, smiling like a cat. 'Five nights? Six? Won't be enough.'

And . . . *SMASH*.

'That's *it*!' My director throws her script on the floor. 'I don't care who you are, Mercy! I don't care who your grandmother is, or how many times she calls the theatre's artistic director to apologise on your behalf! Casting you was the worst mistake of my career!'

Nodding, I pick up my handbag from the side of the stage.

'This is *not* who I am!' Verity continues to shriek as I sling it over my shoulder. 'I am not a shouter! You are *toxic*. You are *poison*. You have turned me into somebody I do not like!'

'Yes,' I say flatly. 'I do that. Welcome to the gang.'

There's a silence while I watch the flames lick at my career, as my dreams begin cracking, as everything I've ever wanted turns black and hollow and starts crashing down.

Then my director turns to Eli. 'Get Daisy. Now.'

Eli scurries off and within seconds Daiiiiiiiissssssyyyy has returned to the stage, dressed in jeans and a red jumper, composure strangely regained. She has clearly been watching everything from the wings and knows what's coming as well as I do.

The grand finale.

'Congratulations,' my director says with more authority than I've ever heard from her. 'Daisy, you are now playing Beatrice.'

She nods.

'Mercy Valentine.' Verity turns back to me. 'You're fired.'

53

Oh, I'm not done.

I grab a taxi straight home – I've got a *dinner party* to attend.

With a bang, I slam back into the house.

'There you are,' I hiss at Maggie as she bustles through the hallway in her grey frock, the exact same one she wore last time. 'Nice of you to *finally* rock up to work, Margaret, I assumed you'd—'

Nope, she's gone.

'Mum?' Ben appears from the kitchen, carrying flowers and wearing a suit that's slightly too small for him. 'Hang on, I've found a better vase, just let me—'

'Well,' I sneer, 'if it isn't Mister Second Choice himself.'

Nope, he's gone too.

With a snarl, I spin in a frustrated circle, looking for somebody else to cross my path.

'Max!' Dad yells from upstairs. 'Can you come and get extra chairs?!'

A voice from the garden: 'Bit busy!'

'*BOY*,' my father booms, 'I don't care if you're preparing for the next space landing, you wanna sit in a chair, you get in here and help with the flaming chairs!'

Camera trained on himself, Max comes in from the garden wearing a brand-new tuxedo.

'Oh,' I snip, '*here* he comes, the least talented of the—'

'*NOW, MAXIMUS!*'

'Coming, Father! Blimey, anyone would think we don't have staff,' my brother grumbles, jogging straight past me. 'Just wait until I'm a TV star. They won't be bossing me around then.'

He bounces lankily up the stairs, three at a time.

'Get dressed, Mercy,' my grandmother says curtly, gliding into the hallway in a long lilac gown. 'Something with a little colour, please. That's quite enough of all this black. It's simply morbid.'

I go to growl at her.

'*Excuse me,*' she interrupts, tapping her stick at a passing waiter. 'Where do you think you are taking those bread rolls, young man? What is the point in freshly baked rolls if they are placed on the table before we are all present? Put them back in the oven.'

She follows him into the kitchen, tutting.

'Eff!' Po hops out of the library in an orange dress, tugging on a green shoe. 'Effie, I can't find the other one. Can I wear two different colours, do you think?'

'Here.' Faith pokes her head out of the laundry room. 'Catch.'

She lobs a green heel across the hallway.

'Oh,' I snort, 'how *very*—'

Nope: they've both disappeared.

For the love of God, will *somebody* in this family just stay still long enough for me to destroy them?

There's a knock on the door and I run towards it in relief.

Oh yes, this will do *perfectly*.

'Sorry I'm late,' Roz smiles, wearing a horrendous pink ombre shift dress and holding an enormous lasagne in one arm, a brown anorak in another.

'British recipes are so confusing, I got all the measurements wrong and then I wasn't sure if it was Fahrenheit or Celsius so—'

I open my mouth—

'Oh, how *kind*,' my mother says, sweeping forward in blue silk. 'We always forget to feed the staff.'

She takes the lasagne away from the American.

'Please, *do* come in.' Mum gives her a formal, distant smile. 'Such a pleasure to have you in my home, Roseanne. It is *Roseanne*, isn't it? Don't feel bad that Michael didn't tell you about the dress code, my soon-to-be ex-husband can be so forgetful sometimes.'

'It's actually Rosaline,' Roz says with a muted smile.

'Bit ironic,' I snort as derisively as I can. 'Because we all know that Rosaline gets dumped for—'

'Don't be rude, Mercy,' Mum interrupts sharply, turning towards the dining room. 'Please, do let me take your coat to the cloakroom, Roz, or whatever it is you call that thing you're holding.'

With a catty little Hollywood smile, my mother leads Roz away.

She just stole *all* my lines.

'ARRRGGHHH!' I shout at the top of my voice, throwing my handbag hard on the floor. 'CAN ANYONE EVEN SEE ME ANY MORE?!'

Cheeks flaming, I run up the stairs and into my bedroom. My hands are shaking, my heart racing, all control has completely disappeared.

'Charity?' I say hoarsely. 'If you come back, I swear I'll stop. I'll try to be happy again.'

With a wave of dizziness, I walk to my mirror.

'Charity? Stop being so *selfish*!'

But it's just me.

My face, my rage, my destruction, my pain, my darkness.

Desperate now, I race to my closet. I pull everything out and haul it into a pile in the middle of my room. Tugging off my black leggings and jumper, I rifle through it until I find what I'm looking for. Then I tug the tiny grey flapper dress on. It's too tight, far too short, it smells of dust and makeup smears and memories.

With most of the buttons still undone, I return to the mirror.

'Tee,' I whisper as the room tilts. '*Please.*'

'Yo yo yo,' Max calls from the hallway behind me.

'Mermaid? So the big dinner's in five and Grandma wants me to check you're actually getting changed—'

I freeze, then turn round.

'Umm, dude.' My brother stops in the open doorway, eyes wide. 'DUDE. What are you *wearing*?'

Horrified, my mouth opens.

'*Hahahahahahaha!*' Max snorts, bursting into laughter. 'That is a *hideous* dress, Mermaid. Where did you get that from? Creepy Dolls R Us?' He laughs even harder. 'And no offence, but it looks a little on the snug—'

'GET OUT!' I scream, hurtling towards my brother and shoving him as hard as I can. 'OUT! GET OUT GET OUT GET OUT!'

He falls onto the hallway carpet with an *oof.*

'I was joking!' Blinking, Max scratches his head. 'Blimey! Obviously *somebody's* got their period.' I kick him until he scrambles up with his hands in the air. 'Okay! Okay! I'll go downstairs and tell them you're nearly ready! Keep your wig on.'

My brother disappears and with a howling brain I storm out into the hallway. Max's bedroom is at the end of the corridor. Without pausing, I march straight into the messy, stale chaos and look around.

His laptop is on his desk, still open.

I guess his password in four seconds, move the *MY BIG BREAK!!!* file onto a memory stick and pull it out. Then I run down the stairs and kick the dining-room door open with a loud *BANG*.

Everything is glittery, warm, golden, just as it used to be.

'Mercy!' Grandma says, glancing up from her champagne glass. 'That is an entirely unnecessary—'

She falls silent, seeing the expression on my face.

'Leave the room,' Grandma says to the waiters, hovering round the edges. 'Quickly, please.'

The staff empties out as my family stares at me in shock.

'What's happened?' Effie asks gently. 'Mer, what is it? Why are you wearing the ghost dress?'

'Well,' I sneer, ignoring her. 'How delightful that we've started gathering in here again. A quaint little heart-warming family celebration, I see! Exactly like the old days!'

I glance around the twinkling room at Grandma, Mum, Dad, Faith, Hope, Max, Maggie, Ben, Roz.

'Except, it's *not*, is it?' I laugh brutally. 'Because

someone is missing. Not that you'd be able to tell, because pretending is what Valentines *do*.'

Deliberately, I walk over to the table, pick up a crystal champagne glass and drop it on the solid oak floor.

Smash.

'We fake it.'

Another glass: *smash.*

'We fake happiness.' *Smash.*

'We fake perfection.' *Smash.*

'We fake closeness.' *Smash.*

'Do you know why the Valentines are the most famous acting family on the planet? Because faking it is *all we do*.'

With one arm, I sweep the rest of the glasses off the side table.

SMAAAAAAAAAAAASSSSSSH.

'Mercy!' Grandma cries.

'Oh, go to hell,' I hiss at her, whipping round. 'If it wasn't for *you* and your pride, Charity and I wouldn't have been *on* that television set in the first place.'

She blinks in astonishment and her mouth snaps shut.

'MERCY,' Dad booms, slamming his fist on the

54

[Heartbeat sounds]

Max

Think you know the Valentines?

A rapid montage of glossy magazines featuring the Valentines land one on top of the other.

Max

You don't.

Montage footage:

Hope sobbing on her bed; Faith climbing down fire escape of family mansion with shaved head; Mercy screaming abuse at housekeeper; Michael and Roz kissing in London park; Dame Sylvia refusing to talk to paparazzi; dishevelled Juliet wandering down a hallway, hair knotty and expression lost; Max calling his father, but call is rejected.

                    Max
Lies. Secrets. Grief. A family in pieces.

  THE VALENTINES flashes in black and gold

  Max [direct to camera, close up]
I'm Max Valentine, and I'm gonna show you . . . everything.

55

Dead silence.

Max stands up so abruptly his chair falls over.

'Guys,' he says desperately, holding his hands out like a self-help guru to a crowd of sceptics. 'Don't look at me like that, it's still in the works. I'm prepared to accept editing notes . . . Really, when you think about it, it could be healthy for us, to show we're not—'

'You ass-hat,' Faith says clearly.

Everyone turns to stare at her instead.

'Max, you complete and utter *ass-hat.*' My sweet sister rises from her seat, visibly shaking with anger. 'How could you do this? All this time, you were secretly *filming* us? It has taken *everything I have* to get out of the limelight, and now you're just going to . . . push me back into it again?'

My brother flinches. 'Eff, that's not the way it—'

'You're putting my heartbreak on television?' Hope jumps up with flushed cheeks, her fists squeezed shut. 'But the whole world will see me crying!'

'LIKE HELL HE IS,' Dad booms, lurching up and bashing his fist on the table so hard the cutlery clatters. 'MAXIMUS LAURENCE VALENTINE, YOU ARE CANCELLING THIS PROJECT.'

'I . . .' Mum says weakly, staring at the flickering projector screen. 'I didn't realise . . . I had no idea . . . I . . .'

'Never!' Grandma yelps, leaning on her stick to propel herself forward. 'Never in my entire life have I been so appalled by a member of this family!'

'Look,' Roz starts quietly, 'I think it's important that we all—'

My grandmother turns on her. 'Pipe down, missy! You are not a part of this family, regardless of how hard you are clearly trying to be!'

'SYLVIA!' Dad yells. 'DO NOT SPEAK TO ROZ LIKE THAT!'

'Except—' Hope frowns, deep in thought. 'I *do* look cute, right? I'm a pretty crier, hashtag blessed. And this could be my chance! Plus, if we show how it ends –' she grabs Ben's hand and smiles at him – 'then really it's a very beautiful story.'

Ben frowns. 'Hope, I'm not comfortable being on television.'

'Me neither,' Maggie interrupts. 'For the record.'

'AND YOU'RE NOT GOING ON TV, HOPE, YOU ARE STILL FIFTEEN.'

'But, *Dad*,' Hope complains. 'Charity and Mercy were only *fourteen* when they did that ghost show, so it's totally unfair that—'

'WHY DO YOU THINK WE MADE THE RULES IN THE FIRST PLACE? HOPE VALENTINE, YOU ARE NOT GOING ON TELEVISION AND THAT IS FINAL!'

'This is so *unfair*!' Hope slams a plate down. 'Max! Leave me in!'

'TAKE HER OUT.'

'Leave me in!'

'*You will take me out immediately*,' Faith screams over the hubbub. None of us have ever heard her raise her voice like that before. 'Or I will use every penny I've saved to *sue the living daylights out of you, Max*!'

'I'm so sorry,' Mum whispers at her plate. 'I didn't realise what was going on. I'll try harder. I'll—'

'Do not apologise for this, Juliet!' Grandma bangs her walking stick on the floor. 'This is not your fault!'

'. . . DISINHERITED . . .' Dad is still shouting. '. . . IN ALL MY DAYS . . .'

'Leave me in!'

'TAKE ME OUT.'

'I'm so very—'

'Everyone, if we could just—'

'. . . tacky, destroy everything we have built over a century, cannot believe that . . .'

'. . . really uncomfortable with—'

'IN!'

'OUT!'

'IN IN IN!'

Everyone is standing up and screaming over the top of each other across the dining table.

'Guys!' Max is beseeching desperately, cheeks flushed. 'Listen, let's just sit down and talk about this rationally and—'

Quietly, I start edging out of the room.

All I wanted was to hurt my brother – just an outlet to vent my rage on . . . Except I can't control the damage, can I? That's the point. I never can.

Eyes filling, I find the door handle and watch the

screaming escalate, my healing family breaking apart again.

Blindly, I slip into the dark hallway.

'Mercy.'

I need to go.

'Mercy.'

I need to get as far away from here as possible.

'Mercy, *stop*.'

Quickly wiping my eyes, I turn round to face Faith. She closes the dining-room door quietly behind her and takes a few steps towards me.

'Don't say it,' I snap hoarsely. 'You hate me, I know.'

'It's not going to work,' my sister says gently.

I hesitate. 'What?'

'However hard you push us away, we will keep coming back. Whatever you do, we will still love you. That's what families *do*.'

My throat tightens, closes.

'Will you?' I whisper, because maybe they wouldn't.

Not if they knew.

56

Two years ago

'Charity? Has anybody seen Charity Valentine?'

For the third time this week, there's an urgent rap on the dressing-room door and a harassed-looking production assistant pokes his head in.

'Charity?' he asks hopefully.

'Mercy.'

'Oh man.' He grimaces. 'Your sister was supposed to be on set half an hour ago. Everybody's waiting. Again.'

'She's on the toilet.' I smile apologetically. 'Bad tummy. Oysters. She'll be out in a tick.'

'Right.' He doesn't believe me. 'Well, tell your sister to get on set as soon as she can.'

'Absolutely,' I nod sweetly.

As soon as the door shuts, I grab my phone yet again and type:

TEE WHERE THE HELL ARE YOU? GET A MOVE ON

I freaking *told her* this would happen.

After a solid year of fancying him, Charity finally scored a first date with Blake. They've gone out for a walk, an ice cream, to feed the ducks, whatever. My twin kept prodding me awake at intervals all night to update me on her 'romantic' plans, until I eventually threatened to smother her with a pillow.

It might be cute if it wasn't about to destroy her career.

Our career.

Beep.

OMG Cee we are having the BEST time! I am so in love! Not as in love as Blake is obvs hahahaha xxx

Smiling in spite of myself, I type:

Cool but you were supposed to be back and it's your turn on set – I can't keep covering for you. They're going to notice.

Beep.

I knowwwww but Blake never gets days off and we just want to get to know each other better – you only get a first EVER date once, right? Xxxx

Beep.

PS have I ever told you how pretty and lovely and awesome you are? X

Beep.

PPS Seriously, like, soooooooooo pretty. Xxx

I roll my eyes.

FINE Tee, I'll cover for you again. Just get back in time for us to go home together so nobody suspects.

Beep.

I WILL. I LOVE YOU. Xx

Now I smile.

Yeah, you better. X

As fast as I can, I tug on the grey flapper dress. Rushing to the makeup artist, I get the full treatment: dark eyes, dead skin, short ashy bob wig. Then I hurry towards the film set, consciously lightening my step, relaxing my face and unfurling my shoulders.

'Hey, Tee!' A cute extra grins at me and I grin back. 'Looking especially cute today.'

'Ta very much, handsome.'

With a perky skip, I hop over a camera wire and enter the set.

'Charity!' The director looks up. 'Finally! How are you feeling, sweetheart?'

'Better.' I pat my tummy with a grimace. 'But you might wanna cordon off the entire backstage area, if you know what I mean?'

He laughs, distracted by checking the lighting.

'Which reminds me,' I add in a husky voice, 'why can't you hear a pterodactyl using the bathroom? The *P* is silent.'

I hear a low rumble as the crew chuckles.

'Why do ducks have feathers?' I'm starting to feel slightly giddy, light-headed. 'To cover their butt quacks.'

They laugh again – a warm, enveloping sound, like a hug that doesn't touch you – and I realise with a pang that of all the roles I've ever played, being my sister is my favourite.

'Finally, what did one toilet say to the other? You look *flushed*.' I give a charming bow to my audience. 'So, where would you like the genius to stand?'

'Over here.' The director shakes his head. 'What are we going to do with you, Charity? You're so unreliable. Nothing at all like your twin.'

My stomach twists sharply and I can't stop myself.

'Yet I'm just more lovable, right?' I grin conspiratorially and lean forward. 'Go on, confess. I won't tell anyone.'

'Not true,' the director whispers with a small wink. 'Ssshhh.'

Something inside me falls and smashes.

'O-kay,' I say, quickly attempting to right myself before anyone notices. 'Let's get started.'

The cameras whirr and I try to focus on screwing up the scene so that nobody guesses I'm me.

'CUT!' The director beams. 'Your best yet, Tee.'

Small consolation, I guess.

'What can I say?' I grin, blowing a kiss at the team. I can feel myself running out of gas, shutting down, darkening, my mask dropping. 'Food poisoning works wonders. Laters!'

As fast as I can, I saunter back to the dressing room just in time for my smile to fizzle out like a firework in the rain.

Breathing out, I close the door behind me and lean against it.

'How did it go?'

Charity is sprawled across our cosy Papasan chair with her muddy feet propped up casually on the vanity. I never sit like that; I hold myself rigidly like an unwanted ornament.

'Good,' I say in a small voice, starting to unbutton.

'My first date went *swimmingly*, thank you very much.' She chuckles throatily. 'By which I mean I pushed him in a pond. Blake looks so *adorable* wet, her cheek. 'What's with the out-of-character PDA? You're going to freak me out. Stop it.'

Wiping my eyes with an embarrassed grin, I pull away.

'So . . . swaps?' I check hesitantly.

'Yeah.' Charity grins. 'Swaps.'

57

The house empties out.

The dust settles, and one by one my family leaves. Dad and Roz back to their hotel, Grandma to her swanky Kensington flat, Mum to her bedroom, Faith to the Brixton studio, Hope somewhere with Ben, Maggie to her flat in Putney.

And I'm left alone in the silence. Stranded in a huge home that feels unfamiliar and hostile, like a person I don't know how to be around.

Numb, I wander aimlessly through the hallways.

In and out of enormous deserted rooms, trying to find something to distract me from their emptiness. I amble into the cold, dark kitchen, raid the fridge, pick at leftovers from the uneaten banquet: discover I can't really swallow, my appetite is gone. I try the cinema room again, attempt to watch a film, any film, but realise I can't focus.

Feeling anaesthetised, I go into Charity's bright yellow bedroom, remove the joke Post-Its that Faith stuck all over the room, throw them in the bin.

Then I hole up in my navy bedroom.

Lying on my bed in the dark, spending hours scouring the internet for a fight, an argument, a humiliation – just something that will make me feel an emotion again, *anything*.

On day two, there's an official public statement.

Due to unforeseen personal circumstances, we are sad to announce that Mercy Valentine will no longer be taking part in the upcoming performance of *Much Ado About Nothing* at the Globe Theatre. However, we are proud to welcome a promising newcomer to the role. Understudy, Daisy Morgan, a recent RADA graduate, will be stepping into the iconic role of Beatrice. Last few tickets still available.

Nothing.

Even discovering that Daisy went to my dream drama school and so is technically more qualified than me has zero impact, so I take to Twitter.

Just to clarify, I QUIT. @The_Globe_Theatre

*Don't bother going to see the play. It's LAME.
@The_Globe_Theatre*

*Also, Shakespeare is IRRELEVANT. @The_Globe_
Theatre*

As expected, the slap-backs come thick and fast:

*Everyone knows @MercyValentine was fired for being
a diva. LOL*

*What's in a name @MercyValentine? Clearly nothing
when you CAN'T HOLD ON TO YOUR JOB.*

Still nothing.

So I head to Instagram to try again. It appears
the Birdbrains have deleted and re-uploaded the
photo of us at the sleepover, except this time they've
cropped me out. The pillow fight has been similarly
edited: there's a bunch of hearts stuck over where
my face used to be.

A quick scan through their accounts confirms I've
been completely eradicated.

Nope: I feel nada, not even a flicker.

I make an anonymous account on YouTube and start trolling any celebrity I can find:

That haircut is ugly.

Why do you keep plaguing the world with your music?

YOU HAVE ZERO QUALIFICATIONS IN MAKEUP APPLICATION WHY IS ANYONE WATCHING THIS

I still feel dead inside.

By the third day, I'm so desperate for pain I email Finn:

From: Mercy Valentine
To: Finneas O'Connor

Hi

I wait a few minutes, then try again:

From: Mercy Valentine

So I guess you're not talking to me any more

A *ping*.

From: Finneas O'Connor

Mercy, what do you want?

Finally, the tiniest twinge: I cling on to it like a life-raft.

From: Mercy Valentine

Ooooooh snippy ;)

Ping

From: Finneas O'Connor

Mercy, I will ask you again – what do you want?

He clearly hates me and it hurts – just a tiny little hole in the numbness that I can breathe through – so I push it further:

From: Mercy Valentine

OMG KISSING ELI WAS A JOKE LIGHTEN UP

Ping.

From: Finneas O'Connor

It wasn't, Mercy. I think we both know what you were doing. I like you but I really don't think it's supposed to be this hard, this soon.

It's clearly not a healthy dynamic for either of us.

So let's just leave it, okay?

Finn

I hold my breath and close my eyes.

The hole in me opens up a little more, like a crack in the ground.

Aching, I drag myself to my feet and sling a black coat on over my penguin pyjamas. I've been wearing them now for three days straight and they stink, but it's not like there's anybody here to notice. I walk up and down the corridors, knocking on doors, but nobody answers. Tying the coat belt up tightly, I text John and sit on the front doorstep for the limo to pull smoothly up the driveway.

'Hi,' I say flatly as he steps out and opens the door.

'Hello, Mercy,' my driver says carefully. 'It's nice to see you. Where are we going today?'

Sliding into the backseat, I sit for a few seconds, staring woodenly at the headrest in front of me.

'I don't know,' I admit finally. 'Nowhere. Anywhere.'

John nods and starts the car.

We drive slowly through the quiet roads of Richmond and I see barely anything, but I'm comforted, somehow, by the movement of the limo and the steady purr of the motor, like a baby that can't sleep.

After half an hour I feel myself beginning to drift. I stare at the back of John's balding head, so familiar – such an everyday part of my life, yet so unacknowledged – and there's suddenly something I have to say.

'I'm sorry,' I whisper as he indicates right.

'What for?' John asks calmly.

'For being such a cow to you.' I close my eyes and feel the sway of the car as we take a slow, steady corner. 'For being so demanding. For making you pick me up at random times of night and drive me to get kebabs. For forcing you to wait for me for hours and expecting you to drop everything for me at a moment's notice. For being so entitled and rude, and never asking how you are.'

There's a silence as the car thrums along a narrow road.

I'm so drowsy now I'm nearly asleep.

'I've got a kid, you know,' John says finally into the quiet. 'A daughter. A year younger than you.'

My eyes open guiltily. 'I . . . didn't know.'

'She lives with her mum.' He rubs his nose with his finger. 'I don't see her as much as I'd like to.'

Another flash of guilt. 'No thanks to me, huh.'

'That's not what I meant,' he corrects gently. 'What I'm saying, Mercy, is that I would hate to think that she was out there, at night, with no way to get home again. With nobody looking out for her, or knowing where she was.'

A lump suddenly rises to my throat. 'Oh.'

'It's okay to need people, Mercy,' John says, looking at me through the rear-view mirror. 'We all do.'

The ground inside me opens up a little more and I feel one emotion rise up through it.

Eyes filling, I lean forward.

'Thank you,' I whisper. 'That's what I meant to say.'

He smiles back at me. 'You're welcome.'

58

It's dark by the time we return.

John waits patiently in the driveway – presumably in case I need to leave again – and I slip back into the empty house, feeling fragile and delicate, like something I could easily smash.

With the lights off, I head silently into the dining room. There's just enough moonlight to see what I'm doing, so I turn off the still whirring overhead projector, pack it away neatly in the huge bureau; remove the remaining non-broken glasses and put them back in a box. Maggie's done a good job of cleaning up, but there's still a little crunching underfoot so I sweep again. I carry the few remaining side plates to the kitchen and grab a cloth to wipe down the table a second time.

I'm just picking up a silver napkin ring that's

rolled into the corner when I see a dark figure in the open doorway.

With a lurch, I jump halfway out of my skin.

'Mum?' I narrow my eyes at it. 'How long have you been standing there?'

She takes a step forward and the moon catches on her silver sequins; she flashes like a lightning bolt.

'A while,' she says softly.

Clearing her throat, my mother takes another step towards me and I realise with a heart-spin that she's in full Hollywood glamour mode. She's wearing her favourite shimmering full-length gown, waved blonde hair, red lipstick.

'I thought everyone was out,' I say, looking down again.

'No.' She takes another small step. 'I've been in my bedroom. I had a lot of thinking to do.'

Nodding, I pretend to give the table another wipe so I don't have to look directly at her. I'm not entirely sure what to do with my face, what to say. There's still a distance between us, and I don't know how to cross it. I've never known how to.

427

'I'm sorry,' I mumble in a tiny voice. 'For ruining dinner.'

'You didn't ruin anything,' my mother says, taking another step. 'Darling, that trailer . . . I am so incredibly ashamed of myself. You were all struggling, and I wasn't there for you. I fell into myself somehow, and I couldn't . . . I didn't . . .'

'Have room for other people's pain,' I finish quietly.

'That's just it.' Her face twists. 'But it was my *job* to have room, sweetheart. I am your *mother*.'

My throat tightens, and I realise with a sharp pang just how similar we actually are. I've been so busy trying to emulate my mother's success, her talent, her beauty. It never really occurred to me that in shutting the world out, I was just like her already.

'It's okay.' I faux-shrug.

'It's not okay.' My mum shakes her head. 'It is not okay, Mercy. But I will make it up to all of you, I promise.'

Looking down, I give the table another unnecessary wipe.

'Cool,' I manage.

And I expect her to leave again but this time she doesn't: she lingers in the dining room, lost in thought.

'Aren't you late for something?' I prompt slightly sharply. 'Or are we dressing in black tie for every meal now?'

'Oh!' Mum snaps back to life and looks down at herself. 'Yes. It's an award ceremony for *Pinnacle*. I just thought . . . It's not enough, I know that. But I have to start somewhere.'

'Sure.' I shrug, picking up the final platter and walking past her towards the kitchen. 'The limo's waiting outside.'

Somewhat aggressively, I snap the lights back on.

'Mercy . . . would you like to come with me?'

I freeze.

'If you're not ready, then I understand,' my mother continues in a strange, nervous rush. 'But I've got a plus-one, if you want it.'

And I'm not sure which of us is more surprised when I turn back towards her and say, 'Yes, please.'

59

An hour later, Mum and I step out of the limousine.

'Juliet! Mercy!'

'Smile, ladies!'

'VALENTINES! LOOK THIS WAY!'

The paparazzi swarms around us: screaming, shouting, flashing.

We're both dressed to kill – Mum lent me one of her Tom Ford gowns, I'm wearing the highest Prada heels of my life, my lipstick is flawless and my eyeliner perfect – but for the first time possibly ever, I don't want the attention.

It feels too abrasive; like I'm being rubbed away.

Flinching, I take a step backwards.

'Good evening.' Mum moves smoothly in front of me and smiles. 'What an extraordinary honour it is to be here at the British Academy of Film and Television Awards tonight. This will be the thirtieth nomination for a member of the Valentine family, and I am overjoyed.'

More screams, more pushes, more flashes.

With a small wince, I take another tiny step behind her.

'Mercy!' A photographer leans round and thrusts his camera in my face. 'Is it true that you were fired from the Globe? What "personal situation" are they talking about?'

'You've been caught ranting online again,' another one adds, holding his camera high in the air. 'What does Dame Sylvia have to say about that?'

Another steps in: 'The rumours are that you were unprofessional and arrogant. What's your response?'

Horrified and ashamed beyond measure, I glance at Mum.

'I . . . I,' I stutter. *Flash flash.* 'I—'

'Mercy is a passionate artist,' my mum answers firmly, taking my hand. 'Sometimes that passion can *overspill*, as her grandmother well knows.'

The paparazzi laughs at the burn and I stare at my mum in shock. Did she just do to *her* mum what I usually do to mine?

Handing down the Valentine baton indeed.

'We of course wish the production well,' my mother adds with a serene smile, 'and look forward to seeing it in due course. Now, if you'll excuse me, I have a very special evening ahead of me and I'd like to spend it with my daughter.'

She flashes her dazzling smile directly at me.

And I'm so surprised my famous mother has to call my name three times before I follow her up the red-carpeted stairs and towards the glowing beehive of the Royal Albert Hall.

The doors immediately swing open as we approach – no tickets needed for the Valentines – and we're ushered straight through the foyer into the huge domed hall.

As it opens up around us, I feel my breath catch.

It's magnificent: coated in plush red with lines of purple, like the inside of a beating heart. Stone arches and ornate balconies reach elegantly towards the ceiling, and lights shine in orbs on a flower-filled stage where beats the largest screen I have ever seen in my life.

Orchestral music plays, but it's not loud enough to mute the chatter of the thousands of people already gathered: glittering and beautiful, seated in rows of red-and-gold-velvet chairs.

I can feel my insides flickering like a candle.

This vast room is full of faces I know, faces I've met, faces I recognise: faces I've watched over and over again, in the hope that one day I'll be acting next to them. Actors, producers, directors, screenwriters. The brightest stars in the movie world, gathered together to celebrate the miraculous power of storytelling.

This is everything I hoped it would be, everything I've ever dreamt of, everything I've ever wanted.

It's everything I've just thrown away.

'Mum,' I say in a strangled voice. 'It's true.'

Without a word, she leads me towards the front row of seats.

'What the paparazzi just said about me.' I try again, swallowing hard. 'I was fired for being . . . bad.'

Overwhelmed with shame, I focus on my feet.

'Juliet Valentine!' A famous actress whose films I have adored since I was a tiny child catches Mum's glittering arm. 'Oh, my talented beauty! We weren't sure if you would make it! What a relief to see you looking so much better. How have you *been*?'

'Grieving,' my mother says calmly. 'Very unhappy and really quite selfish. Thank you for asking.'

The actress pats her arm sympathetically and pulls away.

We keep walking to our seats.

'Mercy,' Mum says in a low voice, glancing over her shoulder. 'You are not – and never have been – *bad*. You are a grieving seventeen-year-old who needed support and love, and your parents were not there to give you any. That's on me and your father, not on you.'

The ground inside me creaks and opens up a little more.

I nod and my eyes prickle, abruptly wet.

'Now.' We reach the end of our line of seats and my beautiful mother frowns. 'I believe this is us, darling. Do we have everything we need before the show starts? I've realised, I'm – as Hope would say – absolutely *ravishing*. Shall I call a waiter?'

'Let me,' I say quickly. 'I can go get us drinks and snacks.'

'Fizzy water, Mercy.' She lifts one eyebrow at me. 'Maybe a bit of sparkling orange if you want to get really crazy.'

I smile faintly. 'Okayyyy, Mum. Blimey.'

'Oh, don't worry,' she laughs. 'Same goes for me.'

And I have to spin and walk down the aisle as fast as I can, wrist pressed to my cheekbone, so I don't start crying with happiness and ruin my makeup. Because I've loved having nobody to answer to, I've loved the freedom, I've loved the parties.

But I think I love having my mum back more.

Trying to hide a slowly erupting grin, I burst through the doors of the foyer and look around the open buffet for the nearest staff.

'Excuse me?' I say, tapping a tux-clad waiter. 'Do you think I could grab those glasses of orange juice and a handful of whatever that pink gooey stuff is? I'm here with *Juliet Valentine*.'

My insides swell so sharply I say it again, for good measure.

'Juliet Valentine is my mum,' I repeat proudly. 'She's up for Best Director and we're celebrating.' I go to take the two glasses then hesitate. 'What are those oyster things? Actually, why don't you just give me the tray?'

With my hands full, I turn back towards the hall.

Three familiar heads appear in the distance, and I feel my happiness wobble.

'Guys?' I head towards them. 'What are you doing here?'

Vee, Mee and Dee continue talking.

'Guys!' With difficulty, I nudge my way through the glittering crowd and stand behind them, still holding the tray. 'I didn't know you were coming this evening.'

They keep talking.

'Hello?'

Slowly, my friends turn round to stare at me. They're so dressed up they look like they've raided the Harrods jewellery department. Dior is actually wearing a full-blown *tiara*.

'Oh, look,' Nova says flatly. 'It's the house wrecker.'

'Apparently she's *surprised* we're here.' Amethyst lifts her perfect little nose and smooths down her pink satin gown. 'Because we're not important enough to be invited to a fancy awards ceremony without her help, right?'

'Right,' Dior smirks, fiddling with a massive diamond earring. 'It's just not a *party* without Mercy Valentine.'

Sneering, they turn their backs on me again.

My mouth has gone dry.

'Haha.' I clear my throat. 'Look, I get that you're still mad. I totally understand. The sprinklers were an accident. I thought it would be fun, but it was . . . a poorly thought-through prank. I sincerely apologise.'

Nova shrugs without looking at me. 'Whatever.'

'Yeah,' Dior agrees smarmily, adjusting her sparkling crown. 'Like, *so* whatever, it hurts, you know?'

'Come on,' I frown. 'Can't we just put it behind us now? You're my friends.'

Now Amethyst looks directly at me. 'Are we, though?'

'We *used* to be,' Nova says sharply. 'We used to be friends, back when you were somebody worth knowing. Now you're just an embarrassing mess, Mercy. An unemployed psycho stuck-up *waiter*.'

'What?' I look in surprise at the tray in my hands. 'No, this isn't—'

'Dating *stage crew*.' Amethyst rolls her eyes.

'We started a new group text,' Dior smirks, adding somewhat unnecessarily: 'Without *you* in it.'

My throat closes and I take a step back.

The lights in the room flash brighter, three times,

and then abruptly dim. A tannoy announcement politely asks all guests to take their seats: the ceremony is starting.

'And now that Charity's gone,' Nova adds, 'we don't think there's much point in hanging out with you any more.'

'We liked her more,' Amethyst explains.

'A *lot* more,' Dior echoes.

They hold my gaze and I take another step back: don't say it please don't say it don't say it don't say it—

'It's just a shame she died and we all got left with *you*.'

60

Two years ago

'Stop smiling, Tee.'

'I'm not smiling.'

'You are.' I laugh and ping a hair elastic across the car. 'You're grinning from ear to ear and it is *very* un-Mercy-Valentine like, so you're going to have to stop it if you want to pretend to be me today.'

Charity laughs and pokes me with her foot.

'You smile too, Mer. Strangers might buy your tough-girl act, but *I* know that deep down you're a soft cotton-candy kitten full of sunshine, sequins and rainbows.'

'I flaming am not.' I pull a ghastly face and lean

over to cuff her round the head. 'I'm fierce and terrifying and don't you *dare* tell anyone different, okay?'

'Won't need to.' Tee smiles, stretching out lazily. 'The right people will work it out for themselves.'

We grin at each other.

'Hey,' I say suddenly, leaning forward. 'We're on the wrong sides of the car. I'm always on the left, remember?'

'Ugh.' Charity rolls her eyes. 'Really? This is unnecessary attention to detail, Cee. Nobody will notice.'

'If you're going to do something properly . . .' I swap sides and shift her over with my bottom then reclick my seatbelt. 'There. Much better.'

'You're the worst.'

'I'm the best.'

'Debatable.'

'Certifiable.'

Laughing – me in purple, her in red – we settle into the journey home. Our normal chauffeur's got the weekend off, so we're being ferried back in one of the studio's much smaller cars, by a very quiet guy who isn't nearly as friendly as John.

Surreptitiously, I study my twin's face as we take a corner.

The broad smile is still there: breaking out, disappearing and shining again like the sun between clouds. Honestly, I'm kind of fascinated. We've always shared so many emotions, but this one is entirely unfamiliar. I can't even pretend to know how it feels.

'What's it like?' I ask abruptly.

'Hmm?' She slides glowing eyes towards me. 'What's *what* like?'

'A first date.' I flush slightly. 'How did it . . . feel?'

'Are you for real?' My twin laughs loudly. 'Little Miss I Hate Love is interested in romance all of a sudden?'

'Shut up.' I kick her. 'I'm *curious,* that's all. It seems like a dangerous sickness, and I feel obliged to check that you've not become clinically insane.'

'You're so kind.' Charity rolls her eyes, thinks about it for a few seconds then beams at me. 'It felt good.'

'*Good?*' I wait for a little more detail then chuckle. 'That's it? Wow. You're a real poet, Tee. Blake must have properly swept you off your feet today.'

Tee smiles with that strange, secret smile, and I'm suddenly blown away by just how shut out and lonely I feel.

'It was *good*, that's all. I'm happy.'

The sunshine blazes through the back of the car window and illuminates her: a haze of curls and the outline of her cheek, the hot glow of her lips and eyelashes.

Her happiness is part of me.

Which means I'm happy now too.

'Succinct,' I grin with an eyeroll, as the car begins to slow down for a red light. 'Remind me to get allllllllll the boring romantic details from you, like, literally never.'

Charity laughs loudly.

And neither of us see the other car approaching the junction.

Neither of us see the other driver, texting on his phone.

Neither of us see the lights change.

And neither of us see the car plough straight into us, on the side I would have been on if I had just been me.

61

I stagger backwards.

As loud applause erupts, I shove the waiter's tray at a random woman and stumble through the crowd, knocking against walls and celebrities, lurching out into an empty corridor.

'Hello?' An assistant calls after me urgently. 'Miss? You can't go that way. The ceremony has started and we're locking the doors, so if you could please make your way to your—'

Panicking, I break into a run. I push at side doors to the left and right until one finally gives, barrelling into an empty staffroom full of plastic chairs and a large flickering television.

'Welcome,' a woman on it announces, 'to the seventy-second annual ceremony for the British Academy of—'

I close the door softly behind me.

I sit on the floor.

I scratch the scab on my hand until it starts bleeding.

We all got left with you.

We all got left with you.

We all got left with you.

We all got left with—

'SHUT UP,' I scream, starting to cry. 'SHUT UP SHUT UP SHUT UP SHUT UP!'

Because this time the voice is mine.

62

Two years ago

A cut on my hand.

That's the only damage I have. A small laceration on my right fist from the windscreen glass. I'm sitting alone, in a hospital room that smells like a clean toilet, surrounded by posters about washing my hands and checking for lumps.

And all I can do is wait.

For someone to arrive, for news. I stare at the two doors on either side of the room, not knowing what either will bring. People come and they go but they're never mine; they're never for me.

Finally, one door opens. My mother looks older than she has ever looked before.

Wobbling, I stand up.

'Are you hurt?' She takes two brief steps towards me. 'Tell me quickly – are you hurt?'

I shake my head.

'Is there any . . .?' A hesitation. 'Do we know if . . .? Has anyone . . .? Is there any news?'

I shake my head again.

Mum's face breaks and in one motion she almost falls across the room: closing the gap, gathering me inwards.

I lean against her numbly.

'Oh, my darling,' she whispers, stroking my hair. 'Oh, my poor, poor darling.'

Then she suddenly freezes, pulls away – realising who I am, understanding that I'm in the wrong clothes – and everything in me drops, because this hug is not mine.

This love is not for me.

And the other door opens.

63

I keep crying.

Staring vacantly at the television screen, gouging at my destroyed knuckle, sobbing in big, ugly jags; the brutal truth crawling into the empty spaces inside me, just like it does every single night.

My sister died because of me.

She died because she was more fun, more playful, easier to be with, less intense. She died because I wanted what she had, so I took it. And there isn't a single person in my life who doesn't secretly wish it was the other way around.

'And the winner is . . . Juliet Valentine!'

Wiping my eyes, I blink at the huge screen. The camera is scanning the hall, searching for my mother's beautiful face, which I guess is exactly what I've been doing for years.

'Mercy.'

And it keeps searching, focusing on an empty seat as the applauding crowd turns and looks for her too.

'Mercy.'

Trying to find something that isn't there.

'Mercy, look at me.'

Twisting, I turn round and stare at my mother. She closes the door gently behind her.

'You won,' I say numbly.

'I don't care,' she says softly, walking towards me in her glittering gown. 'At this moment, I have never cared about anything less in my entire life.'

Slowly, she sits on the floor next to me.

I close my eyes.

'I was on the wrong side of the car,' I whisper, no longer able to hold it in. 'It was my idea to swap over that day, Mum. It should have been me that died.'

My mother takes a sharp breath inwards.

Opening my eyes, I look blankly at the shining television.

'And I don't blame you.' My voice gets even softer. 'I don't blame you for pulling away at the hospital, when you realised I wasn't her.'

They're still calling my mother's name.

'But I need her too,' I continue, my voice rising and falling. 'I've always needed her. Charity made me . . . lighter. She made me a better person. Except now she's gone, all that's left is *this*. She took all the good in me, and now I just feel . . .'

I search for a word that's big enough.

'*Tilted*,' I say in a small voice. 'And all that's left is rage. Rage at me, at you, at her, at everyone. There's so much rage inside me; there's nothing else left. It's all burnt up, charred, black.'

My mum looks at me with soft eyes.

'I hate myself,' I whisper, rubbing a trickle of blood across my hand as the room drowns. 'I think I probably always have.'

With a small cry of pain, I put my forehead on my knees and wrap my arms round myself, emptied.

I'm open, finally, my ugliness laid bare.

There's a silence.

Next to me, Mum takes off her shoes, puts them gently on the floor next to her, curls up into her knees too.

'Juliet Valentine apparently cannot be with us tonight,' a voice above us says. 'So, congratulations,

Juliet. And now, we move on to the category of Best Actor—'

My mother clears her throat. 'Do you know what you were like when you were little?'

I shake my head.

'You were such a funny, intense little thing.' She smiles wistfully. 'Always glowering, always watching. You tried so hard, at everything, but you never wanted anyone to see you trying. It was like you needed to be tough, right from the start.'

My stomach twists. 'That's kind of my point.'

'And you were *fierce* too,' she laughs. 'My gosh, if anyone crossed you or somebody you loved, you were like a tiny warrior with a flaming sword. Fearless. Honest. Brave.'

I swallow. 'Or a bad-tempered psycho.'

'Oh no. Please never say that.' Mum frowns at me. 'Those are words people throw at girls and women they can't control. There is *nothing* wrong with standing up for yourself, Mercy. Nothing wrong in saying what you want and how you feel. In fact, it's a rare talent. Not that you need another one.'

My eyes fill. 'But Charity—'

'Charity was my sweet joker,' she says, her eyes

warm. 'All she wanted to do was play, and be loved, and make people laugh. And she needed people. When she fell over, she instinctively lifted her arms to be cuddled.'

I smile faintly.

'But you were different,' my mother continues. 'You didn't want to be touched, my darling. Especially when you were in pain. I'd watch you curl into yourself, pull away so you could be alone.'

There's a pause and I lift my head.

Mum looks straight at me – sees me, really sees me – and I can feel something starting to swell in my chest. Something tight, suddenly unravelling.

'Mercy,' my mother says in a soft voice, 'that's why I pulled away. Not because I confused you, but because I *didn't.*'

I unravel a little more.

'Why on earth would I want you to be any different?' Mum smiles. 'You are exactly as you should be. You are fiery and brave and honest, and I love you unconditionally.'

With a sob, I put my hands over my eyes.

'I just—'

'Unconditionally,' my mother repeats.

'But—'

'*Unconditionally,*' she says firmly.

And with a dizzying sensation like an hourglass turning, I suddenly feel my entire life and everything in it swing upside down. All these years spent thinking I wasn't enough.

Trying so hard to be other people.

Believing I couldn't be loved if I wasn't.

Hesitating, I slowly lean over and rest my head tentatively on my mother's shoulder, like a butterfly landing. I feel her wait a few seconds, and then put her hand on top of my head.

'I still hear her sometimes,' Mum says quietly. 'I hear her now.'

I look up, blinking wetly. 'What does she say?'

'She says she loves you. She says you're still her favourite.' A small laugh. 'And she says that she can't wait to see what you do next, because your life is going to be so, so *good.*'

I smile. 'What a poet.'

Then I lean into my mum and let her wrap her arms round me.

64

I sleep for days.

Going straight home, shutting the curtains and lying flat on my back like a depleted vampire. A voice inside me whispers *enough,* and this time I listen, even though it's my own.

After all, I've got two years of sleep to catch up on.

I wake in bleary fragments, faintly aware of quiet activity going on around me. Hope, napping on the bottom of my bed like a puppy; Faith, bringing in plates of buttered toast; Hope, watching a film on mute while Eff tenderly helps me get into my pyjamas, puts me back into bed and tucks my teddy under my chin.

I submit sleepily, like a child, then fall asleep again.

Slipping into a dreamless dark that doesn't feel like a nightmare any more because it isn't an emptiness I have to fight against. This time I let go, and it picks me up and carries me away to a place where I feel stronger, lighter, safe.

At some point, I briefly turn my phone on.

Nova
OMG Cee, your mum won the award!
Congrats!

Amethyst
Nice one! Want to celebrate?

Nova
Cee?

Amethyst
MERCY

Dior
She's not talking to us :(

Nova
OMG some people are SO sensitive

With my eyelids heavy, I hit a button:

Mercy has left RIDE OR DIE GANG.

I mean, what kind of *friends* would have made that our group name in the first place?

Then I turn my phone off and fall asleep again.

And my strength slowly grows, until finally I feel my tiredness drop away completely and I'm wide awake.

Sitting up in bed, I rub my eyes and groggily stare around my dark bedroom. There's faint pressure on my legs, so I automatically turn on my bedside-table lamp and realise – as the room abruptly lights up with a click – that as I slept somebody has clearly replaced everything I smashed.

'Good evening,' Faith smiles sweetly at me from where her head is resting on my ankles. 'Don't worry, it's dark outside. You won't spontaneously burst into flames or melt.'

'That was *amazing*,' Hope adds chirpily. She's leaning against my wall, reading *Variety* magazine. 'I didn't even know humans could pass out for that long. I thought maybe you were in a korma.'

'Coma,' I correct blearily. 'I haven't drowned in coconut curry.'

Then I stare at my sisters.

There are magazines and books scattered across my duvet, a laptop is open and there's an old black-and-white film running quietly on my television. Clearly both of them have been here for ages. Something in my chest abruptly squeezes shut, then expands again, opening like a flower.

'How long have I been asleep?' I ask faintly.

'Long enough for Grandma to decide you may have bumped your head and could need medical assistance,' Eff says with a grin. 'We had to stop her from marching in here with the emergency services and pulling you out of bed by your feet.'

'I harnessed my inner Mercy,' Po adds proudly. 'And growled at her like a dog.'

I laugh and study my wonderful, brilliant sisters.

There is no tiny part of either of them that I do not adore. Their pains hurt me, their fears are mine to fight; their loves are for me to cherish, their dreams are for me to help them chase. Their strengths are mine, their hearts and losses are mine; their flaws are mine too.

My sisters are me, and I am them.

And – my eyes suddenly fill – they feel the same way about me, always have done.

I can't believe I ever thought I was on my own.

'I love you,' I blurt in embarrassment, suddenly overwhelmed. 'Both of you. I know I don't say it very often, or . . . often enough.'

'Or at all,' Faith laughs, nudging my foot. 'Like, ever.'

'Fair.' I smile and grimace slightly. 'But I do. And I'm sorry I've been such a . . .'

'Grumpy pain in the butt?' Hope offers.

'Aggressive nightmare?' Eff suggests.

'Bad-tempered diva with a scream that carries for miles?' Hope frowns. 'You're going to need to show me how to *project* like that, Mer. I start at my new school in a few weeks, and I need to know how to hold my own.'

'That I can do,' I laugh, flushing deeply. 'Thanks for sticking with me, you silly muppets.'

'As if we ever had a choice,' Faith grins.

'We're stuck to each other,' Hope says airily. 'Like that joke Tee used to make. What's brown and stuck to you? Your brown stick. That's what sisters do. We stick. Like sticks.'

We laugh – eyes shiny and full – and it abruptly feels like Charity is here too: in the girls we have been, and the women we will become. Which means she can't leave, not really, not ever. We each carry a different part of her with us.

With a full heart, I lean back on my pillow.

'Hang on.' I lurch forward again, looking at my watch. 'What *day* is it?'

'Tuesday,' Faith says, picking up a piece of cold toast. 'Can I have this? It's a bit soggy.'

'Oh my God.' I swing wobbly legs out of bed and realise with an uncomfortable twinge that I need the toilet probably more than I've ever needed anything, ever. 'I'm supposed to be somewhere important tonight. I'm going to miss it.'

Groaning, I stagger to the mirror.

Yup. I look exactly like somebody who has done nothing but sleep, snore and fart for three days.

'Can I help?' Po asks, jumping off the bed and clapping her hands as I quickly text John and ask for a lift. 'Is it swanky? Oh my gosh, I am *the best* at making people look glamorous and enigmatical.'

I exchange a sly, amused glance with Eff.

'Yes,' I say, smiling back at my baby sister. 'Hope,

I would be *honoured* if you could make me look as *enigmatical* as physically possible. I clearly need all the help I can get.'

As fast as I can, I pee with relief then hop into the shower. Effie diffuses my hair while I do my makeup, and Hope rummages gleefully through my closet, squeaking in delight.

'This!' She pulls out a black gown, places it with reverence on the bed behind her and runs back in again. 'Or this!' A black shift dress. 'Or this?' A black trouser suit. 'Or . . . actually, never mind about this one, I think I dropped ice cream down it in Los Angeles.'

Full of love, I look at the clothes my sweet little sister has laid out carefully in front of me.

'I was thinking,' I say slowly. 'I might wear red tonight.'

Faith and Hope glance knowingly at each other and beam.

'We were *hoping* you'd say that,' Hope says, pulling out a mid-length, red, fifties-style chiffon dress and holding it out with the air of a professional stylist. 'This one, I do believe, is perfect.'

Heart lurching, I pull it on and stand in front of

the mirror. It's beautiful and old-fashioned. It has a square neckline, long sleeves and a tight waist with a red ribbon wrapped round the middle. It flounces into a huge, red circle, which flares out when I twirl.

And I do: I twirl like the ballerina inside a music box.

Because I look like me again; I *feel* like me again.

'Red like roses,' I tell my reflection as soft, warm happiness rises up from my feet.

'Like lipsticks,' Eff smiles.

'Like hearts,' Po agrees.

Laughing, I kiss them quickly on the cheeks: so fast and so lightly it's barely a graze. They both flinch with visible shock, clearly expecting me to bite them.

Then I grab my bag, slip into my heels and run down the stairs.

'Wait up for me!' I shout back at my sisters. 'I won't be late this time!'

But there's one more thing I have to do.

65

It takes me no time at all to find him.

As always, my brother is standing in front of our giant fridge, examining the contents like an archaeologist at a particularly complicated but fascinating dig.

'Max,' I say, turning the overhead light on.

He pretends not to hear me.

'Max.' I lick my lips and try again. 'Is your stomach ever full or are you basically a human Labrador?'

He takes a large lump of Cheddar out of the fridge, unwraps it like a burrito and closes the door.

'Woof,' he says flatly without making eye contact.

Then he brushes sulkily past.

'Max,' I say, blocking his path by putting my hands on either side of the open doorway. 'I think I probably owe you an apology.'

He stares at me, lifts his eyebrows then takes a huge bite of the cheese as if it's an apple. 'You *think*?'

'I do,' I amend quickly, clearing my throat. 'I owe you an apology. What I did . . . I'm sorry. With the trailer . . . it was wrong. You trusted me with a huge secret, and I broke my promise. You have every right to be angry with me.'

He screws his face up, then his shoulders collapse.

'I *was* angry,' he admits with a shrug. 'Then I was just sad. Then I was angry again, then guilty. Hungry. A bit sleepy. I got a mad headache. Honestly, I've had a full roller-coaster of emotions while you lay unconscious like some rancid princess from a fairy tale waiting for true love's kiss.'

I smile, with a small twinge. 'Which didn't come.'

'Of course not.' Max grins, in spite of himself. 'They realised you'd trash the room and claw their face off for even trying.'

I laugh with a bolt of relief: he's forgiven me. 'Max, I'm so sorry I wrecked your big break.'

'You didn't.' He rips off another chunk of cheese and now his smile widens to a smug grin. 'The show's still going ahead. Grandma, Dad and Mum had some kind of family mafia bosses meeting yesterday, mediated by Roz. She's really nice, FYI. I like her a lot.'

I open my mouth, and he holds a warning finger up.

'Stop being sassy for like three seconds, Mermaid. Jeez. Anyway, they reached an agreement. The TV company has agreed to take Effie out, leave Hope in and give Grandma approval on every scene before it airs, for a price.'

'Really?' I blink, genuinely stunned. 'How much are they asking for?'

'A huge amount.' My brother lifts his eyebrows even higher. 'To be specific, a regular cameo from their new Executive Producer, multiple Academy Award winner, Dame Sylvia Valentine.'

My mouth drops open. 'No way.'

'Way.'

'Grandma's going to be *in* it?'

'She's going to be more than in it,' Max says, shaking his head with equal astonishment. 'She's going to *narrate* it. She says this constant need to put the Valentine family on a pedestal has done nothing but damage and it's time for the world to see who we really are.'

I suck my breath in. 'Gosh.'

'Language.' Max laughs and pats the top of my

head. 'So I actually owe you one, Mer. But *never* do that to me again, okay? We're family. We're on the same team, okay?'

'Okay.' I nod. 'Same team.'

'Cool,' he says with a smile, eating his cheese again.

And that's it, all anger or bitterness gone. He may hide it, but Max's massive heart is a big part of what has held this family together over the last two years.

I feel a lurch of love for my brother and punch his arm.

'Owww,' he says, holding out the cheese. 'Want some? It's clammy but still solid vintage.'

'You're gross.' I take it off him, ravenous. 'But yes.'

I shove it in my mouth and glance at my watch. If I leave right now, I should just make it in time.

'You look nice, by the way,' Max says behind me as I turn to leave. 'It's good to see you wearing your colour again.'

'Red for *danger*,' I smile and twirl for him. 'In the animal kingdom, it means *stay away.*'

'I'm poisonous!' he laughs. 'Don't eat me!'

'Or simply *everybody, look at meeee.*' I wink at him. 'Like a monkey with a fat red bottom.'

'Which is exactly what you are,' Max grins as I pick up a pen from the side table and lob it at him. 'You know, Mer, in most cultures around the world, red actually means *life.*'

I beam and grab my old scarlet coat from the coat rack. It's a little tight, but it'll do for now.

My brother and I grin at each other.

'I know,' I smile, opening the front door as freedom rushes through me. 'That's exactly why I'm wearing it.'

66

Except this time John isn't there.

Instead of a silver limo waiting patiently in the driveway, there's an old grey Volvo estate with an almighty scratch down one side.

I blink at it, confused. Who the hell—

'WELL?' The window slides open and my father calls out of it. 'ARE YOU GETTING IN THEN, MISSY, OR YOU JUST GONNA STAND THERE WITH YOUR CHOPS HANGING OPEN?'

Even more confused, I take a few cautious steps forward. It's a big vehicle, but my massive dad still looks like he's driving a Playmobil car. The top of his head is literally grazing the ceiling.

'What?'

'I'm here for lift duty.' The engine revs erratically. 'Apparently that's what normal dads do, isn't it? Ferry their kids around. So here I am, being a normal dad. Got myself a normal dad car and everything . . . 'Bout time, right?' he quips, not quite able to look me in the face.

I climb into the passenger seat and stare at my father. He still won't meet my gaze.

'What is this?' I say again, frowning at him.

'Oh . . . it's a short-term rental,' he replies, even though that patently isn't what I meant. 'Don't worry, I'll find something a little more *Valentine*-appropriate. This is all we could get last minute.'

He lifts his eyebrows at the left-hand steering wheel.

'Though I'll never understand why you guys insist on driving on the wrong side of the road,' he adds with an air of indignant frustration. 'Also, it's not automatic, so this should be interesting. Seatbelt please, young lady.'

Stunned, I put my seatbelt on. 'Where's John?'

'I gave him a much-needed holiday.' Dad fiddles with the gears, and the old car crunches and lurches forward. 'He's in the Bahamas. It isn't enough, but he wouldn't accept a kidney.'

It takes my father four attempts to get the security gates unlocked.

I continue to stare at him.

I like to think I'm not a particularly easy person to render speechless, and yet – after seventeen years of trying – my father has finally managed it.

'I—' I start, then stop, swallow.

Nope. I've got nothing.

After the world's most awkward silence, Dad turns on some terrible sixties music and starts driving into central London. I have no idea what happened yesterday but clearly I'm witnessing the fallout. What else has been decided by my grandmother and parents? Are we selling the house, painting ourselves green and moving into a spaceship bound for Mars?

'Dad—' I eventually croak as we reach the Thames.

'Hang on,' he interrupts as the phone propped up in a windshield grip starts ringing. He turns the music down. 'Hold that thought for just a moment and then I'm all ears, kiddo.'

'Hey, love,' he says, clicking on speakerphone. 'Any news?'

'We've got a second viewing in the morning,' Roz says in her warm, calm voice. 'There's another couple interested, but I remain optimistic about our bargaining skills.'

'Awesome.' Dad replies. 'Did you tell them who I am?'

'I did not.' Roz laughs. 'And I very much hope never, ever to do that in my life, thank you. How's the car? I emailed them the paperwork. Did you get there in time?'

'On our way. I'm with Mercy right now, in fact.'

I'm staring at Dad, trying to process all this new information while simultaneously realising how happy my father looks. Not just happy: glowing. At the sound of Roz's voice, his face has lit up like a camping torch. The shrink may have far too many pockets in her trousers, but he is *seriously* in love with her.

'A viewing?' I frown. 'For what?'

'A new house.' Dad glances at me sideways, carefully, and takes a gentle left turn as if I might be made of porcelain. 'I'm moving back to London. Permanently. Enough of being away from home, I think.'

Quietly Roz adds: 'Your father is gonna be around for you a lot more often from now on, Mercy.'

And I'm hit by gratitude so strong I want to burst into tears.

I was so busy chasing my mum, I hadn't realised quite how much I needed my dad too.

Also, guilt: I have been horrible to this cargo-panted woman.

'Thank you, Roz,' I say in a tiny voice.

'Not necessary,' she replies, and I can hear that she's smiling. 'Now I'm going to leave you two to catch up. I've got a British client list to go build, and you guys are *strangely* averse to therapy. Good luck with the play, Mercy.'

Then the phone goes dead, the music stops and the car pulls smoothly up to the kerb behind the theatre. Dad and I sit quietly, both trying to work out who should speak first.

'Dad,' I say finally.

'You were right,' he says, taking a deep breath and gripping the steering wheel hard. 'About everything. I didn't want you on set with me.'

A flash of brand-new, unexpected pain. 'Oh.'

'But not because of the reason you think.' My father turns towards me, and his face is suddenly torn, fragile. 'I was running away, Mercy. The grief

. . . It was too much. I couldn't bear being in that house without Charity. So I threw myself into work.'

I frown. 'Okay . . .'

'At the start, I told myself it was just one job.' Dad swallows. 'Just one film, far away. That would be enough for me to . . . get a grip. Pull myself out of the hole. But it wasn't enough, and nothing changed. So I worked harder. I took another job. Then another.'

He rubs a giant hand across his eyes, then turns to me.

'I failed, sweetheart. I failed as a dad. I failed to protect you or make it better. And the more I failed, the harder it became to come back.'

I've never seen my dad cry – not even at the funeral – but now his dark eyes are wet and shining.

My heart compresses inwards.

'Dad—' I say, putting my hand gently on top of his. 'You don't—'

'I didn't want you on set, Mercy, not because you didn't deserve to be there or because I didn't want to see you.' His voice breaks. 'I just didn't want you to see me failing *again*.'

And I want to be angry: I want to tell him that he's the grown-up, that he should have got over his pain, should have found a way to be there for us, should have tried harder.

But grief isn't like that.

It's a bomb, and when it explodes none of us really know where the pieces of ourselves will land.

'It's okay,' I say softly. 'Dad, I understand.'

With a small bleat of relief, he puts his head on top of our hands and rests it on the steering wheel for a couple of minutes while his huge shoulders move up and down. I wait patiently for him to gather himself together again.

Finally, he lifts his head and attempts to smile at me.

'You want a job?' He wipes his face, sheepish now. 'Because I'm about to start directing a new film in London and I hear you're unemployed. I think it's maybe time the best actress in the family was offered a little classic nepotism, right?'

I laugh. 'Thanks, but no thanks. That's something I have to achieve by myself.'

He nods and looks at the Globe. It's getting busier and busier outside the theatre. Crowds are gathering for the opening night of *Much Ado About Nothing*: excited, bubbling, looking forward to the performance.

I zip up my coat, lift my chin.

'You want me to come in with you?' Dad follows my gaze and sits up straighter. 'Because I swear, if anybody says a single unkind word to my daughter this evening, I'll—'

'You'll?' I prompt with a twinge of affection.

'Never you mind.' My father grins widely at me. 'Let's just say in America we have a *much* less dignified way of dealing with these things.'

'I've got this, Dad,' I say, opening the car door and climbing out. 'They're my consequences to face.'

'I'm proud of you, kiddo,' Dad says, leaning across the passenger seat. 'And I'll be waiting here for you. Reading a newspaper. Repeatedly looking at my watch. Muttering about how I've got nothing better to do with my life than provide a free taxi service for my errant teenagers. That kinda stuff.'

Another weird flush of intense relief.

'You don't have to wait,' I say anyway.

'I'm your dad, Mercy.' My father smiles at me with a face full of love. 'And someone much wiser than me told me that's what dads do.'

67

I guess karma is never easy.

And it kicks in almost immediately – all my bad behaviour, coming back to bite me. With my head down, I slip round the theatre crowds and make my way to the back door: locked.

I try another door: locked again.

Mortified, I go round to the front with my hood pulled low over my forehead, looking desperately for a way in that doesn't include making a scene or finding another fire extinguisher.

This time, I don't want to distract anyone from the main event.

'Oh, *what*?' A blonde girl in the queue is studying a sign plastered across the show poster. 'Mercy Valentine isn't in it any more? I literally only bought tickets because I used to watch that ghost show as a kid.'

'Doesn't matter,' her friend consoles. 'Apparently she's gone well off the rails now anyway.'

'*Exactly.*' The girl screws her nose up. 'I was hoping for some decent drama but otherwise it's just *Shakespeare.*'

With my head down, I approach her, my cheeks burning.

'I'll take it,' I say, dipping my head still further. 'The ticket. If you don't want it, I'll give you . . .' I rummage quickly through my handbag, pull out an indeterminate wad of cash and thrust it at her.

'Are you kidding?' The girl's eyes widen and she rips the money out of my hands. 'Fine. Sold.'

She lobs her ticket at me and bounces off, squeaking in glee.

'No way.' Her friend frowns, bending to try to look under my hood. 'You're *not* . . . Never mind, of course not.'

Shaking her head, she hurries off to catch up with her friend.

Relieved, I take their place in the queue. With my hood pulled low, I'm hoping nobody recognises me. Why would they? I'm not wearing black; I'm not scowling; I'm not trying to ruin everything.

Finally, I reach the entrance doors of the Globe.

The girl checking my ticket lifts her eyebrows, but nods and says nothing, pointing me towards the front of the standing stalls. Gingerly letting my hood down, I get as close as I can to the stage and wait as the rest of the audience fills the theatre, holding my breath as they jostle, push, find their places. From this angle, the wooden stage is glowing and empty, and when I look up the sky is a deep, starless navy.

Then the lights in the auditorium flash and the crowd falls silent.

My breath draws in.

And I watch with a full heart as my play starts without me.

'I learn in this letter,' Leonato says, walking regally onto centre stage, studying a piece of paper, 'that Don Pedro of Aragon comes this night to Messina.'

Swallowing, I edge forward: Piper has quietly entered the scene with Daisy, who is wearing a blue dress, remade for her. It fits her flawlessly, and with full hair and makeup she looks like a perfect Beatrice.

She lingers at the back, listening carefully to a messenger, and when she takes a few swift steps towards him I feel my stomach lurch in surprise. Her movements are quick, bird-like, nothing like the slow, wandering gestures I've become used to.

'I pray you,' she says in a sharp voice I've never heard before either. 'Is Signor Mountato returned from the wars or no?'

She *is* a perfect Beatrice.

And when she lifts her chin defiantly, I hear it.

I hear her eagerness and impatience, the heart pounding in her throat and the barely concealed, eager jitteriness. I hear the excitement in her voice, and my stomach flips again.

Verity was right. Beatrice *absolutely* fancies Benedict before the play has even started.

'O, he's returned,' the messenger grins.

Daisy laughs, a deliberate brittleness. 'I pray you, how many hath he killed and eaten in these wars? But how many hath he killed? For indeed, I promised to eat all of his killing.'

And it's right there, the timeless giveaway: she's making every conversation about Benedict.

'You tax Signior Benedict too much,' Leonato reproves lightly.

And all I can think is, but *of course* she does.

What's she going to do? Admit that she can't stop thinking about him? That she's pined the whole time he's been away, that she hasn't slept, can't think of anything else? It would be such weakness, such vulnerability. It would be *humiliating*.

I turn my attention back to the stage.

'I see, lady –' the messenger shakes his head sadly – 'the gentleman is not in your books.'

'No.' Beatrice blushes. 'An' he were, I would burn my study.'

Amazed, I push through the crowd to get nearer the stage.

Under the stage lights, her pale face is luminous. As I turn briefly to look around, every single person in the audience is focused on her, completely entranced.

With a clatter of footsteps, Eli saunters on to stage and I feel another tremor of surprise. He's entitled, he's jaunty, he's . . . brilliant.

'I wonder that you will still be talking, Signor Benedict.' And with a pang I recognise it all: the

478

barriers and the self-defence, the internal struggle. 'Nobody marks you.'

'What!' Benedict grins and lifts an eyebrow. 'My dear Lady Disdain! Are you yet living?'

As if he hasn't spent every single moment thinking about her, as if she's not *clearly* the very first person he's looked for when he's home.

And the play swings forward, pulling me with it.

Stunned, I stand unmoving and watch as a story I thought I knew hits me like a brick to the face. All this time, I thought Beatrice and Benedict were tricked into falling in love. But they were in love before the play *even started* – they were just too scared to admit it.

By the time the final scene opens, my eyes are full and my cheeks hot. I've somehow moved right to the front of the stall, my nose nearly pressed against the stage.

'Do not you love me?' Beatrice smiles playfully, all her hostility gone.

'Troth, no,' Benedict lies, smiling. 'No more than reason.'

'Why,' she starts to laugh. 'Then my cousin

Margaret and Ursula are much deceived, for they did swear you did.'

He starts to laugh too. 'They swore you were almost sick for me.'

'They swore that you were well-nigh *dead* for me.'

And as Beatrice and Benedict giggle with the exact same sense of humour, it hits me that love isn't a *trick*. It's not a placebo. It's not a submission or a conquest. It's not a darkness that consumes, or a trap that slams shut on you; and it is definitely not a weakness.

It doubles, instead of halving.

You face the world as two, not one.

Daisy was right.

This play is romantic as *hell*.

'Come,' Benedict concludes, nudging Beatrice jokily. 'I will have thee; but, by this light, I take thee for pity.'

'I would not deny you,' Beatrice rolls her eyes. 'But, by this good day, I yield upon great persuasion, and partly to save your life, for I was told you were in a consumption.'

'Peace!' Benedict laughs. 'I will stop your mouth.'

Eli grabs Daisy and kisses her, hard.

480

And as the audience around me breaks into impulsive, raucous applause, I abruptly turn and start pushing my way through the crowd, my stomach fizzing, my heart on fire.

Finn.

I have to find Finn.

68

Where to even start?

I push through the cheering crowd, scanning the balconies for familiar bright green eyes. Would he be watching the show from there? Or backstage?

Slipping into the empty hallway, I find a side door.

With a quiet *click*, I enter the dark, deserted theatre wings. The entire cast is on stage, taking their bows to ecstatic applause. I check for Finn, but he's not up there either.

I try a few closet rooms, just in case he's packing set away.

Nope.

Then I head towards the rehearsal room, my anxiety steadily becoming desperation. It's the opening night. He can't have *missed* it, can he?

'Finn?' I call, my cheeks on fire. 'Finn!'

Behind me there's a rousing cheer and the door

bursts open. The jubilant cast swells in: cheering, singing, high-fiving. 'Friar Francis' is chucking his wig jauntily in the air; Rosie is already taking photos; 'Don Pedro' is making a beeline towards the after-show buffet.

They rush past me like a wave over an insignificant pebble and I feel an abrupt roll of sadness.

This is not my celebration.

'Hey.' I spin, scanning the exalting group. 'Has anyone seen—'

'Mercy!' Piper draws to a stop next to me, pink with success. 'What are you doing here?'

'I wanted to see the play. It was brilliant.' I flush hot. 'Have you seen Finn?'

'No. Not all evening, actually.' She shakes her head and glances quickly over her shoulder. 'Um, you shouldn't be here, Mercy. Verity's not going to be happy. The way you left . . .' She grimaces, although not without sympathy. 'I mean, we all have bad days sometimes, but you really . . .'

'Threw my toys out of the pram,' I finish for her grimly, embarrassment mounting.

'Into a fire.' She smiles. 'And poured petrol on top.'

'I know,' I admit, smiling back sheepishly. 'For

what it's worth, I'm genuinely sorry. The things I said . . .'

'Oh.' Piper lifts her eyebrows. 'I wouldn't worry about that. We're professional actors. You're not the first dramatic celebrity we've worked with, and you won't be the last.'

'Pipes!' Rosie shouts across the room, pointedly ignoring me. 'Come on! Eli's about to make a speech!'

Suffice it to say, he's already standing on a table.

'Hello?' Elias Bingo-Wings tings his glass. *Ting. Ting. Ting.* 'Could you all gather?' *Ting.* 'Thanking you kindly.' *Ting.* 'Now we're all present and paying attention, I'd like to take this very special moment to thank my—'

'Speaking of dramatic celebrities . . .' Piper rolls her eyes subtly. 'Take care, Mercy. I hope you find Finn. Check the store cupboard. I've seen him napping in there before.'

With a bounce, she forgets me and joins the rest of the cast.

The store cupboard? Why would Finn be sleeping in a store cupboard? Why would *anyone* be sleeping in there? More importantly, why isn't he in here, celebrating opening night with his cast mates?

Anxious now, I run into one of the small corridors.

'Finn? Where—'

'Are you FREAKING KIDDING ME?'

Slowly, I turn to face an absolutely incandescent Verity.

Puce, she takes fierce steps towards me.

'Hang on,' I start meekly, holding my hands open in submission. 'Before you throw me out, Verity, I just want to say—'

'Oh, I think you've said quite enough already.' She laughs brutally. 'Getting you to *stop* saying things is the real directorial talent, Mercy. Well, you're not ruining tonight. Security? SECURITY?'

Scowling, she turns to search the empty hallways.

'It was a great performance,' I say quickly, before she can change her mind and rugby-tackle me. 'Really amazing, Verity. I mean it. The crowd loved it too.'

'No thanks to you,' Verity snorts in contempt. 'Your little "don't bother going to see the play" tweet had over forty thousand likes, according to our PR department.'

I flush. 'I'm sorry.'

'Yes, well, it had the opposite from intended effect.' She sniffs. 'We are the Globe Theatre. We do not need a fading teen starlet's *approval*. In fact, your disapproval made it a nigh on sell-out run. So thanks for that.'

I flinch, even though it's totally deserved.

There's a click, and behind Verity a door swings open and Daisy wanders slowly out, her huge eyes glowing and a bunch of congratulatory lilies in her hands.

'Oh!' She stops suddenly. 'Mercy!'

The transformative light in her face flickers for a moment.

'Hi, Daisy.' I smile gently. 'Congratulations.'

Now she looks even more torn. 'You saw it?'

'I did,' I nod. 'You were incredible. Subtle, original, funny. Honestly, you totally blew everyone away. You're a star.'

Verity rolls her eyes, clearly unconvinced by my sincerity.

'Do you really think so?' In slow motion, Daisy smells the flowers. 'I can't quite belieeeeeeve it's real, even now. The truth is, I was chuffed just being the Second Watchman.' Then she looks up. 'I don't thiiiiink I played Beatrice as well as you would have, though. It's youuur part.'

Verity snorts again and I ignore her.

'It's not my part, Daisy.' I smile, no longer sure why I found her so irritating. 'It was always yours. There is *nothing* I could teach you.'

We beam at each other and I feel a sense of closure.

'How lovely,' my ex-director snaps. 'Now, if you don't mind, I've got a cast to celebrate with. See you there, Day.'

Still grumbling, she stomps off down the hallway.

Daisy makes a move to follow her.

'Umm,' I say, scratching my throat as a hot tendril of embarrassment creeps up my neck. 'Daisy, I . . . don't suppose you know where Finn might be, do you? I've not been able to find him anywhere.'

'I haven't seen him.' She frowns thoughtfully. 'Actually, we were just saaaaaaaying that it's weird he didn't show up. Obviously he didn't have any work to do tonight, but we'd have thought he'd waaaaaant to celebrate.'

'I'd have thought so too,' I say, now even more worried.

How am I going to find him? I don't know where he lives, and I don't even have his phone number.

Daisy looks at my crestfallen expression for a few

seconds, then opens her handbag and begins to rummage carefully inside it. Finally, she pulls out a crumpled piece of paper and a pen, checks her phone and scribbles something down.

'Heeeerrrrre,' she says, thrusting the paper at me. 'Finn's address.'

I stare at it in surprise.

'We all exchanged details the first week,' she explains. 'Go and find out if he's okaaaaay. He's been horrible since you . . . left.'

Even now she can't say *were unceremoniously fired for being a diva witch from hell.*

'Wait, he has?' My spirits abruptly lift off the ground like a hot-air balloon. 'You're not just saying that? Like . . . *how* horrible?'

'Oh my gosh.' Daisy's eyes widen. 'Soooooo horrible. Sarcastic. Rude. Bad-tempered. Really, really awwwwwwful. He's like a totally different person.'

I feel a wide, happy grin spilt my face in two.

Finn still likes me.

'Thank you,' I say, clutching the paper tightly.

'You're welcome,' Daisy smiles at me, then looks back down at her flowers. 'And, Merrrrrrcy? Thank *you.*'

69

'So?' My father looks curiously at me over his newspaper as I climb into the Volvo. 'How'd it go?'

'Good.' I nod distantly.

Then I un-crumple Finn's address, smooth it out and stare at it for a few seconds. I'm starting to feel lightheaded.

'Where to next?' Dad asks loudly, switching on the engine. 'My taxi services are at your disposal.'

I cough and mumble the location written on the paper.

'What was that?' My father narrows his eyes as if it'll help him hear me better. 'Acton? What on earth do you want in *Acton*?'

'Umm.' I clear my throat. 'A boy.'

'A BOY?' Dad explodes, slamming his hands down on the steering wheel. 'YOU WANT ME

TO DRIVE YOU ALL THE WAY ACROSS LONDON FOR A BOY? ARE YOU MAD? WHO IS HE? WHAT DOES HE DO? WHO ARE HIS PARENTS? DO I NEED TO MEET HIM? YOU'D BETTER BELIEVE I'M GONNA NEED A TALK WITH THIS YOUNG MAN, FIND OUT HIS INTENTIONS.'

With my nostrils flaring, I stare at my father.

He stares back.

'How did that sound?' Dad winks. 'Suitably paternal, protective and terrifying?'

'Indeed.' I laugh loudly. 'Top marks.'

'Jokes aside,' Dad says, plugging Acton into his satnav and taking a left turn. 'You're my girl, Mercy. I hope whoever this boy is, he's worth it.'

I look back out of the window at the London streets rolling by and smile.

'Oh,' I say with absolute certainty. 'He is.'

Finn lives in a cul-de-sac right by Acton train station. There's nowhere to park, so Dad pulls the car onto the pavement round the corner.

Swallowing, I climb out and hesitate.

'You've got this,' Dad says encouragingly, pulling

his newspaper off the backseat. 'And I won't watch, promise.'

With a nervous grimace, I impulsively take off my red coat and sling it into the backseat. Whatever happens next, I want to look awesome for it. Then I smooth my dress down and follow the address, round the corner and up the stairs.

The door is off-white, plastic and feels weirdly impermanent.

Hands starting to shake, I knock.

Silence.

A disappointed swoop of my stomach. I knock again.

Silence.

I'm just about to give up and try again tomorrow when I hear a few footsteps and a slight rustling. I don't know how, but I know it's him.

'Finn?' I say, knocking again. 'It's Mercy.'

Silence again, but this time I can feel him standing quietly on the other side of the door.

'Please, Finn. I need to talk to you.'

'This isn't really a good time,' he says in a tight, flat voice. 'You should go.'

'Are you okay?' I panic, all hurt wiped out by

worry and fear. 'Why weren't you at the play opening? Has something happened?'

A pause, then he says in an even flatter voice, 'Wasn't really feeling it. Can you leave me alone?'

My hot-air-balloon feeling instantly pops.

'Sure,' I say shortly, turning to go. 'Whatever you want.'

But my feet won't move and I realise I can't. I won't. I will not leave him like this. He's in pain, and I can feel it. I've pushed Finn away so many times and he's come back. It's my turn now to do that for him.

Jaw clenched, I get my phone out and email:

From: Mercy Valentine
To: Finneas O'Connor

Please open the door.

I hear his phone *beep*, and a second later:

From: Finneas O'Connor

No.

So I take a deep breath: then I'll do it like this.

From: Mercy Valentine

Ever since my twin died I've felt like half a person. I blamed myself, and felt like all the good in me went with her. You've seen me at my very worst. I know how it feels to love somebody so completely you lose yourself when they go, and I couldn't risk doing that again.

But the thing is, I don't feel like a half with you.

You are funny and brilliant and kind and so insanely hot it sets my ears on fire, but . . . you don't always have to be. I will still like you.

You are just as lovely, even when you're in pieces.

Please open the door.
X

With my eyes squeezed shut, I press SEND. There's a *beep*.

And I wait for what feels like forever, resting my fingertips on the plastic door, willing it to open, letting Finn know I'm still here.

Eventually, I hear a rattle. The chain on the door clicks, and it opens. Finn's eyes are pink and his cheeks are pale. He looks exhausted, like he's been crying, and so, so sad.

With a tight heart, I take a step forward.

'What's happened?' I say gently, a knot in my throat. 'What is it? How can I help? Just tell me, and I'll—'

I pause and look past him into the tiny flat.

'Oh my God,' I say.

70

The flat is totally empty.

Not in an 'I've just moved in' kind of way; not in an 'I'm a boy and I don't understand the mood-setting advantages of flowers and candles' kind of way.

In a no-furniture, no-family, about-to-be-demolished kind of way.

With a grim expression, Finn beckons me in.

Blinking, I walk through the rooms in silent bewilderment. The living room has floral wallpaper, but it's completely blank: any art removed, empty nails still hanging. In the middle of the floor is a crumpled sleeping bag, next to a green plastic fold-out chair with a kettle propped on top of it, and an empty Pot Noodle container that smells faintly of curry. The only light is coming from a plastic lamp perched precariously next to them.

I keep walking. The kitchen has been completely gutted.

No fridge, no oven, no microwave.

The two bedrooms are empty, four little rectangular dents in each carpet where beds used to go. The wardrobe door is swinging open, only empty hangers left inside. There's a tiny bathroom with the fittings still in place, but when I turn the tap, no water comes out. When I flick the switches, no lights come on.

It's like nobody lives here but, clearly, they do.

'What's going on?' I say quietly, turning back to Finn.

'Well.' His face is so strained it looks like it's made out of wax. 'Just living my best life, obviously.'

I look more carefully at his clothes. He's wearing the same wrinkled jeans and dusty jumper he wore when he made me drop him at the theatre. He was there, that morning, lying down on the balcony. What did Verity say? *Finneas O'Connor? He practically lives here.*

And that's when it hits me: *he was.*

'Where did everything go?' I ask quietly.

'Sold,' he shrugs with a faint, dry smile. 'I'm

guessing, anyway. The debt collectors came this morning to take the last of it and turn off the utilities. Which is good, because taking a cold shower was becoming a guilty luxury.'

I stare at him. How is he still *joking*? 'Where's your family?'

'My mum died when I was a little kid,' he says, sitting down heavily on the sleeping bag. 'My father . . .' A short, hoarse laugh. 'Let's just say his gambling has reached a brand-new low.'

I stare at him. 'No siblings?'

'Nope.'

A wave of sadness for him, followed by shame. He's been going through this the whole time I've known him. I was so busy focusing on my own grief it never occurred to me that Finn might need someone too.

Quietly, I sit down on the sleeping bag next to him.

In silence, I gaze at him until he catches my eye.

'So.' He shrugs. 'Thoughts?'

'Umm.' I look around at the vacant flat, then at the empty Pot Noodle. 'I'm starting to feel really awful about making you pay for those French croissants.'

He laughs grimly. 'And coffees. Don't forget the coffees.'

I flinch. 'They were six euros each.'

'Seven, actually.' Finn looks directly at me with his bright green eyes and I feel my stomach turn over, the way it always does with him. 'Don't feel too sorry for me, Mercy Valentine. Remember, *I'm* the one still with valid employment right now.'

'Touché,' I smile. 'It's going to be okay, Finn. We'll think of something.'

'Yeah.'

There's a short pause, then Finn adds: 'I mean, it helps to know that I'm *so insanely hot I set ears on fire*. That's probably a skill I can monetise. Do you have any good contacts?'

Now I laugh loudly. 'Shut up, idiot.'

'No, really.' He grins. 'Maybe I could join some kind of circus. The Brilliant, Kind, Funny, Ear-flaming Finneas O'Connor! Or was it the Kind, Funny, Brilliant—'

Finn holds his finger up and gets his phone out of his pocket.

'Hang on, let me check the exact wording.'

'Oh my God.' Embarrassed, I grab the phone and

chuck it across the sleeping bag. 'Stop. Are you going to be quoting that email to me for the rest of time now?'

'Of course not.' He gives me an indignant look. 'Only for the first year or two, and then I very much hope you'll send me some more compliments so I can update the file.'

I laugh as happiness lurches through my chest.

The first year or two? Does that mean . . .?

'Are you sure,' I check with a sudden flicker of doubt, 'that you can bear to be seen with an unemployed, dramatic diva with a terrible reputation, no career, no non-black clothes that fit her properly any more and a *scream that carries for miles*?'

Finn thinks about it for a long, lonnnngg moment.

I push him with my hand.

'Hey,' he asks finally, pushing me back with a grin. 'I opened the door, didn't I?'

And my joy is so bright, so weightless, I feel it explode, blasting the night away.

Instead, I lean in to kiss him softly.

And as we kiss – as our lips touch and our cheeks flame – suddenly nothing feels so empty any more and nothing feels so dark. I'm not alone, and it feels like I have space for his pain, and for mine. I have space for our happiness, and our sadness; our excitement and our hopes; our disappointments and our celebrations.

I finally have space for it all.

After what feels like forever, but also not long enough, Finn pulls away slightly and lifts his eyebrows.

'Does this mean I can have my postal van back now? It's still in your driveway.'

I laugh and kiss him again.

'Sure. Consider your van no longer a hostage.' I pause, my cheeks flushing. 'So, we're doing this? Me, you? Properly? Like . . . a relationship?'

'Looks like it,' he smiles, nudging my nose with his. 'Get ready to bicker in Ikea about cutlery and cry in the bath, Mercy Valentine. I, for one, am excited.'

I hold my hands out to him, open.

He takes them both.

'I'm excited too,' I tell him.

'Snap,' he smiles.

I smile back and kiss him, hard. 'Snap.'

71

Eight years ago

The marquee empties out.

One by one, our glamorous guests take their leave from the anniversary party, and we hear the cleaners swoop in, vacuuming, folding away the tables, scooping up flowers and the leftover drinks.

Obviously, we were sent to bed hours ago.

But that wasn't going to happen, so now we're all sitting on the winding mahogany stairs in our pyjamas, watching out of the stained-glass windows as Bentleys and Land Rovers and Jaguars roll down the driveway. Max is perched on the top step with his elbows on his skinny knees, fluffy-haired Faith is flopped on the second, me and Charity are sitting together below them, and finally Hope, her head nodding, trying her hardest to stay awake.

'Come on, Po,' Eff whispers, standing up. 'I think the party is over now.'

Hope's eyes shoot open. 'No! I'm not sleepy! I'm just giving my eyelids a quick break!'

We all laugh.

'Ooh,' Max says, suddenly perking up. 'I reckon if I get out there before the cleaners leave, there might still be some cake left.'

'I'll come,' Faith yawns, standing up. 'Maybe I can save some of the flowers.'

'Well, if you're all going,' Tee says, hopping up as well. 'I am too.'

'And me!' Hope struggles to her feet. 'Can somebody carry me?'

'Thought you weren't sleepy?' Max laughs.

'I'm not *sleepy*,' Po clarifies indignantly. 'I am precious and lazy. There's a difference.'

'Obviously you're coming, Mermaid,' Charity adds flashing me a grin. 'Army of two, remember?'

'Three,' Eff laughs.

'Four,' Max grins.

'Five!' Hope squeaks.

We all laugh and start running down the stairs, any inclination to sleep vanished.

Then Max abruptly comes to a stop.

The rest of us pile into his back, nearly knocking each other over. Curious, I peer over Charity's shoulder and see Mum and Dad, standing in the candlelit hallway in their finery, carrying plates piled high with elaborate food.

'Six,' Dad says, lifting his eyebrows.

'Seven,' Mum smiles. 'I'd say we've got a full-blown squad.'

They gaze up at us, their faces soft and warm.

'Here,' my mother says, holding out a plate of profiteroles, which is immediately snatched away by my brother. '*Something* told me you weren't in bed as instructed.'

'Hey,' Dad laughs, holding out his plates too. 'In fairness, our troop of performers deserve a little treat. It was a big opening night, this evening. That murder mystery play . . .'

'Good, right?' Charity puffs up. 'Mercy wrote it.'

'I—' Po squeaks, then yawns widely.

'Directed, is what she was going to say,' Eff says, giving her a gentle kiss on the head.

'It was *wonderful*,' Mum says, picking Hope up. 'By far the best anniversary gift we have ever been given. Thank you, my darlings. Now I think it's time to put my Valentines to bed.'

Slowly, she starts climbing the stairs, Po's fluffy head nodding on her shoulder. Dad puts his arm round Charity and guides her up as well. Still chewing as fast as he can, Max follows; Eff quickly grabs a few lilies from a vase and glides behind them.

I stand in the hallway for a moment, a lump in my throat.

'Mercy?' Mum says, as they all turn to look at me. 'Coming?'

And as I stare up at their bright, beautiful faces – the people I love most in the world – it suddenly feels like I want to catch this moment like a bird and hold it in my hands.

'Yes,' I say, climbing the stairs after them. 'Wait for me.'

72

Four months later

'Is everybody ready?'

I look round at everyone gathered in the cinema room.

Faith and Scarlett sit together on one of the double sofas, holding hands and beaming at each other shyly when they think nobody is looking. Mum is elegantly perched on the edge of a leather lounger, a gold champagne glass in her hand. She's put on a little weight and is starting to look rosy and curvy again, lighting up the room with her famous mega-watt smile.

Mum winks at Dad and he grins fondly back at her.

Then he squeezes Roz's shoulder as she leans

forward and says something to Grandma. I don't know what it is, but it makes my grandmother laugh loudly, covering her mouth with her hand.

Hope and Ben are both somehow squeezed onto a single cosy armchair, her fluffy head leaning on his shoulder, while he radiates pride. Maggie glances at the couple affectionately from the back of the room, where she's quietly decanting popcorn into bowls.

Max adjusts his silver top hat from in front of the huge screen.

'I *said*,' he repeats more loudly, raising his eyebrows, 'IS EVERYBODY READY?'

'Oh!' Mum nods quickly. 'Sorry, darling. I thought it was rhetorical.'

'Let's have it then!' Dad claps his big hands together. 'We're all on tenderhooks!'

'It's actually *tenterhooks*, Dad,' Hope interjects with an elaborate sigh. 'I learnt at school that a tenterhook is a sharp hooked nail that you use to fasten cloth to a tent, which means it's pulled tightly.'

We all look at her in simultaneous shock.

'Blimey,' Max breathes. 'Education, who knew?'

'Sooooo,' Po adds triumphantly, revelling in the

moment. 'We use it as an expression because it makes you feel *tents.*'

Now everyone laughs.

'Great segue,' Eff says, reaching over and pinching Hope's cheek lightly. 'Well made, little one.'

Our little sister puffs her chest out like a tiny robin.

'So, this is live?' Roz gestures at the huge screen, taking a popcorn kernel and popping it neatly into her mouth. 'We're seeing it at the same time as the whole world sees it?'

Max glances at his watch and grumbles, 'Not if everyone doesn't show up on time we won't.'

Now everyone looks at me.

'Hey!' I shrug and hold out my hands. '*I'm* here. I cannot be held responsible for the tardiness of other people.'

There's a *bang,* and the cinema-room door opens.

'Sorry!' Finn breezes in, an enormous box of chocolates clamped under his arm. 'Turns out they were under a pile of Mercy's dirty laundry. Cannot believe I didn't look there first.'

I grin at my sexy boyfriend.

Yeah, I know. We're still very much together, and very much in love.

Four months and counting – who knew?

'It's not *dirty*,' I faux-grumble, moving over so Finn can sit next to me. 'It just gets a little hot and sticky under the studio lights, that's all.'

He flings a long arm round my shoulder. 'That makes no sense, Mer. You're in costume on set.'

'The stink and makeup rub off on my normal clothes too.' I smack him lightly. 'Why are you like this?'

'Why are you?'

'I asked first.'

'Dunno. Too much time with you?'

We grin and kiss each other on the lips.

After I swallowed my pride and went to every single audition Persephone could get me into, I finally (okay, pretty quickly) landed the lead role in a British period drama film. I've been working my butt off – long hours, late nights – so when an opportunity for a screen set-builder turned up, I passed it over to Finn.

Now we're working together again, my career is back on track, he's found a new flat and . . .

Let's just say it's good. It's really, really *good*.

'*Gross*,' Scarlett laughs, throwing popcorn at our

heads. 'Are we here to watch a new hit TV show or what?'

Finn and I break apart, grinning, our cheeks hot and red.

'We sure are,' Max says in excitement, clicking the remote control so that the huge screen lights up. 'Okay, it's the ad break. Does everyone have their social media open? I'm going to need *full family publicity,* please. All of us. That includes you, Grandma.'

'Absolutely not,' she says drily as everyone obediently grabs their phones. 'The line has to be drawn somewhere.'

Then she looks at me.

'Although I *might* Twitter a little when Mercy gets her first big award,' she adds with a proud smile. 'From what I hear, it's very much on the cards.'

I smile at her and then bow my head, embarrassed, while Finn lifts my hand and kisses my healed knuckle.

'It's starting!' Hope interrupts, pointing at the screen as the adverts finally stop. 'Look, look!'

With a full heart, I gaze around the room.

Impulsively, I stand up.

'To Charity,' I say clearly, holding my orange juice high in the air.

Everyone lifts their drinks too.

'To Charity,' my family says simultaneously, smiling. And as the room gets brighter, as the shadows and the darkness fall away, I see a reflection of a girl in the framed movie poster on the wall next to me: dark hair, dark eyes, a face full of pride and happiness.

She's smiling too.

With a crackle, the screen blasts to life.

And in gold lettering, curled round a pink heart, it simply says:

Acknowledgements

2020 was a strange year.

Nobody saw a worldwide pandemic coming, but – in being literally shut away from other people – Mercy's isolation became very real to me: in many ways, this is a book of hope and strength that only 2020 could have created.

With that in mind, I am immensely grateful for those who frequently reached into the solitude to drag me back to the surface. Pacifically (as Hope would say), Kate Shaw, my stalwart agent and champion, who remains a beacon of encouragement, affection and support, and Lizzie Clifford – the genius editor I have worked with for a full decade, who never fails to step in when I need her: to untangle, to smooth, to redirect and to ignite. To both of my literary rocks, I cannot offer enough thanks.

But it is to my sister, Tara, that I have dedicated this final book.

The Valentines is – first and foremost – a love story to sisters. The three books are designed to work together as a jigsaw puzzle: an exploration of the complex, intense relationship between siblings. My little sister is both my best friend and the person I fight with most frequently: she is the person I call first when I'm crying, when I have good news, when I'm overwhelmed. We are an 'army of two' (credit to the awesome 00s band, the DumDums). She has shaped me, and I have shaped her: we are the people we have become because of each other. And it is my sister who has stepped in during lockdown to keep me afloat. If 2020 achieved anything good, it was to help bring me closer to the bright, strong, brave person I rate most highly in the world.

So, Tara: thank you. In calm or stormy weather indeed.

I'd also like to extend huge gratitude to my brilliant and dedicated team at HarperCollins, who – while working remotely – also helped to bring this book to life. Ann-Janine Murtagh, Charlie Redmayne, Nick Lake, Samantha Stewart, Michelle Misra, Jess

Dean, Laure Gysemans, Mary O'Riordan, Elorine Grant, Kate Clarke, Elisa Offord, Beth Maher, Alex Cowan, Geraldine Stroud, Jo-Anna Parkinson, Louise Sheridan, Sam White, Robert Smith, Carla Alonzi, Sarah Mitchell and Aisling Smith. I can't wait to party with you all in person soon.

Before the first lockdown started, I was lucky enough to spend a day backstage at the Globe Theatre with the Royal Shakespeare Company. As a Shakespeare enthusiast and postgrad, this was a dream come true for multiple reasons, not least because it helped me bring Mercy's passion (and mine) to life. So huge thanks to the RSC for letting both me and my fictional brilliant-actress character fulfil a lifelong ambition.

To my family, I have missed you so this year. Mum and Dad, you never fail to amaze me with your generosity, love and consistent grace and sense of humour. Autumn, you are turning into a little girl just as independent and luminous as your mum, and I am so proud of you. Grandad, I'm so lucky to have a gentleman like you (not a nobleman!) in my life. To the rest of my family: Zero, Ghost, Caro, Louise, Adrien, Vincent, Vero, Charlie, Simon, Ellen,

Freya, Robin, Lorraine, Romayne, Dixie, Grandma, Judith. This year has only taught me how much I love you, and how much I want to hug you all when this is over.

Finally, to my readers. If nothing else, the past year has shown us how warm, how positive and how strong we all are: together and alone. Thank you for coming on this final Valentines journey with me. You are – and always have been – the reason I write.

With love and hope for the future, always,

Holly xxx

Turn over for a sneak peek of Hope's story in Happy Girl Lucky, *the first book in the Valentines series . . .*

FADE IN: REGENT'S PARK, LONDON, A SPRING MORNING

HOPE, fifteen, stands with her back to the sunshine, blue silk dress fluttering in the breeze. Her hair glistens, her posture is excellent and you can tell right away that she is the star of this film. In front of her is A HANDSOME BOY.

BOY
(*entranced*)
We've never met before,
but somehow it feels like we know
each other already.

                    HOPE
You feel instantly familiar to
            me too.

                    BOY
        (*even more entranced*)
Do you believe in fate,
    beautiful stranger?

                    HOPE
                  (*shyly*)
Of course I do. Everything
happens for a reason.

                    BOY
Then . . . perhaps *you* are my
            reason?

BOY holds out his hand. 'Teddy
Bears' Picnic' music starts playing.

                    HOPE
This is all happening so *BEEP*
            fast . . .

BOY

And yet we've waited our whole lives. Now *BEEP* take my hand and together we will – *BEEP BEEP BEEP-BEEP—*

BEEEEEEPPPPP

Blinking, I stare at the hand reaching towards me.

'You want toppings on this?' the BOY continues, yawning through his nostrils. 'We got chocolate sauce and chocolate sprinkles. Strawberry sauce and nuts, but that's extra. Or butterscotch sauce or toffee sauce. Chocolate flakes are extra too, so are toffee pieces and –'

I sigh. He's getting this script *all* wrong.

A few seconds ago, I was the romantic heroine poised to run away with my true soulmate – now I appear to be in a meeting with Willy Wonka's accountant. As usual, I *infinitely* prefer my version.

'Yes, please –' I smile sweetly as the car behind me starts beeping its horn again. 'Actually . . . never mind. Plain is just fine.'

'That's one pound thirty, then.'

Smiling harder so my dimples show, I hand the money across while gazing over the counter as intensely as possible, using all my advanced actressing skills to communicate complex, award-winning emotions.

The BOY stares back. 'You're ten pence short.'

'Whoops!' My eyelashes must have been fluttering too fast to see properly. 'Here you go.'

Our fingertips touch lightly and I stare at them, waiting for a flash of light, a few sparkles, maybe a bit of casual levitation. Up close, his fingernails have a thin line of black under each one, there are bright red spots marking his cheeks and his apron has melted chocolate smeared on it. Although I'm actually in black jeans and a neon cropped jumper – and it looks like it's about to start raining – so reality isn't exactly doing either of us a favour.

But there's *definitely* Potential. I just need to harness this new cinematic direction – fast.

'So,' I say as the car horn starts blaring again, 'what's your star si—'

'HOPE! WHAT ARE YOU DOING? YOU WERE SUPPOSED TO BE LOOKING FOR A

TOILET! DO YOU HAVE CONSTIPATION OR
WHAT? GET IN THE CAR RIGHT NOW OR
WE'RE GOING WITHOUT YOU!'

OK, the word *toilet* is absolutely not going in my
big opening scene; I am also editing out *constipation*
immediately.

The BOY's eyes slide over my shoulder, then
widen as he spots the huge luxury car parked behind
me.

'Whoa,' he says, abruptly waking up. 'Is that—'

'Yep.' I take a step backwards. 'Thank you so
much for this ice cream, kind stranger. I shall
treasure it forever and ever, until it melts or gets
eaten.'

Quickly – while he's still watching – I take my
hair out of its tangled knot and give my black curls
a quick, charming shake.

Then I glance adorably back over my shoulder.

HOPE
I'm afraid I must leave you here,
but this moment will be engraved
upon my heart for the rest of
time ...